The Middle Ages Come to Life ... To Bring Us Murder.

A Play of Isaac

"The player Joliffe appeared occasionally in Frazer's delightful series featuring the nun Dame Frevisse. Now he has his own story . . . In the course of the book, we learn a great deal about theatrical customs of the fifteenth century, including intricate details of stagecraft, costume construction and the like. In the hands of a lesser writer, it could seem preachy; for Frazer, it is another element in a rich tapestry." —*Contra Costa Times* (CA)

"Careful research and a profusion of details, especially those dealing with staging a fifteenth-century miracle play, bring the sights, smells and sounds of the era directly to the reader's senses. There's also a fine sense of history, all woven together in a medieval tapestry of rich colors.

"Looking over Ms. Frazer's impressive list of novels already to her credit, I can see a lot of pleasurable reading ahead. I especially look forward to meeting Joliffe and the players again." —*Round Table Reviews*

"The mystery, and the events surrounding it, are played out quite naturally through Joliffe's unquenchable curiosity. For lovers of mystery and lovers of history, this is a find; a mystery backed by solid research. I hope to see much more of this likable group in future volumes." —*Romance Readers Connection*

"A terrific historical who-done-it that will please amateur sleuth and historical mystery fans." —*Midwest Book Review*

continued . . .

The Outlaw's Tale

"A tale well told, filled with intrigue and spiced with romance and rogues."　　　　*—School Library Journal*

The Bishop's Tale

"Some truly shocking scenes and psychological twists."
　　　　—Mystery Loves Company

The Boy's Tale

"This fast-paced historical mystery comes complete with a surprise ending—one that will hopefully lead to another 'Tale' of mystery and intrigue."　　　　*—Affaire de Coeur*

The Murderer's Tale

"The period detail is lavish, and the characters are full-blooded."　　　　*—Minneapolis Star Tribune*

The Prioress' Tale

"Will delight history buffs and mystery fans alike."
　　　　—Murder Ink

The Maiden's Tale

"Great fun for all lovers of history with their mystery."
　　　　—Minneapolis Star Tribune

The Reeve's Tale

"A brilliantly realized vision of a typical medieval English village . . . Suspenseful from start to surprising conclusion . . . another gem."
　　　　—Publishers Weekly (starred review)

The Squire's Tale

"Meticulous detail that speaks of trustworthy scholarship and a sympathetic imagination."　　　　*—The New York Times*

A Play of
Dux Moraud

Margaret Frazer

BERKLEY PRIME CRIME, NEW YORK

THE BERKLEY PUBLISHING GROUP
Published by the Penguin Group
Penguin Group (USA) Inc.
375 Hudson Street, New York, New York 10014, USA
Penguin Group (Canada), 90 Eglinton Avenue East, Suite 700, Toronto, Ontario M4P 2V3, Canada
(a division of Pearson Penguin Canada Inc.)
Penguin Books Ltd., 80 Strand, London WC2R 0RL, England
Penguin Group Ireland, 25 St. Stephen's Green, Dublin 2, Ireland (a division of Penguin Books Ltd.)
Penguin Group (Australia), 250 Camberwell Road, Camberwell, Victoria 3124, Australia
(a division of Pearson Australia Group Pty. Ltd.)
Penguin Books India Pvt. Ltd., 11 Community Centre, Panchsheel Park, New Delhi—110 017, India
Penguin Group (NZ), Cnr. Airborne and Rosedale Roads, Albany, Auckland 1310, New Zealand
(a division of Pearson New Zealand Ltd.)
Penguin Books (South Africa) (Pty.) Ltd., 24 Sturdee Avenue, Rosebank, Johannesburg 2196, South
Africa

Penguin Books Ltd., Registered Offices: 80 Strand, London WC2R 0RL, England

This is a work of fiction. Names, characters, places, and incidents either are the product of the author's
imagination or are used fictitiously, and any resemblance to actual persons, living or dead, business es-
tablishments, events, or locales is entirely coincidental. The publisher does not have any control over
and does not assume any responsibility for author or third-party websites or their content.

A PLAY OF DUX MORAUD

A Berkley Prime Crime Book / published by arrangement with the author

PRINTING HISTORY
Berkley Prime Crime mass-market edition / August 2005

Copyright © 2005 by Gail Frazer.
Cover design by Leslie Worrell.
Cover illustration by Brigid Collins/Arena Works.
Interior text design by Kristin del Rosario.

The Edgar® name is a registered service mark of the Mystery Writers of America, Inc.

ISBN: 0-425-20434-0

BERKLEY® PRIME CRIME
Berkley Prime Crime Books are published by The Berkley Publishing Group,
a division of Penguin Group (USA) Inc.,
375 Hudson Street, New York, New York 10014.
The name BERKLEY PRIME CRIME and the BERKLEY PRIME CRIME design are trademarks
belonging to Penguin Group (USA) Inc.

PRINTED IN THE UNITED STATES OF AMERICA

10 9 8 7 6 5 4 3 2 1

Maydyn so louely and komly of syte,
   I prey thee for loue thou wyl lystyn to me;
To here my resun I prey thee wel tythe,
   Loue so deryn me most schewe to thee . . .

Anonymous,
Dux Moraud

Chapter 1

The summons from Lord Lovell came while they were packing their goods away for the last time before taking to the road again. The playing had gone well. There was no reason for alarm, but out of long habit a quick, assessing look passed among the five of them. Their small company had been Lord Lovell's players for hardly three months. For years before that they had been lordless, with no protection in their travels and work except other people's goodwill and their own wits.

So wariness still came readily, and before the servant was further than, "Lord Lovell has asked you come . . ." Basset, Ellis, and Joliffe were looking at each other, silently asking why, and Rose's face was gone very still, and even half-grown Piers had frozen out of his happy talk into watching his mother and the others as the servant finished, ". . . to him, Master Basset, if you please. And the one of you called Joliffe."

With lordly graciousness, no outward sign of alarm, and

a slight bow of his head, Basset said, "It is our honor and pleasure to obey."

Rose immediately came to straighten the upright collar of his doublet and twitch the folds of his surcoat to hang better from his shoulders. She was the only woman in the company and keeper of all their clothing, both for their plays and otherwise. Not that there was much "otherwise" about them. They had been a poor, small playing company for a long while, with almost everything they earned spent to keep them barely going from village to village to sometimes a town, not on such things as new clothing or too much food. To come under Lord Lovell's patronage and protection had been their best stroke of luck. "Ever," Basset had said, and he would best know, having formed the company years before Joliffe had joined.

So when Lord Lovell had made them his company of players and bade them come to Minster Lovell at Michaelmas this year of God's grace 1434 to divert both his household and his officials come for the end-of-harvest reckoning, they had come and were just ending their week here. They were too small a company to have much choice of plays, and filling that much time with suitable ones had been difficult, but by eking it out with Rose's tumbling and Ellis' and Piers' juggling and Joliffe's skill with the lute, they thought they had done well, especially against the general gloom that had come with yet another year's bad harvest. The summer that had started bright and fair had gone to rain and cold by St. Mary Magdalen Day, first delaying the harvest, then rotting too much of it in the fields. Last year had been lean after a bad harvest. This year, with a second bad harvest to follow the other, would be leaner. The players lived only on what other people would give for their work, and when other people had little to give, the players tended to have nothing. Lord Lovell's patronage—and the money that went with it—had come just in time. As they had walked beside their cart toward Minster Lovell, with yet more rain pattering into the road's mud and the hedges and ruined fields around them, Basset had said what they all knew. "We'd not have made it through another year like last."

Now Lord Lovell wanted to see two of them, and while they all thought they had done well enough that he was pleased with them, "The last thing you ever take for certainty is anyone's goodwill," Basset had told Joliffe in his early days with the company. "You may have done everything you could and earned it ten times over and still not get it." Which Joliffe was remembering as he followed Basset away from the shed they had been sharing with their cart and horse. In the servant's wake, they crossed the manor's outer yard, went through the cobbled gateway into the smaller inner yard and across it not to the wide way into the great hall—tall and newly built with golden Cotswold stone—but to a lesser door in the older wing of rooms directly across from the gateway. Word was that Lord Lovell would be having those rebuilt sometime soon, too.

"And pleasant it must be to have the money for putting up new when the old isn't falling down yet," Ellis had grumbled when Rose mentioned she had heard it. He had been stitching a new patch onto their old tent at the time and not been happy at his work.

"Lord Lovell is doing well enough by us," Basset had said back. "Don't you complain about his money."

"Not so long as enough of it comes our way," Joliffe had added. But fear that an end of it might be coming their way was in him and undoubtedly in Basset, no matter how straight-backed and at seeming ease they went together into the low-beamed room where Lord Lovell awaited them, standing at a glassed window that looked out at an orchard.

He turned as they entered, a man of medium height with a long swoop of a nose and eyes set rather too near it,

dressed in a floor-long houpelande of deep blue wool, its
thick folds gathered low on his waist by a wide belt set
with silver, its end hanging past his knees. Between the
French war and his many lands across England, he was a
wealthy man, who—from what Joliffe had seen here—
failed in no comforts for himself or his family. At a ready
guess, the room was where he did business, with a wide
table set to catch the best light from the window, a row of
scrolls laid at one end of it with pens and inkpot beside
them, and chests and a closed-door aumbry along one wall
where other scrolls and documents could be kept. There
was a single chair beside the table, with a wide, curved seat
and carven arms and back, and as Basset and Joliffe made
their deep bows to him, marking the gulf between his high
place in the world and their low one, Lord Lovell sat down
and regarded them with a benevolence that somewhat
eased Joliffe's mind. He did not look like a man about to
unhire them.

Nor was he. Instead he smiled and said, "With one thing
and another, I've had little chance to say how well pleased
I've been with your company, Master Basset. That you
could raise laughs so often after this glum harvest-time is
tribute to your skill, besides that my lady wife was most
particularly moved by your play of *Cain and Abel*."

Basset bowed again. "Our pleasure in pleasing you is
twice-doubled by knowing she was pleased."

"My steward delivered your quarter's money to you?"

"He did, my lord. Thank you for this chance to thank
you for it myself."

"I've noted, though, that you've added no one to your
company. I thought by now you would have."

They did indeed need and want to have a larger company. With only three men—with Joliffe usually playing
the women's roles—and a small boy, the plays they might
do were limited; but Basset said, "As yet we've had no

place for someone else. Joliffe"—Joliffe bowed—"is re-working plays to that end, but until then another player would not earn his way, I fear."

Lord Lovell took several silver coins from the flat leather purse hung from his belt beside his dagger, laid them on the table, and pushed them toward Basset. "Would that help toward taking on another man? Or boy."

Basset glanced easily at the coins, as if they were not as much as the company might have earned in a very good month, and said smoothly, "Your lordship has someone in mind?"

Lord Lovell barked a pleased laugh. "Sharp, Master Basset. Very sharp. Yes, I've someone in mind. He's a younger son of one of my bailiffs. Thus far, he's not proved suited to anything his father has set him. After watching your company, he claims he wants to be a player. His father, for lack of anything else to do with him, has asked if I might place him with you."

Standing where he was, Joliffe could not see Basset's face but he kept his own carefully brightly interested in Lord Lovell's words, and probably Basset was doing the same—hiding his sure dismay at the likelihood of being saddled with some moonstruck youngling of surely no skill and possibly few wits—though Joliffe would willing grant that a certain degree of witlessness was necessary in any-one who became a player. Otherwise they'd not choose to be a player.

"In truth," Lord Lovell finished, "no one knows what else to do with him."

Whether Basset could do anything with him was beside the point, since there was no wise way to turn down what Lord Lovell asked of them; and putting the best front to it that he could, Basset bowed and said with apparent willing-ness, "I'll be pleased to give him a chance."

Lord Lovell nodded, satisfied. "I can have my clerk

draw up a formal contract of apprenticeship while the boy packs."

Quickly Basset said, "By your leave, my lord, no contract."

"No?" Lord Lovell asked, surprised. A successful lord, like a successful merchant, knew the benefit of contracts.

So did Basset, but, "Someone is either a player or they're not, my lord. It would be shame to bind the lad and find he hates the life. Besides that, there are skills I can teach anyone, but there are other things that are either in a man or not, and only time and trying will tell. Binding with a contract will make no difference."

And if the boy proved impossible, being rid of him would be the easier if there were no contract. But Basset did not say that, and if Lord Lovell thought it, he let it go, too, simply said crisply, "Well enough. I'll have him sent to you as soon as we're done here. Now, there's another matter." One that he was less easy about: he paused to shift one of the scrolls lying on the table a little to one side and then back to where it had been before he looked up, not at Basset but past him, for the first time fully at Joliffe. "Last summer. That business at the Penteneys. You found your way through the tangle before anyone else did."

There was much to be said for a player's skill at keeping one thing on his face while his mind raced through any number of very other thoughts. Just now Joliffe held his face to a mild interest while in his mind he quickly shifted what he had supposed about the matter at the Penteneys. Yes, he had sorted out the tangle but those who knew that were few and he had not thought Lord Lovell was among them. Keeping his surprise to himself, he simply bowed, and said mildly, "Yes, my lord."

Lord Lovell shifted the scroll again, to one side and back again, and this time did not look up as he said, "That had much to do with my interest in taking on your company as my own. I wanted to be able to call on your wits if need be."

With the slightest twitch of their heads, Joliffe and Basset shared a glance. They were both shifting their thoughts, and by the smallest of nods Basset told Joliffe the game was his for now. Putting a careful edge of interest to his voice's mildness, Joliffe said, "And now there's need, my lord?"

Lord Lovell looked up at him. "Now there's need. As players, you can go unquestioned to places anyone else I might send would be suspect. You can be in the midst of a household, seeing things, without anyone wondering why you're there."

"Where would you have us go, my lord?" Joliffe asked, even-voiced, showing reasonable interest and keeping his instant wariness from sight.

"One of my feofees"—holding land from Lord Lovell in return for service if called on for it—"Sir Edmund Deneby, is readying a marriage between his daughter and the nephew of another man I know and am friendly with. It's a reasonable marriage. I've encouraged it. The only thing is that the girl was betrothed before but the man died not long before the wedding."

"Suspiciously, I take it?" Joliffe asked, the guess not difficult.

"He fell ill of a flux that couldn't be stopped. Such things happen." Lord Lovell said it easily but was not at ease about it. He might be unable to say in clear and certain words *why* he was uneasy but nonetheless he was.

"No one else fell ill?" Joliffe asked. Since they were in this with no way out, he might as well know more. "He was a hale man but it came on suddenly and killed him too quickly?"

"You know about it?" Lord Lovell asked in quick return. "You've heard something of it?"

"No, my lord. Those simply seemed the most reasonable

things to make you uneasy about what might otherwise seem straight-forward mischance."

Sitting back in his chair, Lord Lovell smiled and rapped his knuckles against the tabletop. "There! That's what I want. Sharp wits looking at this thing." He looked to Basset. "Master Basset, I'm sending your company to Sir Edmund as a sort of betrothal present. He and Master Breche are presently at Deneby Manor, working out final matters before the betrothal, settling the contract for Mariena and Amyas' marriage. Amyas. A fool name. What did they think he was going to be, some hero out of a French romance? Anyway, I've had dealings with Master Breche and I've backed this marriage, so no one will wonder if I send my players there for this while before the marriage."

"How long will we have?" Basset asked.

"As I understand it, they're in the last of the betrothal talks. Everything should be agreed within a few days, the betrothal will be made, the banns immediately given on the three following days, and the marriage held the day after the last of them."

That was a quick moving toward the marriage. The usual way was for the banns announcing it to be read at the church door for three Sundays in a row and the marriage to follow sometime soon after. It was possible—though rare—to do it more quickly and, "Why the haste?" Joliffe asked. "Is that part of your suspicion?"

"No. Master Breche has merchant interests abroad. He's due to be in Calais by Martinmas. Amyas is his heir. He wants him settled before he goes."

"Is the girl Sir Edmund's heir?"

"There's a son. Much younger. So she's not the heir, but Sir Edmund is giving a good dowry with her and she'll have considerable lands from her mother when her mother dies."

And her brother might die. Then she would have everything, if—"Is the estate entailed in the male line only?"

Joliffe asked. Because that would mean the property could go only from male to male, never to a daughter, however sidewise that might take it, even to remote cousins.

"No," Lord Lovell said, with a level look at Joliffe that said he understood what lay behind the question. While a well-dowered knight's daughter was a very good thing, a daughter who was heir to all that knight's property was even better, and here was someone with only a younger brother in the way to that. But even without that, it was likely a good marriage just as it was, because by way of it, a merchant's heir would rise into the gentry and a knight's daughter acquire a wealthy husband.

Besides, it seemed that Lord Lovell feared for the bridegroom, not the brother.

Even as all that chased through his mind, Joliffe asked, enjoying this chance to question a lord, rather than merely obey. "Is there more you could tell us about what has you uneasy?"

"I would there were. As it is, the best I can offer is that you just go there, make of matters what you can, and let me know."

"How do we let you know, my lord?" Basset asked.

"My lady wife and I are coming to the wedding. We'll be there the day before and I'll make occasion to talk to you. If there's any reason not to go forward with the marriage, I can deal with it then."

Unless the bridegroom died sooner, Joliffe thought but did not say; but found Lord Lovell adding, level-voiced and looking straight at him as if reading his mind, "In the meantime, if you see need to keep anyone alive, please do so." He pulled a scroll toward him, dropping his gaze to it, dismissing them with, "I'll have Gil sent to you directly."

Joliffe followed Basset in deeply bowing and retreating from the room. A servant waiting outside went in as they left, probably to receive an order about this Gil with whom

they were going to be saddled, but neither Basset nor Joliffe said anything until they were in the middle of the
yard, away from anyone to hear Joliffe ask, "What do we
tell the others?"

Without slowing or looking at him, Basset said, "What
my lord told us. That he has a boy who wants to be a player
and we're to take him on, and we're being sent as a betrothal gift to this Sir Edmund Deneby."

"And about the other?"

"Nothing."

The briefness of Basset's answer told how he felt about
the business set on them.

"We've been asked to do worse," Joliffe pointed out.

"And when we refused, we lost our then-patron and
have been living narrowly ever since," Basset pointed out
in return.

"But this time we've accepted," Joliffe said cheerfully.
"We'll do what we can, which probably won't be much,
and there'll be an end of it. Although," he went on thoughtfully, "if my lord thinks I'm going to hurl my body in front
of an assassin's dagger or suchlike to protect this Amyas
Breche, he can think another thought about it."

"Watch what you don't wish for," Basset muttered. "You
might get it. What we need to talk about is this thought
Lord Lovell has that we can do his spying for him because
of the Penteney business."

Because that matter had been much Joliffe's doing, he
started somewhat uneasily, "I—"

"Later," said Basset. "When there's time."

The others were waiting for them with all the hampers
and baskets packed into the cart and the mare Tisbe hitched
between the shafts. While Joliffe went to be sure of her
harness' straps and buckles, Basset explained about this Gil
that was to join them.

All in all, the others took it not so badly as they might.

Ellis said, "He'll be the one who was all but falling into the playing area with staring at us, whatever we did here."

"If it is," Rose said encouragingly, "at least he's neither lame nor ugly."

Over Tisbe's back, Joliffe said, "A player can do with being ugly. Look at Ellis."

"I'll look at you with a stick the next time you're in reach," Ellis returned without heat. "That'll help your looks, anyway."

"It's what his voice is like and whether he's trainable," Basset said.

"Even Joliffe has been mostly trainable," Piers said from where he sat on the cart's tail, legs swinging.

"I get enough of that from Ellis," Joliffe said. "Don't you start."

"You give enough of that to Ellis," Rose said. "All of you stop it." She was Basset's daughter and Piers' mother and Ellis' love and often sounded as if she would willingly knock all their heads together if she had the chance. "Father, you haven't noted the cart."

"The cart? What's wrong with the cart?"

"Nothing's wrong," Rose said. "Look."

Piers helpfully pointed at the cart's curved canvas top. The high-sided cart carried all the properties needed for their work and what little else there was in their lives. Sturdily made to begin with and carefully kept these many years, it rarely failed them, but it was the canvas cover over curved wooden struts that kept the weather off everything, and despite the best of mending, it was simply wearing out. Patched, blotched, and gray with use, it told all too well how low the players' fortunes had sunk these past few years. Except that instead of that cover there was another one now—crisp with newness, without patch, blotch, or mend to be seen, and brightly painted gold and red in the bold, curving, nebuly lines of Lord Lovell's heraldic arms.

Both Basset and Joliffe must have very satisfactorily gaped at it because Rose and Ellis and Piers all burst into laughter together; and while Joliffe stood back to admire it and Basset circled the cart, staring, Ellis said, "The man who brought it said it was Lord Lovell's gift. He left a cask of paint, too, for us to paint the cart red to match when we've a chance."

Still staring, Basset breathed, "Blessed St. Genesius." The patron saint of actors.

"You really didn't see it?" Rose insisted.

Basset shook his head, picked up Piers from where he had fallen off the cart-tail with laughter, and said without taking his eyes from the splendor that had so suddenly overtaken them, "I never did. I was thinking about where we're going." He blinked and gathered his thoughts. "Do you know, I don't know the way to Deneby Manor. We'll have to ask."

"I know the way," said someone from the outer corner of the shed.

They all turned to look at the boy standing there with a long bundle clasped to him with both arms. The same boy—as Ellis had guessed—who had been at everything they had performed at Minster Lovell this week. Until now there had never been reason to note more than that about him, but that had changed and Joliffe made a first, quick assessing of him. Older than Piers by a few years, he was pleasant-featured enough, with straw-brown hair and a well-limbed body, compact enough that it might never take him through a gawking, awkward time. All that, at least, was to the good. More, including his voice and whether he was trainable, would have to wait. Basset was saying, surely while making his own judgment, "You do? To Deneby? That will be a help. You're Gil, I take it?"

The boy ducked his head in awkward acknowledgment, thought better of that, and tried a slight bow from his waist

instead, more awkward because of the bundle clutched to
him. As he straightened, his gaze flickered to all of them
looking back at him, and Joliffe remembered his own first
moment of joining Basset's company. That had been before
the disaster had come on them, so there were more people
looking at him—five men and Rose and another woman—
but the feeling must be the same for this Gil as it had been
for him: the lone outsider being judged by a close-grown
group who knew each other, did not know him, and were
unsure they wanted to. Basset had done then just as he did
now—said with hearty goodwill, "Welcome, young
man—" and went on to make them all known to him. "Ellis Halowe, who does our villains and heroes, depending
on which we need. Joliffe Ripon, who mostly plays our
women's roles as well as anything else that's needed. My
daughter Rose, who'll keep you clothed and teach you your
share of the cooking. Her son Piers, who'll make trouble
for you, just as he does for the rest of us."

Gil smiled and nodded at each of them. They smiled
and nodded back.

"It's your last name we don't know," Basset said.

"Densell, if you please, sir," Gil said.

"Well, Gil Densell, it's time we were on our way. That's
all your gear?" Basset asked. "Put it in the back of the cart.
Show him where, Piers."

"There's a meat pie on the top," Gil said. "For all of . . .
us." He offered that "us" uncertainly. "From my mother,"
he added, abashed.

"Then doubly welcome," Basset said heartily.

Young Gil would learn soon enough, thought Joliffe,
that food from anyone for any reason was always welcome
among them.

But even now, with Piers showing Gil where to stow his
bag and no reason left not to be on their way, Rose said,
"There's one more thing."

Joliffe, going to Tisbe's head to start her away, turned back to see Piers handing his mother a folded cloth that must have been lying at the cart's back. He and his mother and Ellis were all smiling as if to burst, and before Joliffe or Basset could ask why, Rose shook out the cloth and held it up, showing it was a tabard of strong red cloth painted with Lord Lovell's badge of a silver wolf-dog—playing off Latin *lupellus* and Lovell—stitched on its front. Slipped over the head, the tabard would hang loose in back and front and by the Lovell badge tell to the world whose players they were.

"From Lady Lovell," Rose said. "There's one for each of you and Piers and Ellis, too."

"The Lord and St. Anne and the blessed Virgin love her," Basset breathed, staring much as the Israelites must have stared at the manna from heaven. "I . . ."

Words failed him. Joliffe did not even try for any. A few months ago they had been near to ruin and now they were a lord's players, with all the marks of honor that could go with being so.

"We'll wear them," Basset said. "As we leave. To let my lady know we honor her gift."

"And then put them away for later," Rose said firmly. While Piers tossed folded cloths to Ellis and Joliffe, she went to her father and slipped the tabard over his head, settling and straightening it as she had his surcoat. He struck a pose and she nodded at him, smiling approval. Then she turned to Ellis, waiting for her help though he did not need it; and when she had the tabard on him, her hands lingered on his shoulders, and he put his hands over hers, the both of them smiling at each other with smiles far different from what she had shared with her father.

Joliffe, putting on his own tabard, held in his own smile at sight of them. The affection between them was too often an uneasy thing and it was good to see them being simply glad of each other, brief though it lasted before Rose had to untangle Piers' head from his tabard, saying to Gil while she did, "I'm afraid there's none for you yet."

Lifting his chin, the boy said cheerfully enough, "That's no matter. After all, I'm not a player yet."

Joliffe began to have hope of him.

Chapter 2

The day's rain held off until the players were a mile or more from Minster Lovell. Their tabards were safely stowed in one of the hampers by then and they had their cloaks on and their hoods up against the soft drizzle that would likely last all day but was better than a downpour. Drizzle took longer to soak through thick-woven wool.

According to Gil, who had been there with his father a few times—"When he still thought he might make a bailiff of me," the boy said simply, with neither triumph that his father had failed nor bitterness that he had tried—the manor of Deneby was north and east from Minster Lovell, a day and a half's travel at the cart's pace. "We'll be there early tomorrow afternoon," he said. "All going well."

The boy might be addled enough to want to be a player, Joliffe thought, but he was at least sensible enough to add that "all going well." And he made no word of complaint about the rain or the walking either, and that was to the good, since walking and rain were both inevitable in a player's life. Unless, Joliffe amended, a player prospered to the point of affording a riding horse—which was so rare a thing as to be a laughable thought—or else fell so ill he had to ride in the cart—which God forbid. A player could no more afford to be ill than he could afford a riding horse.

At least this Gil looked healthy enough, striding steadily beside Basset. With Minster Lovell behind them, they had all taken their usual places around the cart: Basset on one side, Ellis on the other, Joliffe at Tisbe's head, Rose and Piers behind. Sometimes it went other ways; sometimes they walked together or in various pairs, and in good weather Piers often roamed forward to Ellis' side or his grandfather's or Joliffe's, but today he kept beside his mother, slogging with the rest of them, and Basset had called Gil to his side to talk with him while they walked.

Joliffe remembered his first walk and talk with Basset, when Basset had skillfully drawn him out with questions and at the same time given him to understand what his place in the company would be and, for good measure, gave him his first lesson in playing. "Your voice and your body do your work," he had said. "Your voice and body. They're the tools of your trade. However sharp your mind is, boy—and I suspect yours is sharp enough you've cut yourself more than once—it's no good to us if you can't work your voice and body into whoever you need to be in a play, and you're going to have to be everyone there ever was if you're going to be in this company—from sweet maiden to old man, from angel to devil, to everyone and everything between. We've no use for someone who can only be himself."

Remembering, Joliffe smiled to himself. He had learned, and he was good, and he took pleasure in both the work and in being good at it. He smiled, too, because his years of almost always playing the woman or girl in any play

they did were maybe done. He was become somewhat old
for playing maidens. If Gil proved any good at all, he was
more than welcome to become every maiden there was in
all their plays.

Their plays. Despite his boots were in mud and rain was
dripping off his hood's edge past his eyes, Joliffe smiled
wider at the thought of what he could do with their plays if
Gil proved good. When their company had broken up and
shrunk, he had reworked what plays of theirs he could to fit
the few of them that were left, with him and Basset and
Ellis often shifting to play two or more parts apiece in a
single play. Too many of their plays, though, could not be
altered enough to be playable by so small a company and
had languished these years in the bottom of the box where
their scripts were kept. With even one more player, possibilities opened up and through the summer, after Lord
Lovell had taken the company for his own, Joliffe had begun to work over the plays, seeing what could be done.

Now, with Gil to be maybe of their company, he could
think more directly about possibilities, ignoring Tisbe while
he did, knowing full well she did not need him. The mare
had been with the company long enough that she knew her
business. Set out along a road, she simply kept on going. If
she came to a crossroads and no one told her otherwise,
she stopped until told which way to turn. If she came to a
bad stretch of mud, holes, ruts, or rocks, she waited for
someone to guide her and the cart carefully past it. When a
village or town came into sight, she slowed until told whether
or not the players meant to stop and make ready to perform
there or else go straight on. This last year, things being as
bad as they were with the ruined harvest, they had played
everywhere they came to, needing whatever farthings or
foodstuffs were given them in return.

Supposing any were given at all.

With Lord Lovell's coins in their purse these past few

months, they had done a little more choosing; and today, with more of Lord Lovell's coins in hand and some place particular they were supposed to be, they simply traveled on. Not that there were many places to pause the way they were going, north and east through the wide forest of Wychwood, but by late afternoon they were beyond it, and with early dark drawing in because of the rain, they stopped for the night in a village where the reeve agreed they could shelter in his barn in return for performing for his family after supper.

That was a good enough exchange. "Though we don't have to give as much as we might, since we're feeding ourselves," Basset said over the players' own supper of Gil's meat pie and a leather bottle of ale brought from Minster Lovell. "This is excellent pie, young Gil. Our thanks to your mother and welcome to you."

Basset lifted his handleless cup as he said it and the others followed suit. Gil grinned and lifted his in return. "My thanks to you," he said. "For taking me on."

"We'll see how thankful you are in a week or so, once Basset has put you to work," Ellis said. But he was smiling. He tended toward black-browed frowns more than any of them, but even he was presently in good humour, being well-fed, well-sheltered, and with money in hand.

As the players had expected, after supper they found most of the village crowded into the reeve's house. There was not much space left for them to play but they were used to that and began with some juggling by Basset, Ellis, and Piers. Then Joliffe played his lute (his juggling skills were execrable) while Piers sang in his bright, clear child's voice. Basset's sleight-of-hand tricks followed, accompanied by a running exchange of practiced insults between Joliffe and Ellis that rocked their lookers-on with laughter and approving shouts.

Rose kept aside, near the door with Gil, and slipped him

away as Basset began his flowered closing speech of thanks to all, interrupted by Joliffe and Ellis snipping insults at each other behind his back until with a roar he chased them both out the door, leaving Piers to make the final bow all by himself with a flourish of his feathered cap and a wide, triumphant smile before running after the others, leaving shouts, laughter, and clapping behind him.

All the brightness of performance was gone from them, though, while they laid out their pads and blankets on the barn's packed-earth floor by the small light of a single tallow candle in a lantern. With no one to see them, they moved with the tiredness earned by a day's walking and an evening's work, and Gil asked somewhat shyly, "Do you have to do that all the time? Play at the day's end?"

"Often," Basset said. "Nor it doesn't do to give less for these things. Next time we come this way, they'll remember us, and better they remember well than ill. Value for value."

"And at the end of a rainy day there isn't better value than a dry place to sleep," Rose said. "Piers, don't you dare lie down in those wet hosen." She had set up a drying rack around the small clay pot that carried their fire and was hanging all their hosen over it. Fed with a little of their hoarded charcoal and the dry sticks they kept in the cart against wet days, the fire heated the pot; the pot, then covered to slow the fire to a smother, gave off warmth most of a night—too little warmth to be much use against cold nights but grand for drying wet hosen, and dry hosen were far more pleasant to put on in the morning than were damp.

Piers stripped his legs bare at his mother's order, yawning while he did. Ellis, already sitting on his blankets, was rubbing his bare feet as if they ached, while Basset lowered himself with a groan onto his bed; and Gil asked, "You seemed not tired at all while you were playing. How do you do that after a day of walking?"

"Being half-mad or else an idiot helps," Joliffe said, spreading his still-damp cloak over his blankets.

"Then you should be better at it than any of us," Ellis muttered.

"Pretend I've just thrown my pillow at you," Joliffe said. His pillow being a small oblong of straw-stuffed canvas and somewhat hard.

"Pretend I've just thrown it back at you," Ellis said around a yawn. He slid between his own cloak-covered blanket and straw-stuffed sleeping pad.

"We're players," Basset said, answering Gil. "That means that when we're pretending to be someone, we feign feelings that they have, not our own. Tonight we were 'the jolly players,' full of mirth and fun. At Minster Lovell you saw Joliffe as the fair Marian and Ellis as bold Robin, most wonderfully in love with one another. Do they look to be in love with one another to you, now that you know them?"

Joliffe made mime of gagging, and from the depths of his blanket, Ellis snorted. Rose, kneeling, just finished with tucking Piers into his own bed, turned and reached, smiling, across her own bed toward Ellis, who put out a hand and briefly clasped hers. With her was where his love lay, and hers with him, however rarely it came to more than wishing between them.

Gil looked as if he were sorting through a great many thoughts as he crawled into his own blankets.

In the morning Basset's value for value was rewarded. The rain had stopped in the night and a yellowish dawn was trying to happen through thinning clouds as they started out, cloaks and leather shoes still damp and stomachs only somewhat satisfied with the barley gruel and the bit of yesterday's bread that Rose had portioned them for breakfast. But as Tisbe turned the cart into the village street, headed the way she had been going yesterday, a woman came out from one of the houses, hurried toward Basset, thrust a small loaf of bread into his hands, and said, "For last night. Our own thanks. 'Tisn't much, but it's something."

Loaf in one hand, Basset swept off his hat with the other and made her a low bow. "Good lady, that it comes from your fair self makes it precious beyond gold."

She laughed at him but was blushing, pleased, as she retreated to her cottage. Only when the village was behind them did Basset say to Gil at his side, "Folk know when you've given fully and fairly to them. Some will take it all and give little or nothing. Some pay what's asked and no more. Some, like that good woman who owed us nothing, give something more precious than a silver coin from a lord." Because in a dearth-time like this year, silver coins might sometimes be more readily had than bread. "It's still warm from her oven," Basset said. "Shall we have it now or save it?"

The vote was entirely to have it now. Warm, fresh bread was too good a thing to let go cold for later; and though divided among the six of them, the little loaf did not go far, the pleasure of it raised spirits.

The drying weather raised spirits more, nor did it seem there'd been so much rain here: the going was none so bad, with rarely need to heave the cart along through a mudhole. Basset had taken one of their scripts from the box and tucked it inside his doublet before they had started today. Now he brought it out and set Gil to reading it aloud, first to find out what possibilities his voice had, then to begin training him both to understand what he read and how to make the most of it.

"These aren't just words you're reading, lad. These are people talking. You have to understand not just what they're saying but why they're saying it. Because if you

don't understand why they're saying it, chances are your
listeners won't understand it either, and nothing loses you a
crowd like them not understanding what you're doing. And
if you lose your crowd—"

"You lose your money," chorused Joliffe, Ellis, and
Piers from ahead, aside, and behind. It was a lesson they'd
heard more often than almost any other.

Ignoring them, Basset went on, "You lose your money.
Which can mean no food for your belly or roof for your
head that night."

"Which we don't always have anyway," Ellis put in.
"You've been lucky so far."

"Remember when—" Piers started.

"We'll remember later," Basset said, probably not trusting what Piers would choose to remember. "Right now I
want to work him." And through the rest of the morning's
miles Basset did.

The rest of them closely heeded how it went, not for the
sake of the lesson itself but to judge what they could about
Gil, because besides that they needed him to be good, they
needed to know something about him. They all lived too
much together, day in and out and nights, too, to add to the
company someone with whom they could not live—a com-
plainer or a whiner or someone given to quarrels or naturally glum, unable to find an often desperately needed
laugh when things were bad; or someone too weak in body
to keep up their traveling pace; or too weak in voice to be
of use; or too stupid to learn.

They already knew Gil could keep to the walking well
enough, and before the morning was out, they found he was
both clear-voiced and fairly quick to catch what Basset
wanted from him. He was also cheerful at it. How cheerful
he would be after a few weeks on the road was another
matter—one that would have to wait those few weeks for
answer, Joliffe supposed.

They paused along the road to eat their noontide bread and cheese and ale. The sun was weakly out but the grass was still too wet for sitting on. Rose and Piers sat on the lowered tail-gate of the cart. The rest of them made do with standing, and when the first edge of hunger was off and everyone's chewing had slowed, Basset said, "So, young Gil, how far would you say we are from Deneby?"

With all of them looking at him, Gil seemed to find his bread and cheese suddenly far too dry in his mouth; but he chewed and swallowed and said, "My guess is about two hours' walk, Master Basset. But that's just a guess."

"That's good enough," Basset assured him. "Suppose you tell us, though, before we get there, what you know about this Sir Edmund Deneby and his people. There's a wife and a son and the daughter whose marriage they're working toward, yes?"

"Mariena," Gil said. "I've seen her. She's lovely." From the way he said the word, her loveliness was still warm in his memory, and Joliffe felt a twitch of wariness. They didn't need a lovesick boy mooning after their host's daughter. Gil shrugged. "Her brother is just a boy. But then there's Lady Benedicta." His voice went altogether the other way from how he had spoken of her daughter.

"Hard to please, is she?" Basset asked.

Gil paused over his answer before saying slowly, "I don't know what she is. I never had anything to do with her, nor my father either. I only saw her at meals in the great hall. A hard-favored woman. The sort you don't want ever mad at you?"

He made the last a question, as if uncertain that it told Basset enough. Basset acknowledged with a nod that it did and asked, "What of Sir Edmund?"

"He's a good sort, my father says. Straight-forward. No twisting about. His people like him."

Basset nodded some more, satisfied with that. "Well done. Thank you."

Well done, indeed. It never hurt to know ahead of time what sort of people they were going to play for. From what Gil said, Joliffe judged that Sir Edmund would probably be easy to please but his wife might be a trouble; but among Basset's sayings about trouble was the palpable truth, "If there isn't one, there's another," and they had had to deal with troublesome wives before now. Sometimes it took no more than doing a play that ended with a wife having the upper hand. Sometimes it took other than that. They would have to wait until they were at Deneby to judge, but at least they were forewarned.

While they passed around the leather bottle of ale for the last time before moving on, Basset said, "I'm thinking that we should stop in Deneby village before pushing on to the manor. There's a village, isn't there, young Gil?"

"About a quarter mile from the manor house itself," Gil readily supplied.

"Better yet," said Basset. "I say we stop there for the night, to learn what else we can about what's what at Deneby. Play something, then spend a few hours of the evening at the alehouse, and move on in the morning to present ourselves to Sir Edmund and all."

There were general nods to that before Ellis asked, "Play what?"

That was always a closely considered question, because an ill-judged choice, no matter how well played, could put them into trouble in some places or, here, set them off on the wrong foot before they were even at the manor.

"Not a farce about marriage," Rose said. "Not before we know how feelings are running about this one."

"Nor about stewards," Basset said, and explained to Gil, "Making sport of stewards and reeves and any other manor officers is always an easy way to laughs in villages, but we're going to be here too many days together and there's no use in finding out too late the steward overmuch minds being laughed at."

Gil nodded with ready understanding. "That play you did about the priest, then? That had us all laughing."

Basset briefly considered but said, "Best not. We might want the priest's friendship while we're there."

"A saint's play," Joliffe said. "That won't offend anyone."

"So long as it's not one about the virtues of virginity," Basset said. "Virginity not being what's on people's minds at Deneby these days. But, yes, one of the slap-and-fall-about saints plays should do. Are we ready to move on? Gil, why don't you walk ahead with our good Tisbe, and Joliffe and I can talk about which play will serve."

That was reasonable enough; but when Basset sorted it so that Rose and Piers were walking beside the cart, and he and Joliffe well behind it as they set off again, Joliffe knew they were going to talk about more than which play to do. Nor did Basset waste time but said when the others were enough ahead not to hear him, "We'll do *St. Nicholas and the Thief*. There. That's settled. Now, about this spying we're to do."

"It's not my fault," Joliffe tried.

"Of course it's your fault," Basset said without heat. "You made clever this summer and got yourself noticed. There's nobody to blame for that except you."

"Maybe we could blame Lord Lovell? He's the one who's done the noticing."

"No one ever got far in the world by blaming a lord for anything. No, it's all of it your fault and that's settled. It's what we're to do about it is the question."

"Be such poor spies Lord Lovell doesn't ask us to do it again?"

"And maybe lose his interest in us? No, honest work is

honest work. You and I will do what we can, keep the others out of it if possible, and hope for the best."

"Spying is honest work?"

"Starving may be more honest," Basset said with sudden grimness. "But if I'm choosing, I'll forgo the starving, thank you."

"Basset, I *am* sorry for this," Joliffe said, serious.

But Basset waved both that and his own grimness away with one hand, saying, easy again, "Sorry butters no parsnips, boy. Not that it would much matter if it did. I've never been partial to parsnips. We'll do what we can and it will have to be enough. Just like with everything else in life. Come. Let's tell the others who we're going to be this afternoon."

Chapter 3

Deneby village was a long curve of road with houses pushed up against it along both sides, their gardens and byre-yards behind them. There was no green, only a widening of the street between the churchyard and an alehouse, and the players chose there for their play. Gil had his first lesson from Ellis, Joliffe, and Rose in how quickly the simple wooden frame could be set up beside the cart and the cloth hung from it to make the back of what was instantly then their playing area, while Basset made a grand, booming speech that brought people to see what they were doing and Piers went skipping up and down the street, playing merrily on a recorder to draw more folk from their houses.

Despite it was mid-afternoon, there were enough Deneby women and children and men not out to the fields—too soaked as the fields presently were for autumn plowing or planting—to make a good gathering, and to them Basset announced that he and his company were

come from Lord Lovell especially and particularly to perform for their lord and lady toward the lady Mariena's
wedding day but that first and here and now they would
play, for the delight and bettering of all good folk here, a
tale of St. Nicholas.

While Piers played and jigged in front of the curtain,
Basset went behind it, for Rose to help him quickly into
St. Nicholas' long robe while Ellis put the bishop's mitre
on his head. Joliffe handed him the episcopal crozier and,
all dignity, Basset strode out and around to the curtain's
front to take up a pose as a statue of St. Nicholas on a
cloth-covered box. Piers scampered out of sight the other
way, past Joliffe—gowned and wimpled as a woman—
coming on with a small, closed chest that "she" set in front
of the "statue." While "she" was making prayer then to
St. Nicholas to guard her wealth while she was gone, two
riders came along the street and drew rein to one side of
the crowd to watch and listen. Joliffe finished his speech
and went from sight around one end of their curtain; was
hardly out of sight when Ellis as a Thief went out around
the other end, intent on the chest of treasure.

Joliffe took the chance to look at the riders. One was a
half-grown boy in a short scarlet riding tunic and green,
rolled-brimmed cap, riding a rather fine bay gelding. The
other was a burly, plain-faced man more plainly dressed
and more plainly mounted. From that, Joliffe guessed the
boy was likely Sir Edmund Deneby's son, out for an afternoon ride, and the man an accompanying servant. Then it
was time for him to go out again and on with the play. It
must have pleased because at the end, when Gil and Piers
went around with their caps held out for any coins anyone
might want to give, the boy took a coin from his belt-hung
pouch and leaned from his saddle to drop it into Piers' cap,
calling over the heads of the villagers starting to drift
away, "I want another play."

Basset turned from popping a walnut from behind the ear of a laughing child clinging to its mother's skirts and bowed to the boy, but answered, "My lord, I regret to say we cannot please you with that at present."

"Do another one!" the boy demanded.

Basset bowed again, no less respectfully, but answered, "You ride a fine horse, good sir. You'll surely understand then that we players are like good horses. We must not be over-worked if you want us to go on being good. Besides"—Basset swept his hat and himself into another low bow—"you'll see us tomorrow and for some few days afterwards. We're sent by Lord Lovell to entertain your family for this while toward your sister's wedding."

The boy did not question Basset's knowing who he was, but stared at him as if deciding whether he was telling the truth or not. He must have decided Basset was, because he said with a sudden smile, "Good! I'll tell them you're coming. You can play at supper tonight!"

"Please you, my master, we'll welcome that you'll herald our coming and thank you for it," Basset said. "But we mean to stay the night here in the village and arrive at the manor fresh with the day."

The boy regarded him carefully before the smile took firm hold again. "I see. I'll tell them that then. That you're coming."

Basset bowed to him again. "That would be most good of you, my master."

"Until tomorrow," the boy said lordliwise and rode on with his servant.

By then all but the most curious of the villagers had dispersed and now the few left went away, leaving the players alone to pack away their goods, giving Ellis chance to ask while he and Rose were folding the hanging small and tight to go back in its hamper, "Why the night in the village?

Why not go on to the manor tonight and save the cost of a night's lodging?"

Basset, standing by to take the wooden pegs as Joliffe and Gil knocked them out of the wooden frame and Piers held it steady until it could all come down, said, "We're going to be here a week or more. I want to know more about Sir Edmund and his people before we're in the middle of it all. An evening in the village alehouse should tell us all we need to know." He cast an eye at the sky. "Besides, I think the rain is done for a while. We can set up our tent, and maybe only have to pay for supper."

Leaving them to finish packing up, he went to ask in the alehouse about supper and where they might set up their tent for the night and was assured they were welcome to use of the common land lying at the village's end. Common land was kept untilled, with every villager having right to graze a set number of livestock there. The village pound was set there, too, where strayed animals were kept until their owners paid the fine to have them back. A milch cow presently imprisoned there lowed mournfully while they set up their tent, but as they finished, a girl came with stool and pail and set to milking it. Done with his share of tasks, Ellis strolled over to lean on the fence and talk with her. Joliffe, circling the tent to be sure all the tie-downs were secure—Gil tied firm knots, he found—saw Rose cast a long look after Ellis. Hurt and longing and anger were so mixed in her face that Joliffe momentarily felt an answering anger at Ellis, but in truth he would have been hard put to say for which of them he felt the more sorry. There was love between Rose and Ellis, deep enough it had kept Ellis with her when he could have been long gone to a less desperate band of players than they'd become until Lord Lovell took them on. The trouble was that, so far as anyone knew, Rose's long-vanished husband, Piers's father, still lived, meaning she could not freely give her love and herself to Ellis in the way they both wanted.

Sometimes she did give way, did give herself completely to him, let him give himself completely to her, and those were good days. Mostly, though, she held out against her desires and his, and sometimes in those times his need went wandering and he found elsewhere what he could not have from her. Then she was hurt and did not always hide it, and the rest of them had to live with that.

Joliffe, on the whole, wished her husband would happen into their way sometime. Then they could kill him and settle matters once and for all.

The girl went away with her pail of milk, and Ellis came back to say, "She says there was a new brew of ale made just yesterday and that generally the ale is good."

"I suppose you told her you were good, too," Rose snapped.

"I told her we'd be in to try the ale this evening," Ellis said, sounding somewhat startled. He always seemed startled by Rose's ill-humour at him. How he could be after all these years Joliffe did not know, unless it was by a willful forgetting—which did not better the matter in the slightest.

Leaving Gil to guard the cart and Tisbe staked out to graze nearby, the rest of them went back to the alehouse in the gathering shadows of early evening. The supper of pottage of late season vegetables was filling if not grand and afterward they sent Piers back with a bowl of it to Gil for his supper and Rose's order for Piers to go to bed when he got there. He wouldn't, but he'd take care to be in bed by the time she returned and that would serve well enough. Then the players settled down to finding out what they could about the household at the manor.

It helped that the ale was all the milkmaid had promised. Good ale made for good talk, and after Ellis and Basset did a brief juggling of bright leather balls between them, the villagers' first wariness eased, letting Ellis and Basset fall into talk with them. Joliffe and Rose kept somewhat aside from them, listening to other talk but joining in little, so that all together they might find out as much as might be of how folk thought about the Denebys, because it would be a different way of looking than Lord Lovell's. Lord Lovell was lord over Sir Edmund, but here Sir Edmund held sway over much of these people's lives. Even those who had already bought their freedom from serfdom and no longer owed him service still lived on land he owned, worked fields that were his, came before his manor-court when there were troubles. A bad lord made for a sad, ill-humoured village, and that would be warning to the players of how much harder their task in pleasing him might be.

The crowd this afternoon had been pleasant enough, though, and talk in the alehouse tonight was easy, neither full of complaints nor sullenly afraid to make such as there were. One man grumbled over a fine lately put on him in the manor-court for taking fish from a stream, but his friends told him, friendliwise, to shut up, he'd had no business taking them from that part of the stream and he'd known it, and Sir Edmund had been easier on him than he could have been.

The heaviest talk was of the poor harvest, but that was eased by other talk of hoped-for feasting at the wedding.

"Not but what he'll want to take some of it out of our stores," the man who'd been fined over fish grumbled, "and leave us with less when we've not much anyway."

"Shut your mouth, Jem," one of his friends said, still friendliwise. "You don't know aught. He's sent to Oxford and Cirencester both, they're saying, for what's to be bought there, rather than having anything off us."

"We're to have our own feast here for the marriage and at his cost," a woman said loudly. "So give over your complaining, Jem. It's not Sir Edmund's fault you're bad at thieving and were caught."

While everyone, except Jem, was laughing at that, a round young man in a priest's black gown appeared in the outer doorway and was greeted with a general raising of cups and bowls and welcoming calls of, "Father Morice!" and "Where've you been?" and "Come in out of the chill," with various folk shifting on benches to make place for him. He stood smiling and nodding to one and all, familiar and friendly, while he looked over the company and then, with smiling words and slaps on the shoulders of folk as he passed, made his way to where Basset and Ellis sat with a few other men.

Basset and Ellis both rose to their feet and made him respectful bows, to which he returned a slight bow of his head and said in a clear, easy voice, knowing perfectly well he was listened to by everyone, "You're the players, yes? May I join you?"

Basset bowed again and Ellis and the men shoved sideways, clearing a place beside Basset. Both priest and Basset sat, the alehouse talk rose up again and closed over whatever their talk might be, and Joliffe and Rose raised eyebrows to each other. The Church had never quite settled how it felt about players. Their craft could be used the same way that paintings on church walls were used: to tell godly stories and show the error of sinful ways, but against that was set the lingering suspicion—and sometimes outright certainty—that the ways of wandering, lordless, landless men were likely to be as sinful as anything their plays might claim to be against.

So it was much each churchman's choice how well or ill he regarded players and happily this Father Morice seemed among the happier-minded sort. Joliffe couldn't watch how things went between him and Basset for long, though, because a village fellow was inching somewhat too close

along the bench to Rose on her other side, with an interested look and his hands beginning to stray her way. A fight
being among the last things the players wanted, Joliffe
gave the man no apparent heed but draped an arm over
Rose's shoulders with seemingly absent-minded affection.
Understanding what he was at, she leaned against him in
return and held up her bowl of ale for him to drink from it.
The village fellow eased away and turned his heed to the
woman on his other side, whose lowering stare at Rose
turned to smiles at him.

Instead, it was Ellis' hard stare across the alehouse Joliffe
met, but Rose saw it, too, and twitched her head slightly
sideways, meaning Ellis to understand there was reason for
Joliffe's arm around her. Ellis flicked a glance at the now
disinterested village fellow, slightly nodded back at Rose,
and returned to his deep talk with the woman who had lately
crowded onto the bench between him and the next man, all
their hips against each other but her eyes for Ellis.

Under her breath, disgustedly, Rose said, "Men."

"Hai," Joliffe protested.

"You, too," Rose said and shifted, without making show
of it, from under his arm as she turned to the woman for-
merly glowering at her and struck up talk across the man
between them.

The last Joliffe heard was Rose asking if anyone in the
village might be willing to do laundry for pay. "Just keeping
these men mended takes all my time," she said—unfairly,
Joliffe thought; but the other woman nodded with full understanding and started a friendly answer, while the man between them began to look uncomfortable. Leaving Rose to
it, Joliffe rejoined the talk of the other men around him.

Basset made to leave not long thereafter when Father
Morice did, the two of them talking together all the way to
the door and out, Father Morice giving wordless, good-
humoured waves and nods to all the farewells called out to

him. Joliffe, Rose, and Ellis broke off their own various talk and followed them, finding them still talking outside in the spread of yellow light from the lantern hung beside the alehouse door. Beyond the light's reach, the over-clouded darkness was like a black wall, save for another lantern hanging beside a door across and farther along the street. As the players joined Basset, Father Morice was pointing that way and saying, "There's my door. Might I offer you a light to see you on your way?"

"My thanks," Basset said, "but I think my daughter has provided for us."

Used to the deep country darkness that came with night-fall, Rose had indeed brought their own lantern with its panes of thin-cut horn. It had been between her feet in the alehouse and now she handed it from under her cloak to El-lis, who lighted its candle-stub at the alehouse lantern's while Basset made them known, each by name, to Father Morice, who said how much he looked forward to seeing them play. Then he and Basset made their cordial farewells and he went homeward with confidence through the famil-iar darkness between the alehouse and his own doorstep.

With less confidence, the players headed back toward the common, enclosed in their own yellow circle of lantern-light, fretted with their shadows so the ground was uncer-tain underfoot. Nor did they talk until they were as sure as they might be in the dark that they were alone, when Ellis, holding the lantern high but his other arm around Rose's waist, said, "The priest came in knowing all about us, but did I hear right that he'd been at the manor all day, dealing over this marriage business?"

"He was and didn't much want to talk about it," Basset said. "Tired of it, I suppose. But, yes, everyone has heard we're here and will be there tomorrow because, as we well guessed, the young man who wanted us to play again is Will Deneby, Sir Edmund's heir. He's also Father Morice's

student, though presently unlessoned while Father Morice
helps with the marriage talks, and Father Morice speaks of
him with affection and some praise as an estimable and
worthy young man."

"You drank too much," Rose said. Observing, not accusing. An over-flourish of words was always sign that
Basset had gone somewhat beyond sober limits.

"I did, but the last several cups were paid for by our
good Father Morice . . ."

"Which ensures him being 'good Father Morice' for
some time to come," said Joliffe.

". . . and while you younglings indulged in idle listening
to all and sundry, I plied our priest for information at
length about Sir Edmund and his family."

"Did you learn anything?" Ellis demanded.

"That Sir Edmund is a generous lord, who sits his own
manor-court," when that task was often left to a manor's
steward or bailiff or reeve, "and against whom there are no
great complaints."

"But . . . ?" asked Joliffe, not of what Basset had said,
but of the shadow faintly behind the words.

"But," Basset echoed. "Yes. But. I don't know the but.
Nor am I sure it's against Sir Edmund. And of Lady Benedicta, the wife, Father Morice would not talk at all beyond
granting her to be a gracious lady, a good lady, a—"

"A lady he'd best not say anything bad about?" Joliffe
suggested.

Although Joliffe could not see Basset's face in the shadows, there was a thoughtful frown in his voice as he answered, "Maybe that. Or maybe she's a lady about whom
nothing can be said at all, she is so slight a being, of naught
but gowns and gauds, of little wit and less—"

"What about this marriage?" Ellis asked. "Are we going
to be playing to people who are glad about it or unglad?"
Because there were few things more disheartening than

playing to folk set into a determined dark humour, not only unready to be diverted but sometimes ready to be angry at anyone who tried it.

"Ah, the marriage," Basset said in the mellow tones that told he was about to wax eloquent.

Rose, as able as anyone to see it coming, said briskly, "Hush. We'll be waking Piers. Tell us tomorrow."

"Tomorrow," Basset said. "The other day that haunts our dreams and hopes for evermore. The day that—"

"The marriage," Ellis whispered fiercely, not willing to wait for tomorrow.

"Happiness all around," Basset whispered back, "and everyone in haste to have it happen."

Which left only the matter of why Lord Lovell had set them to spy here, Joliffe thought.

Chapter 4

The manor of Deneby was set in a wide valley among low, sheep-cropped hills thickly banded along their foot by a stretch of forest. The village with its squat-towered church sat near the valley's lower end, the hedge-bordered great fields spread out around it, with Sir Edmund's manor house farther on, marked by a round tower above a tight cluster of slate-roofed great hall and thatch-roofed lesser buildings, all surrounded by a tall stone wall and a wide moat fed by the stream.

Moats could be stinking things, stagnant and foul, but the stream's flow had this one running clear. Joliffe could see the green ripple of water plants and the shadowy movement of fish in its depths as the company crossed over the wooden bridge from road to manor gateway. Ahead of him Basset and Ellis were juggling bright fountains of balls and behind them Piers and Gil were deeply bowing and sweeping their hats to either side as if already being applauded by the folk just beginning to gather into the yard to see them arrive. Joliffe came playing his lute behind them, dancing a little to his own lively music, while Rose brought up the rear with Tisbe and the cart. Over breakfast Basset had talked of getting yellow and red ribbons for Tisbe's harness, to match the cart's hood now it was so grand, but presently Tisbe was her plain self, while the rest of them had put on their best street-garb—parti-colored tunics and hosen, gaudy-dyed shoes, over-large hats for Basset, Ellis, and Joliffe, a parti-colored gown for Rose. Piers had been outgrowing the tabard that usually served over his daily clothing at these times—"He grows too much from one day to the next to bother the cost of making him better just yet," Basset had grumbled months ago—but still had his cap with a green popinjay feather and today along with the men and his mother was wearing the proud Lovell tabard.

To Gil, because there had been neither time nor any chance to do better for him, was left Piers' old tabard, laughably too short on him but the best they could do at present. All the way to the manor he had been pulling down on its lower edge as if somehow he could make it cover more of his other clothing; but now that there were people to see him—servants and other household folk gathering into the manor yard—he'd begun to use the tabard's shortness, bringing laughter at himself with a flaunt of hip here, a buttock-revealing bow there, a sudden feigned shyness and renewed tugging at the tabard when he caught a girl's gaze on him.

Joliffe had started the day heavy with wondering what they would find once they were at the manor hall. For all that everything had seemed well enough in talk in the village, Lord Lovell was no fool, to be seeing trouble where there wasn't any, and to that had been added worry at how Gil would be. Because no one else had been showing their probably like-worry, he had kept his own to himself, but now—watching Gil caper and play to the lookers-on—his own spirits rose past pretended merriment into true. If Gil proved to be anything like so good as he so far seemed to be, they would owe Lord Lovell far more than they already did, whatever bother there might be with Denebys in the meanwhile.

Supposing Gil was what he seemed and not a spy set on them by Lord Lovell.

That was a thought Joliffe wished his mind had not bothered to have.

Their little band of merriment drew up in the middle of the yard beyond the gatehouse. Perhaps fifty yards from end to end and almost as wide, the yard was surrounded on three sides by various byres and sheds and stables, while directly across from the gateway was the high-roofed, tall-windowed great hall, not so new as Lord Lovell's lately built at Minster Lovell but fine enough to tell the Denebys were no slight family. The round, stone-built tower seen from down the valley, standing at the hall's right end, was older than the hall, with stark, plain lines and narrow windows, its one outer door a full story above the ground, all for better defense when defense was more an everyday matter in England than it presently was. The door was reached by worn stone stairs sheltered by a penticed roof slanted out from the stone wall of the tower, with a stone porch at the top that had originally been small, to keep enough men from gathering there for any strong assault on the door. With assault no longer a likelihood, a wider porch had been made of wood and extended past the tower into a covered walkway to the roofed upper gallery running the whole length of a long, new building along the yard beyond it. By the line of doors both along the gallery above and at ground level below, Joliffe guessed there was a whole wing of rooms there, more comfortable than whatever had been in the old stone tower.

By all that, Sir Edmund looked to be a prospering

knight with a firm hand on matters around him, making him well worth Lord Lovell taking trouble over his business, since much of a lord's worth and reputation depended on the worth and reputation of the men allied to him and Sir Edmund looked to be an ally worth the having.

Basset tossed his juggling balls to Ellis, shifted his manner to dignified, and strode forward alone to meet the man coming toward them from the hall doorway, servants clearing a way for him. He was a hollow-chested fellow with the drawn-in face of a man not in the best of health. Joliffe judged by his simple over-gown that he was not Sir Edmund, was probably the household's steward, and to him but likewise for all to hear, Basset boldly announced that he and his company were come at Lord Lovell's bidding as a gift to give sport and merriment and goodly plays for the delight of Sir Edmund Deneby, his household, and guests this happy time until his daughter's wedding.

"And afterward, too," Basset finished with a low bow and sweep of his hat, "if it should be Sir Edmund's gracious pleasure."

The steward replied in kind, with thanks both to Basset and Lord Lovell, adding assurance of Sir Edmund's grateful pleasure at their being here. That, Joliffe thought, was the kind of welcome being a lord's players got you and far better than many they'd had over the years.

Basset and the steward fell into quieter talk then—the steward apologizing that with the guests and their people already here and those expected later, the players must be given somewhere less to stay than otherwise they might. Basset replied that so long as it was somewhere they could be private to ready themselves for Sir Edmund's pleasure and keep the goods of their craft safe and secret, they would be well satisfied. It ended with a deep bow from Basset and a lesser bow from the steward before he called one of the servants to him, directing they might have use of

the cartshed beyond the carpentry shop, since the great cart
was gone to Oxford—"To fetch the wine for all the feasting
to come," he said—leaving plenteous space for their own.

Basset smiled his respect, stepped back with another
bow, and turned to follow the waiting servant. The rest of
the players followed them both, Ellis making a high dis-
play with the bright balls and Piers leading Gil in a mad-
footed dance to match Joliffe's merry strumming on his
lute while Rose and Tisbe were content with simply following them.

The carpentry shop sat at the far end of the yard, with
a cart-wide gap between it and the stables that led into a
small yard wide enough to bring out and turn the several
carts lined side by side in an open-sided, earth-floored
shed backed against the manor's outer wall. As Ellis
rounded the corner into the cart-yard, he let fall the balls,
catching them all into his arms. Piers likewise ceased
dancing the moment he was beyond sight of the main yard
and Joliffe ceased to play and dropped a hand on Gil's
shoulder to let him know he could stop, too, saying, "Save
yourself for when there's someone to pay for it."

"There's where you can be," their guide said, pointing
toward an empty place at the farther end of the shed.

"What of our horse?" Basset asked. "Will there be sta-
bling for her? Or grazing?"

"Master Henney didn't say. Doubt there's room in stable anyway. Maybe best you keep her here?" the fellow
ventured.

Basset thanked him and slipped a farthing into his hand
in farewell. It wasn't much, but the man beamed at him and
went away, leaving the players looking at each other,
smiles slowly spreading across all their faces.

"This," said Basset for all of them, "is shaping very well."

It was. An honorable reception, a private and dry place to
stay, steady work for a week or more, their meals assured.

Even Ellis, who was given to seeing the darker possibilities in anything, was whistling as they set to their settling in. While Joliffe unhitched Tisbe, Basset and the others debated how best to put the cart into the shed. Fit was no trouble. The "great cart" must be much the size of their own, and the shed was high-eaved enough there was not even need to remove their tilt. Whether to put it in forward or back was the question and finally they decided on back, because it was through the back their hampers of all their goods could easiest be got at, and when they were not here, the cart could be shoved against the rear wall, making everything harder to reach for anyone who shouldn't be there. Not that a determined thief could be stopped by the tilt's canvas or crawling over the forward seat and through the tied curtains behind it, but the idly curious would be kept at bay and there was small likelihood of theft here, because any thief could be too easily found out in the guarded bounds of the manor. But "Better safe to start with than sorry afterwards," Basset said.

"And the shoving the cart back and pulling it forward whenever we go and come will keep you fit," Joliffe said cheerfully, waiting aside with Tisbe while Basset, Ellis, Piers, and Gil began to shift the cart.

Rose came to him, took Tisbe's reins from him, and said in her best mother-voice, "Go and help."

Grinning, Joliffe obeyed.

With the cart in shelter, they changed into their plainer clothing before doing more, not that there was much more to do. With neither room between their cart and the next—nor need under the close-thatched roof—to set up their tent, they only put up the poles with a cloth hung between them that gave Rose a place of her own against the shed's back wall to sleep and dress. For the rest of them, they pulled their bedding out of the cart and stacked it underneath, to be laid out later, both under their cart and between it and the one beside it. "Which happily is not a dung cart," Basset observed.

"Can we have a fire here, do you think?" Rose asked. An open-sided cartshed would not keep as warm around their firepot as a full barn did.

"A very small one should be well enough," Basset said. "In a pit and covered when we're not here."

"Joliffe can collect the wood for it when he takes Tisbe to graze," said Ellis.

Joliffe did not bother to quarrel at that. They would probably be allowed some hay while here but taking Tisbe to graze, too, would both let her fatten a little during her time off from hauling the cart and give him a chance to be somewhat alone while with her. He was not as given to company as his fellow players, and they knew as well as he did how sharp-humoured he could become if he did not sometimes get away. For him to take Tisbe to graze suited everyone.

"The question will be *when* you can take her," Basset said. "We've somewhat of work ahead of us. My thought is to set young Gil to it as soon as might be. What do you say to trying *The Steward and the Devil* tonight? That's good to start with, I think."

He looked around for their assent. Though there were memories that went with playing *The Steward and the Devil,* they all nodded. Gil, having seen it at Minster Lovell, knew it and asked, "I'll be a demon?"

"You will," Basset said. "We still have the large tabard for it?" he asked Rose.

"The tail, too," she said.

"After dinner, then, we'll rehearse you," Basset told Gil, as from the hall someone began to ring a handbell, calling people to the mid-day meal.

The Steward and the Devil was a straight-forward play and one they often did, with Basset playing three parts,

Ellis the Steward, Joliffe the Devil, and Piers as a small but
lively demon who came on at the end to drive the Steward
off to hell. As another demon, Gil would only have to copy
what Piers did—something they had done before when
they'd briefly had to include someone else in the play. Before this morning, Joliffe would have looked on it as a way
to find out how Gil would do before an audience, because
to think of being a player was one thing, to find a group of
strangers staring at every move you made was another, and
more than one would-be player had found himself brought
to a mind-blanked halt at his first moment of it. But coming
into the yard this morning, Gil had carried on as well as
any of them, making it likely he'd do well enough as a
leaping demon following Piers' lead. What would happen
when he was given words to say could be another matter,
but as Basset too often said, "The moment's troubles usually suffice for the moment," and Joliffe put all else aside to
ready for his first sight of Sir Edmund's family and guests,
among whom there might—or might not—be a murderer,
who might—or might not—be going to kill again, depending on how right Lord Lovell's suspicion was.

Or wasn't.

The wide doorway into Deneby's great hall sat at yard-
level rather than over a cellar or undercroft and up any
stairs. When the players came from behind the carpentry
shop, people already crossing the yard toward it turned curious looks their way, and there were some exclaims and
pointing from a small flurry of women hurrying along the
gallery above the yard, but the only person who spoke to
them was a small man who stepped forward to meet them
as they neared the hall. Subdued in manner, gowned in a
plain, brown, ankle-length surcoat and with ink on his fingers, he looked to be a clerk—the steward's clerk, Joliffe
guessed as the man said, "Master Henney said I should see

you to your places in the hall, and ask your names, asking your pardon not to have had them earlier."

He spoke stiffly, very much on his dignity in dealing with them. Other people's dignity at their expense being something to which the players were well-used, Basset merely thanked him graciously and gave their names but at the end asked in return, "And you are?"

That briefly discomposed the man. Servants did not ask such questions back. But that was partly why Basset had done it. Where players fit in the world was never clear, but, whatever they were, they were not anyone's servants. Even Lord Lovell was their patron, not their master. Respectful acceptance of someone's higher place was one thing. Being servile was another. Lacking servants' advantages of set wages and certainty of food and shelter, Basset did not see reason to accept any servants' disadvantages that he could avoid. "If we're going to pay the cost of being players," he had once said, "we might as well have the profit of it, too."

"Even if that and a penny will buy maybe a loaf of bread," Joliffe had said back and been lightly clouted along his head and told that that was not the point and to mind his tongue.

But besides all that, it would be helpful to have the clerk's name, and after an uncertain moment, the man gave way to Basset's polite waiting and said, "I'm William Duffeld, clerk of accounts to Master Henney, Sir Edmund's steward here, whom you have met."

"A fine man," Basset said. "Now, Master Duffeld, would you know if he would permit us to have a small and careful fire where we're staying?"

Duffeld hesitated. "It's the cartshed you're in."

He sounded as if his concern was more for the wooden carts and thatch roof, but Basset readily, cheerily agreed,

"It is indeed the cartshed, and therefore a small fire, kept well-covered when we're not there, will do no harm to anyone and be a comfort to us, the nights drawing in chill and damp this time of year. In truth, as you can see, it would be more than a comfort to us. Our taking a rheum will do our playing no good, and if we do not play, we do not serve Lord Lovell's purpose in having sent us here."

Joliffe did not doubt it was the use of Lord Lovell's name that made the difference. Duffeld hemmed a little but then agreed they might have a small fire.

"And wood for it," Basset said, smiling. "Or allowance for us to gather some for ourselves when we graze our horse. If we may do so."

That was well-done, too. No one would know better than the steward's clerk, whose duties included writing down each day's tally of food and wood used in the household not only by its members but for all guests, the cost of hay and wood. Having already granted them a fire, he was now offered an easy way not only away from wood for it but less hay for their horse, too. The man's calculation was quick. He shortly nodded and said, "I must needs ask Master Henney for a certainty. I'll tell you later what he says, but likely that will serve well. Now if I may see you to your place?"

Basset graciously allowed that he might and they followed him inside, into the low-ceilinged screens passage, its wooden wall shielding the hall from drafts from the outer door. On the left were the butlery and pantry, separated by a passageway to the kitchen. Opposite, a wide doorway through the screen wall opened into the great hall. Wide and long and open to the high rafters, the hall had a low-rimmed long hearth in its middle, flanked by two lines of trestle tables facing each other, running the hall's length to the low dais at the far end and the high table where Sir Edmund, his family, and best guests would sit. They were not come in yet but such of the household as dined in the hall were taking their places along the benches on the outer side of the long tables. Being Lord Lovell's players got Basset and the rest of them a little higher than the very end of one of the tables, only a few of the household's lowest put below them, but since there had been times when they had been denied any place at table at all, they valued the difference.

Basset sat highest, next to an older maidservant with whom he was soon in talk. Joliffe sat next to him, although Ellis had been in the company longer and should have sat there; but Ellis preferred to sit beside Rose, who by rights could have sat above Joliffe, too, but she thought it best to sit beside Piers, and they all—except Piers—agreed he should be at the bottom for the sake of his humility. Not that Piers had ever shown a shadow of anything even distantly resembling humility. That he presently held back from too openly showing his pleasure at being seated above Gil along the table was as near to grace as he was likely to come, to Joliffe's mind.

Joliffe, who didn't much care where he sat so long as it was not at the high table or in the midden, was merely glad to have Rose and Ellis occupied with each other and Basset immediately in talk with the maid, because that left him free to look well around the hall and household. Those who dined here would be the household officers and clerks and better servants, not stablehands and kitchen help and suchlike. These were the people closest to the Denebys and how they behaved would tell much about Sir Edmund and Lady Benedicta. A careless, ill-mannered master tended to have careless, ill-mannered servants. A master with a heavy hand and foul humour had, at best, sullen, wary folk around him or, at worst, people as foul-humoured as himself.

Here, Joliffe was eased to see, folk were well-kept, with easy talk among them and their looks at the players only

curious, not wary or worried. All that boded well, and so
did the signs of Sir Edmund's prosperity around the hall.
The well-plastered walls were freshly painted a rich earth-
red. The wall-hanging behind the high table, painted with
men and women in a flowery meadow, hawks on hand and
hounds among them, was not only large but of good qual-
ity and likely London-made. There were open shelves
standing at one wall, displaying a fine array of silver plat-
ters and goblets and plates against a green damask cloth
draped shelf to shelf from top to bottom. The rushes covering the floor were fresh, the wooden tabletop in front of
him scrubbed clean, and the high table covered by a shin-
ingly white cloth. Everything told that Sir Edmund not
only prospered but used his prosperity well, both for his
own comfort and to impress his guests. A man so well-
given to outward seeming as Sir Edmund looked to be
would probably not be behind-hand in well-rewarding the
players, too, the more especially because they were here at
Lord Lovell's behest.

All that was left to see were Sir Edmund and his family
and guests, and they were entering now through the doorway behind the high table, at the dais' end. First were two
older men who had to be Sir Edmund and the wealthy Master Breche in what looked like friendly talk together as they
went to the two tall-backed chairs at the middle of the table.
Joliffe watched as they delayed sitting down while each
urged the other—to judge by their gestures—to be seated
first. Then they laughed and the man whom Joliffe guessed
to be Master Breche sat first, a stout-waisted man in an
amply cut, long, loose gown of grey wool thickly furred in
black at throat and wrists. He had a merchant's look to him,
while the other man was younger than Joliffe had expected
Sir Edmund to be, in perhaps his late thirties, with a calf-
long, deep crimson gown belted low on his lean waist and
dark hair sleekly cut, his manner graceful as he turned to

seat a woman on the bench to his right while a servant ush-
ered the others to their places along the table.

Basset had been making use of his talk with the maidservant. He leaned away from her to say low-voiced to Joliffe,
"That's Sir Edmund in the red and his lady wife with him."

Joliffe's first thought about Lady Benedicta was that she
was beautiful. There were women on whom their beauty
came young and did not last, and women on whom beauty
came only with the fullness of years, and women on whom
beauty, in the world's sense, never came. However she had
been when young, Lady Benedicta was undeniably beautiful now. Her wide-cauled headdress draped with a short
veil hid her hair but even the length of the hall Joliffe could
see the fine line of her high-arched dark brows above wide-
set eyes and fine cheekbones in the perfectly proportioned
oval of her face. Her trailing gown was of a red brighter
than her husband's, the standing collar closed high under
her chin showing off her long throat the way the long lines
of the gown's thick folds from the green-dyed leather belt
just below her breasts showed off her slender form before
she sat gracefully down.

"That's their daughter, Mariena, on the other side of
Master Breche," Basset said. He cocked his head briefly toward the maid's whisper, then added, "And her betrothed-
to-be beside her."

Joliffe switched his admiring consideration from Lady
Benedicta to them. The young man bowing the girl to the
place beside his uncle before sitting down on her other side
had looks that were nothing beyond the ordinary, but with
youth to recommend them, he was comely enough. The
girl, though . . .

Like her mother, Mariena held the eye. Whether her
beauty was the kind that would last there was no telling,
but at present she had it in plenty, with the same arched
brows and pleasingly proportioned face of her mother, but

as pale and rose as a maiden's was supposed to be. In token
of her maidenhood, her hair—dark like her father's—was
uncovered, and although from where he sat Joliffe could
not tell how long it was, he would have wagered it went to
her waist and more. And a slender waist it was, shown off
by a pale green gown loosely fitted but boldly cut and
curved to leave the sides open far enough down to reveal a
summer-blue undergown close-fitted over breasts and hips.

Young Amyas Breche would be getting a very comely
bride.

Chapter 5

Beside Joliffe, Ellis was looking the same way with openly much the same thought because he said, "There's someone worth their looking at."

Joliffe returned, "If she does anything like so lovely as she is . . ."

Ellis started to laugh but Rose pushed an elbow subtly but firmly into his ribs, silencing him and Joliffe both with a dark look.

They were diverted then by servants coming with the first remove, carrying the first dishes up the hall to the high table with some ceremony. With less ceremony, other servants brought in and set out large bowls of mutton, turnips, and squares of cheese in a thick gravy along the lower tables, one to every two people, for them to spoon onto the thick-cut rounds of day-old bread that served in place of plates at each place. With hunger's first edge eased, Joliffe leaned his head toward Basset and said, "So that's Father Morice beside Amyas Breche, and young Will at the other end of the table. But who's the couple between Will and Lady Benedicta?" A young man and woman with "married couple" all but blazoned on them, well-dressed in sober dark blues with no enriching fur.

"They're the Wyots," Basset said. "Harry was Sir Edmund's ward. Sir Edmund set up his marriage with a merchant who wanted to marry his daughter into the landed gentry." He lowered his voice and leaned a little nearer Joliffe to add, "And that's all Bess here would say about them."

His tone suggested that the *way* she had said no more had told more than what she'd said. An unhappy marriage then? Forced on an unwilling young man who might have preferred to marry Mariena but instead been given to the merchant's daughter? The merchant's daughter was not ill to look at but she was, to put it at the best, plain, and with her married woman's wimple and veil encircling her wide-cheeked face and covering her hair she looked the plainer, contrasted to Mariena. How much did Harry Wyot resent being married to her when he might have had Mariena for his wife?

Come to that, if he was worth a wealthy merchant having him for son-in-law, why *hadn't* he been worth Sir Edmund marrying him to Mariena? There were questions to be asked there.

Another question was why were he and his wife here now?

With disgust, Joliffe realized he was settling easily to the work Lord Lovell has asked of him. It did make everything more interesting, though, and through the meal—and a good meal it was, too, with cod seethed in spiced milk and a frumenty of barley in broth coming next—Joliffe watched, not too openly, the folk at the high table. Sir Edmund and Master Breche kept mostly in what looked to be good-humoured talk with each other, though Sir Edmund occasionally, briefly, spoke to his wife, while Master

Breche exchanged a few comments with Mariena. She was mostly in talk with Amyas on her other side, and very close-headed talk it was. From where he sat, Joliffe could not be sure, but he thought that whenever Amyas passed the goblet they shared, she touched his hand, a not altogether unsuitable gesture since they were about to be betrothed but bold enough that Joliffe began to think she did not object to the match being made for her. Assuredly the young man did not. His attentions to her only faltered when he had to turn and serve Father Morice on his other side for courtesy's sake.

For his part, the priest who had been so ready with talk last night in the tavern today ate with firm heed to his meal and little to the two young people beside him. At the other end of the table Will had it somewhat better. He could have been as odd-man-out as Father Morice, but young Harry Wyot was much in talk with Lady Benedicta, serving her from the dishes set between them and sharing a goblet, so that serving his wife and sharing a goblet with her fell to Will. Being so young, he had to stand to slice the meat and lift it onto her plate and spoon the vegetables and sauces that went with it, all of it better than the plainer stuff served along the lower tables. He did his duty with steady solemnity and in return Mistress Wyot received his courtesy with solemn courtesy of her own and talked with him when she might have ignored him or scorned him for no more than a half-grown boy.

Joliffe found himself liking the boy for his effort and the woman for her kindness, but it was still Lady Benedicta's loveliness and Mariena's beauty that most often drew his eyes, so that only gradually did he become aware of someone's eyes on him. Set at the bottom of the hall, the players and the household folk at the facing table were served by lesser servants whose duty was to get the food on the tables with no bother of ceremony about it. That suited

Joliffe well enough, but he finally began to note that the
woman serving them tended to linger a little longer over
the business than necessary; and when she asked him if she
should bring more bread and he looked full at her, he found
her fullness of breast leaning toward him more than need
be, delaying the lift of his eyes to her face. That did not re-
pel him either. In fact, her smile was very welcoming and
he swallowed before saying he needed no more bread.
"Thank you anyway," he added.

"You've but to ask for what you want," she said, still
smiling as she straightened and headed away with a pleasant swing to her hips.

Down the table, Ellis snorted on a badly smothered
laugh. Rose preferred to pretend she had seen nothing but
did it in a silence that told what she was thinking. Piers,
typically, was more interested in his food, but Gil was
leaned forward to stare along the table at Joliffe in open-
eyed wonder. Joliffe kept his dignity, refusing to know
about anything but the food in front of him until Basset
hastily put down his spoon and began to rise to his feet.

Looking up then, Joliffe found one of the servants from
the hall's upper end was standing across the table, holding
out a small pewter dish with a fine, thick slice of chicken
breast in a white sauce on it. "From Sir Edmund," the man
announced for the hall to hear. "In token of his pleasure at
your presence and that of your company, with thanks to his
right well-honored lord, Lord Lovell."

He set the plate down in front of Basset, and as the rest
of the players rose to their feet, Basset bowed toward the
high table and said in a carrying voice, "My thanks and
that of my company to Sir Edmund, with our hope that we
may please him tonight at supper with a play."

Sir Edmund lifted a hand and bent his head in acceptance. Basset and all the players bowed to him in return and

sat again and the meal went on. Sir Edmund might be only
a knight but he knew high manners and the grace of ceremony. Their stay here was looking better at every turn.

At the meal's end, while the rest of the players returned
to the cartshed, Basset lingered to talk with Master Henney
about their supper being had early, so they would be ready
to perform during supper or at supper's end, whichever Sir
Edmund preferred. Happily, there was no need for them to
rehearse tonight's play. All of them but Gil could probably
have done it sleeping, and a few moments of work showed
him how to do what little he would do at the end. That left
them an easy time then for Rose to get out the garments for
The Steward and the Devil and the rest of them to talk a little about what else they would do while here before going
on with more of Gil's training.

Joliffe, supposing that Basset and Ellis could see to Gil,
asked if he could spend this uncommon leisure time writing over *Dux Moraud,* an old play among the ones they
hadn't used for a time, while he had the chance.

"Are you still set on trying to make that thing work?"
Ellis said. "It's ugly."

"People will love it," Joliffe returned.

"It's sickening."

"You'll play the duke."

Ellis glowered. Whatever he thought about the rest of the
play, the duke's role was too good for him even to pretend
he would not savor it. Their argument over the play always
went this way, but this time he said, "So you're thinking Gil
would play the daughter and you'd be the wife?"

"Yes."

"Then," said Ellis with great satisfaction, "I could at
least play from the heart the part where I order your death."

Piers laughed. Joliffe feigned a clout along side of his
head, and grinning, got out the small, slant-topped box

where he kept ink and quills and what paper they could afford. With that and a cushion, he was about to go to the cartshed's corner beyond their cart and set himself to work when the boy Will came around the corner of the carpentry shop. The look he gave over his shoulder as he came betrayed he was supposed to be somewhere else, and Basset asked him, friendly enough and much as he would have Piers, "In flight from lessons, young master?"

"From my mother. She said I should spend the afternoon with the women. I told her Father Morice wanted me. He'll tell her later he didn't, but by then I won't have been with the women all afternoon."

"Surely your Father Morice wouldn't betray you," Basset said.

"He's not *my* Father Morice," Will said with an edge of scorn. "He's Mother's. She chose him. St. Augustine's is her church, see."

"Her church?" Basset asked, all mild and encouraging interest, not for the mere sake of talk but because the more they understood about the family, the less likely they were to set a foot wrong. "The manor came to your father by marriage, then?"

"Oh, no." Will was brightening under Basset's easy attention to him. "The manor was his all along, but Mother's family held the church and half the village. The families had meant to marry together for years, because Father's family held the mill by Mother's family's manor. If they married, they could trade properties, you see, and it would all suit better. They kept having all sons, though. Both families. Until Mother. So that's why they married, but she kept the right to choose the priest here as part of the marriage agreement and she chose Father Morice." Will dropped his voice as if to impart a secret, his eyes gleaming with mischief. "Father says Father Morice is a waggle-tongued old woman."

Basset chuckled appreciatively. "So you don't mind giving up your tutor for this week or so?"

"No!" Will was triumphant about it.

Openly musing, Basset led on, "It's a long while they're at this marriage talk."

"It's all the dealing they're doing. Who gets what and gives what. Mother says Master Breche is too much the merchant." Will put scorn into the word. "He'll give up no more than he must and as little as may be and yet still have the marriage."

Joliffe held back from pointing out that Sir Edmund must be "merchanting" just as hard if the dealing was going on this long. Instead, he offered, "Still, Father Morice must be well-witted enough, if Sir Edmund wants his help with it all."

Will laughed. "Father says he finds more fiddling small points to be talked out than a mouse finds wheat kernels in a granary."

So the priest was talkative but sharp enough that he was valued by Sir Edmund. And he liked plays. Basset had done well to gain his good will last night. A priest who took against players and could put his case well would have been a bother, if not an outright problem.

Probably thinking they had had enough out of Will for now, Basset said, "But you didn't come to talk, Master William. You came to see what we're doing, and what we're doing is teaching young Gil here how to be a player. Do you want to watch?"

Will did and went willingly where Basset pointed him, to sit on the ground with his back against a cartwheel, out of the way. Joliffe went beyond the cart to the corner he'd chosen, put down the cushion, and sat himself down cross-legged to his work. By long practice, he could shut out what the others were doing when need be and did so now, only distantly aware of Basset and Ellis showing Gil the

different stances a player might strike, depending on what
sort of person he was playing. In time, if Gil lasted as a
player, he would take the needed stance with hardly thinking about it, but for now it would be all dull and driven
work for him.

Joliffe had decided yet again that whoever had first written *Dux Moraud* had little interest in people, only in
preaching, and was trying to give the daughter something
better to say than "Your will be mine in this, my lord and
father" when ordered to kill the baby she'd had by him,
when Piers gave a whoop of laughter on the other side of
the cart and cried out, "You look like you've split something in your gut!"

Bending over with his head almost to the ground to look
under the cart, Joliffe saw Gil in a straddle-legged stance
probably meant to be heroic but closer to what Piers had
said. Surely stung by Piers' laughter, he jerked his feet together, but Basset said sternly at Piers, "You hold your
tongue. I'd rather work at pulling someone back from over-
doing than at trying to make some stiff-sinewed log of a
fellow move at all. It's easier to trim than add on, as your
mother will tell you about sewing. Gil, give Piers no more
heed than you would a cricket chirping. Ellis, show him
again."

Basset somewhat overstated the case for over-playing,
but this was not the time to damage Gil's confidence. That,
Joliffe well knew from his own young days of Basset's
training, would come later when Gil started to be too cock-
sure of himself. He'd then hear far worse about himself
from Basset than what Piers had just said.

Ellis was just taking a heroic stand again for Gil's benefit when a manservant—Joliffe thought the one who had
been with Will yesterday in the village—came into the
cart-yard. Will was scrambling to his feet even before the

man started firmly at him, "You've been missed, Master Will. Best you come before your lady mother begins to worry."

"Well enough, yes, I'm coming, Deykus," Will agreed hurriedly, but he paused in his leaving long enough to tell Basset, "Thank you for letting me watch."

"Our pleasure and honor, sir," Basset said with a bow that Ellis and Piers and Gil copied.

Will almost bowed back but remembered in time they were only players and settled for raising a hand in farewell as he left.

Joliffe sat up straight again and put himself back to work, but shortly Basset said, "Skirts now, I think," and called, "Joliffe, time to take your turn at this."

"Coming," Joliffe agreed, and while he stoppered the inkpot and cleaned the quill's point and stored everything back in his box, Rose got out two of their damsel-skirts from a hamper, was fastening one around Gil's waist when Joliffe stowed the box back into the cart.

Piers, a little more cautious after his grandfather's warning, ventured, albeit grinning, "Gil's blushing."

"At least he's not whining his head off," Joliffe said, starting to put on the other skirt. "The way you do whenever you have to play Griselda's daughter. You'd swear," he added, mock-confidingly to Gil, whose face was indeed trying to reach the rich color of beets, "that he was being gelded instead of girled."

"It's just as bad," Piers muttered.

"You get over pretending to be a girl a lot faster than you'd get over being gelded," Ellis pointed out darkly, though he was no fonder of playing a woman than Piers was.

Still distracting Gil from his embarrassment, Joliffe went on, "Besides, you'll be surprised how women take to a man despite of it. Or," he added thoughtfully, "maybe because of it. They maybe want to find out how much a man he is after seeing him in skirts."

"And St. Genesius knows you're more than willing to show them," said Ellis.

"Children," Basset said in his schoolmaster-in-classroom voice. "Behave. May we begin?"

Despite his unwillingness at the start, Gil did well at his lessoning. By the end of it, he might not have had a girlish swing to his hips yet but he could drop a creditable curtsy. He did tread on his skirt's hem much, but he fell over only once, and when they had finished, Basset allowed it was a promising beginning.

"Better than Joliffe," Ellis said, sitting aside to watch. "Didn't he turn an ankle, almost break it, while he was learning?"

"No," Joliffe protested strongly.

"I remember mending his hems a great many times," Rose offered. "He kept tearing them out with his big feet."

"Everyone picks on me," Joliffe complained.

"It's because it's such fun," Ellis returned.

Lessons finished, Piers and Gil were sent off to fetch water and some hay for Tisbe. Rose took the afternoon's pause to lie down for a rest, and Ellis set to scraping out a firepit in the packed earth floor. Joliffe, before taking a rest himself, went to check Tisbe, tied to the cartshed's end wall and taking life easy. While he was feeling down her legs and seeing that her hooves were clean, Basset joined him, which was reasonable—Tisbe's well-being was their well-being—but Joliffe supposed that Basset had more than Tisbe on his mind, and straightening from her last hoof, said to him, too quietly for anyone else to hear, "You hauled a good bucketful of information out of Will. We know more than we did."

"Not that any of it seems any particular use," Basset

answered, stroking the mare's neck. "But then we couldn't expect that anything even the boy knows would be all that secret. And maybe we'll be fortunate and there won't be any secrets to find out here after all."

"We can only hope," said Joliffe.

Chapter 6

That evening, the play, done in the great hall by torchlight after supper when the household was at ease and ready to be diverted, went well. Gil joined in the deviling with Piers without stumble or fault. "Almost as if you knew what you were doing," Ellis said, slapping him on the back as they made their way back to the cartshed by lantern-light through a soft rain.

"Now if we can just teach him to talk, he may make a player," Joliffe said.

Gil, too happy to mistake their jibing for anything but the friendliness it was, kept saying, "I did it, didn't I? I did it."

"You did indeed do it," Basset assured him.

"Wait until you've done it fifty times and see how you feel about it," Ellis muttered.

"Don't listen to him," Basset said. "Every set of lookers-on and every place we play is different and that makes it a different play every time."

"Not different enough," said Ellis. Rose poked him none too gently in his arm to shut him up.

At the cartshed they changed out of their playing garb, and while Rose put it all away, Basset started a small fire in the firepit and the others laid out the bedding around it. Joliffe saw Ellis whisper in Rose's ear, but she shook her head to whatever he said or asked and turned her back on him, her eyes downcast. Suddenly deeply glum, Ellis kicked his bedding before lying down.

Gil was already into his own bedding and looked to be gone into instant, exhausted sleep as soon as he was under his blanket. The rest of them took hardly longer at it, with Joliffe maybe the last to go into sleep. He was aware of everyone else's evened breathing around him, anyway, as he lay watching the small firelight's orange flickering among the shadows of the cartshed's rafters and roof, thinking, but not much, until he slept, too.

Morning came as damp and drizzling as last night had been, with no comfort from the burned-out fire and only Piers and Gil seeming ready to take on the day cheerfully despite of all. Joliffe had a wary eye for Ellis, who was gone from yesterday's good humour to sullenness, while Basset groaned when he shoved aside his blanket and moved only slowly and with what looked like pain as he made to climb to his feet. Rose, turning over the fire's ashes to find if any embers remained, looked quickly to him. "Your arthritics?" she asked.

"Not *my* arthritics," Basset said firmly. "I never invited or paid them to come and wouldn't keep company with them if I had a choice." Groaning, he used the near cartwheel to pull himself upright, his back and knees straightening unwillingly, before he went on, still firmly, "*Not* my arthritics. Given chance to choose, I'd reject them utterly."

"I'll get your medicine," said Rose. "Ellis, see to these embers, if you will."

Ellis muttered something about the embers being the
only warm thing around here, but Rose gave no sign she
heard him as she went in at the rear of the cart to fetch her
box of simples. Doctors, like so much else in their lives, cost
too much to be indulged in lightly; Rose kept various herbs
and other remedies to hand, treating the company's slight
hurts and ailments herself when there was need. When
Basset's joints flared into pain they were a little helped by
an ointment of mallow and sheep's tallow. It did not cure
but usually at least eased the pain. This morning, though, it
hardly did even that if Basset's hobble when they set out
toward the hall to break their fast was anything by which to
judge. But his stiffness seemed to ease as he walked so that
he was barely limping by the time they crossed the yard.
Only someone who knew him, watching carefully, would
see he moved in pain.

As was usual in great houses, breakfast was laid out on
a long table in the hall—warm, new bread; cheese; cold
meat from last night's supper; ale—for folk to help themselves, eat standing, and get on with the day, with the steward's clerk Duffeld standing by to see that no one ate more
than their share or lingered when they should be to work.
He kept as sharp an eye on the players as on everyone else
and said to Basset when he passed close to him, "You had
hay for your horse yesterday. You'll be taking it out to
graze today?"

"We will, sir," Basset assured him heartily, as if appreci-
ating a fine thought generously offered instead of a near-
complaint curtly given, and moved on before the man
could say more.

Back at the cartshed, Rose piled everyone's cushions on
top of each other against a cartwheel, so Basset could sit
higher than the ground. That left the rest of them to stand,
squat on their heels, or sit on the dirt, but none objected,
pretending not to see how Basset eased himself onto the

stacked cushions, his mouth tight-held to keep in a groan. If he said nothing, then neither would they, but it was always a worse sign when Basset ceased to grumble about his infirmity. His silence when so obviously in pain meant the pain was gone past complaint into plain enduring.

Once he was set, though, he looked them over and said cheerfully, "Here's how I think today should go. Piers, you and Gil will take Tisbe to graze this morning and collect us firewood while you do. The rest of you, we need more talk over what plays we'll be doing these next few days. Then, Joliffe, I want you to get on with your writing, while Ellis and Rose and I go through the garb and properties to be sure of everything. This afternoon we'll continue young Gil's training."

"It's raining," Piers complained.

"You'll not melt," his grandfather assured him.

"Joliffe always takes Tisbe."

That was true but Joliffe suggested, "It will give you chance to tell Gil stories about us all without us overhearing you."

"And smacking you hard for it," Ellis added.

Piers brightened. "Come on, Gil."

"Before you go, though," Basset added, "do duty with the shovel and find the stable's dung heap."

Piers groaned. When on the road they left certain horse-based problems by the wayside when they moved on. Here, lacking that advantage, Tisbe's dung had to be seen to.

"And Gil," Basset went on, "you might as well fill the water bucket again while he does that."

The boys went, and Ellis looked up from wooing the fire to flames again to ask Basset, "Are you planning to play Gil again tonight?"

"Last night gave him confidence. Now we give him training," Basset said. "He's had a taste of applause. He'll take even better to the work."

"So tonight we do what?" Ellis asked.

"I think . . ." Basset paused, looking from Ellis to Joliffe and back again with a glint of mischief. ". . . tonight we'll do *The Fox and the Grapes*."

Joliffe and Ellis both groaned far more loudly than Piers had. Since the play was done in dumbshow and therefore they had no words to remember, it could have been thought an easier play for them to do, but while Basset told the story—beginning where Aesop had but soon turning it into something else altogether—Ellis, Joliffe, and Piers had to play it out, pretending to be more dismayed and frantic and desperate as the story went further and further astray. By the end the lookers-on were helpless with laughter, and Ellis, Joliffe, and Piers were worn out.

Quite aware of their dislike, Basset went on, "I'm gambling they will finish with the marriage talk today and be ready for a release to laughter. Tomorrow and the days after, while the banns are being read, we can do *The Husband Becomes the Wife, The Baker's Cake,* and *Tisbe and Pyramus*. If more is needed, we can decide when the time comes, but I've thought *Griselda the Patient* for the wedding feast, with Gil taking the Daughter . . ."

"And a well-grown little girl he'll be," said Joliffe.

". . . who has but the one speech, but it should please Lord Lovell to see him already at work," Basset went on. "We'll throw in another speech that lets Piers be the son." Someone in the story they had done without until now, Piers having to be the daughter.

Ellis with a wordless grumble and Joliffe with a nod accepted that, both of them trusting Basset's skill at choosing plays that matched an audience's humour of the moment. A very necessary skill among players and one at which Basset was very good.

"Then," said Basset, "to work. Joliffe, some speech for Griselda's lord if you will. You might even add a few lines to Gil's part. This will be, after all"—Basset put on a grand voice—"his first chance to speak as a *player*."

"And if he makes a dog's mess of it," said Ellis, "most people will be too drunk to note it."

"Especially the happy wedding couple, drunk with delight," Joliffe said.

"Um," Ellis agreed. "I thought she looked well-beddable, too."

Ignoring that jibe, Rose said to her father, "You stay sitting. We'll see to things and you'll tell us if we're doing it right. There's a dress I think will do for Gil but it's in the hamper under the cart seat. Ellis, come. You'll have to take out all the others for me to come at it." Which meant she had not ignored the jibe and Ellis was now going to pay for it.

Joliffe took his writing box and the box in which the company's copies of plays were kept back to the corner and out of the way. Piers and Gil returned with cleaned shovel and full water bucket, collected the basket for bringing back firewood, and leading Tisbe between them, left again. Basset, enthroned on his cushions, oversaw Ellis' and Rose's busyness as the hampers came out of the cart. Behind the cart, Joliffe, without a cushion under him today, was aware of the dirt floor's creeping damp until he lost himself in his work. Soon done with adding lines to the Daughter's single speech for Gil and another speech for Ellis as Griselda's lord, he was resisting the urge to work on *Dux Moraud* again—he was still unsure how to make better believable the duke's turn from depraved depths to utter repentance—in favor something more useable, when Basset raised his voice to say, "Welcome, Master William. You've escaped the bonds of scholarship again?"

Joliffe leaned over to see Will standing under the cartshed's eave, out of the small rain but hesitating to come in as he eyed Ellis and Rose at work while answering

Basset, "For the last time maybe. They're nearly done, they're saying."

"Then doubly welcome," Basset assured him. "Come in, if you will. Two of us are gone, as you see, to graze our horse along the woodshore, but you're welcome to watch what we're doing here. Though you must promise to keep secret whatever secrets of our craft you find out while doing so."

Will promised eagerly that he would and Joliffe returned, smiling, to his work, shutting his ears to Will's questions and Basset's answers about one thing and another. It seemed this was their morning for visitors, though, and the next to come interested Joliffe more. Hearing voices approaching, he looked under the cart again and saw the bridegroom-to-be, Amyas Breche, and Harry Wyot, who had been Sir Edmund's ward, come talking together around the corner of the blacksmith's shed into the cart-yard, followed by the stolid Deykus. Basset stood up to greet them with a bow, as did Ellis while Rose curtsied. Joliffe considered staying where he was and only listening, then decided he would rather see the two men more nearly than the length of the great hall and put aside his work to join the others in time for Basset to introduce him at the end.

He bowed, but neither Amyas Breche nor Harry Wyot gave him much heed, busy with looking over the three open hampers and the array of garb and properties laid out on the closed top of a fourth.

"You get all this into that cart of yours and go around the countryside with it?" Amyas asked.

"We do, sir," Basset said.

"That's a good-looking crown," Harry Wyot said, reaching for it.

"You're not supposed to touch," Will said quickly.

Wyot stopped, surprised. Basset said, fully polite and

apologizing, "It's a rule we have, to keep folk from handling things too much. If you'd like to lift it, though, please do."

Wyot did and said, more surprised, "It weighs so little."

"It's of tin, sir," Basset explained. "A little brass laid thinly over tin is all it is, to make it look of gold. The jewel is glass, of course."

The crown was, in fact, one of their most used properties, kings being always popular on stage, but it would not stand up to hard handling. Wyot set it down carefully. Rose, smiling at him, took it up and put it away in its wooden box while Will asked with a wary look sideways at Deykus, "You haven't come to tell me I'm wanted, have you?"

"No, Will," Amyas assured him. "We've come to escape the women. While my uncle and Sir Edmund do their agreeing together," he said to Basset, "Harry and I have been left to keep much company with the women these past days."

"Until now we're heartily sick of it," Wyot said, "and have escaped."

"That's not it," Amyas protested, laughing. "It's that everything has come around to Mariena's wedding gown and we're far too much in the way."

"Is she going to get a new one after all?" Will said with all a younger brother's indignation.

"Did you think she wouldn't?" Wyot answered mockingly.

"It's tender of her not to want to wear the gown made for her other wedding," Amyas protested.

"It's her way of getting another new gown," Will said, all scornful at Amyas' innocence about such things.

Joliffe, rapidly watching all their faces, thought he saw silent agreement with that statement on Wyot's, but Amyas laughed and shook Will by one shoulder, telling him, "You sound just like a little brother."

Will glowered at him, and Basset quickly took up one of the players' false swords, saying to Amyas and Harry together, "Here's something will make you laugh."

They took turns handling the sword and did laugh at its poor balance, dull edges, and round point, until Amyas, handing it back to Basset, said to Wyot, "Well, it looks as if the rain is stopping. Maybe we'll be able to go hawking this afternoon after all." He cast an arm around Will's shoulders. "Let's see how things are in the mews with the hawks and all, shall we?"

Arm still around Will, he left the boy no real choice about going, but Wyot agreed to it readily enough and they all went, the man Deykus stolidly behind them. With them gone, Basset eased down onto the cushions again and said, "So that's Sir Edmund's second choice of a bridegroom for his girl. Or third. I wonder . . ."

"What are you talking about?" Ellis asked. "Second. Third."

"Hm?" Basset had been thinking aloud without thinking what the others did not know. "Oh. Seems the daughter was nigh married to someone else a few months ago, except he died."

Basset made it sound of little matter, because in the usual way of things that's all it would have been to them; and all Ellis did in answer was shrug and say, "Maybe best we don't do *Tisbe and Pyramus* here then. No tragic deaths of young lovers." Which Ellis would regret, because he was particularly fine as a tragic young lover and his playing of Pyramus could usually bring at least a few women to tears. Joliffe's suggestion that sometime when they played at a village with a stream or pond, they do a *Hero and Leander* so Ellis could try a tragic speech while drowning had yet to be met with anything but Ellis' irk.

"*Robin and Marian* then?" Basset suggested. "That's merry enough."

Piers and Gil came back with their own Tisbe and firewood in time for the mid-day din... Some of this is even dry," Piers said, setting down the wood with an air of triumph, since dry wood for burning was always troublesome to have in wet weather. The trick was to have enough dry wood to burn to dry the wet enough to burn in its turn.

"You are both noble youths of exceeding skill and shall be rewarded as best beseemth," Basset declared. From the direction of the great hall someone began to ring a handbell. "By being fed," Basset finished. He stood up stiffly, with Ellis' hand under his elbow to help him, but again he seemed to better as they walked toward the hall.

At dinner the talk was that all was finally settled about the marriage, agreement fully made, and that Sir Edmund, his family, and guests were to go hawking along the river this afternoon while Father Morice saw to everything being copied out several times over in a fair hand, to be signed this evening before witnesses.

The serving woman was still giving Joliffe enough heed to show she found him more interesting than all the talk of her master's success, and at the meal's end, while the players were leaving the hall, Ellis and Piers ahead in debate over something, and Rose talking with Gil, Basset said quietly to Joliffe, "Now's the time, maybe, for you to hang about the kitchen yard and hear what you can there."

Joliffe almost protested that. He had been thinking about what he might do to their *Robin and Marian* to include Gil, trying to guess how much of a part he could be trusted with just yet, so that spending time in idle servant talk instead did not appeal. But Basset was right. They had at least to try to find out what they could, to meet Lord Lovell's behest. So instead of protest, he nodded agreement and drifted aside, leaving the others to go on without him.

No one seemed to note him as he strolled into the kitchen yard at the near end of the great hall. Separated from the main yard by a waist-high wattle fence, the kitchen's yard was a world unto itself, with the tall-chimneyed kitchen linked by a covered walkway to the hall's rear door and at its other side what was surely the bakehouse. Between kitchen and bakehouse was a stone-walled well sheltered under a low-pitched roof on tall posts. Joliffe strolled that way. Knowing better than to put himself into harm's way in a kitchen where clean-up after a meal was going on, he leaned himself against one of the posts like someone with nothing else to do and nowhere else to be and waited.

He hadn't waited long before a half-grown girl in a greasy apron came out the kitchen door, carrying a wooden bucket, coming to the well. She smiled shyly at him as she came and he smiled back and went to the well ahead of her, to send the bucket there down into the dark with a splash. He was winding it back up when she set her empty one on the well-rim and said, "You're one of the players, aren't you?"

"I am," Joliffe agreed. He paused in drawing up the bucket to make her a small bow.

She smothered a smile with a dirty hand and made a small curtsy back to him. Joliffe swung the well's dripping bucket to the well-edge and filled hers, let the well bucket go, and handed hers to her. She never took her eyes from him while he did but thanked him as she took it and then, openly deciding to be very brave, said, "I liked the play last night."

"I'm glad you got to see it."

The girl hesitated, decided to be even more bold, and asked, "You aren't really a devil, though?" The part he had played in last night's play. "Are you?"

"No more than I'm the blushing maiden you'll see me pretend to be another of these nights," Joliffe assured her, looking as benign as he possibly could.

The girl gave a bubbling laugh, said, "I'll tell Sia you're here," and went away, back to the kitchen.

Little doubting who Sia was, Joliffe had almost no wait at all before the maidservant who'd been making bold at him in the hall came out, likewise carrying a bucket. Joliffe again sent the well's bucket down and was drawing it up when Sia, with none of the girl's shyness, joined him, standing with her hip hardly a handsbreadth away from his, not touching but temptingly close, just as her lips were temptingly close when she looked slantwise up at him from under her eyelashes and smiled with a sweetness that said she was here for more than water.

Joliffe returned her slantwise look and promise-of-something-more smile and said, "I'm supposed to find out what I can about the household, to help with better choosing what we'll play for them. Will you talk with me a while?"

"Talk?" Her hip drifted slightly toward him, brushing against his doublet. "I'll gladly talk." Letting him know she'd gladly do more than that.

Aware of his own charms though he was, Joliffe thought her lust seemed a general thing rather than particular to him—as if he were a male-body to be used, rather than someone who, in himself, interested her at all. That was fair enough, though, he supposed, since he was here in like hope of using her. Albeit in a different sense from her clear intent for him. It relieved him of any scruple he might have had; he could hardly lead her on when she was already so far ahead of him, and smiling, he nodded for her to set her bucket on the well-rim, pulled the full bucket to him, and emptied it into hers, asking while he did, "Is everyone as pleased about this coming marriage as they seem to be? Can we count on happy folk when we perform?"

"Aye, they're all pleased enough. Master Henney says Sir Edmund and Master Breche have come to an agreement that suits them both, so they're happy. That Amyas likes the look of Mariena and doesn't know better, so he's happy . . ."

"Doesn't know better?" Joliffe asked, smiling into her eyes.

"You know." Sia shrugged one shoulder forward, in a way that shifted one of her breasts toward him. "She's lovely. He'll have her and a goodly dowry, too. What else does he have to think about it? He'll find out," Sia added darkly.

"Less lovely within than without?" Joliffe suggested.

"She likes her own way, let's say."

And who doesn't? Joliffe thought. The trouble was that most couldn't get their own way as often as they liked. "He's not known her long, then?" he asked.

"Just these two weeks while Sir Edmund and Master Breche have been dealing here."

"How did it come about, this dealing? Sir Edmund and Master Breche knew each other but Amyas hadn't met Mariena?"

He had set the emptied bucket down beside hers, his hand still resting on its rim. Sia moved her hand from her bucket's rim to his, just touching his fingertips with her own while she said, "They've only just met, too, Sir Edmund and Master Breche. It was Mistress Wyot's father told Master Breche there was this chance of marrying up. Out of the town into the gentry, see."

"Ah," Joliffe said, sounding as if now he understood it all. He let his fingers stray forward onto hers and stroked gently along them to the back of her hand. "But if Sir Edmund is willing to marry his daughter that way, what about Harry Wyot? Wasn't he Sir Edmund's ward? Why wasn't he married to Mariena? Wasn't he rich enough?"

Sia gave a small, warm laugh. "He's rich enough. But he wouldn't." She turned her hand over, took gentle hold on

Joliffe's, and drew it toward her. "He refused to marry her, flat out."

"Sir Edmund didn't hold his marriage-right then?" The right that let whoever held it choose whom an under-aged heir would marry—taking the profit from that marriage either by way of marrying a child of his own to the ward or selling the ward in marriage to someone else.

"He held it, right enough." Sia was enjoying herself, tattling to someone for whom it was all new. "But Harry Wyot wouldn't marry her. There was yelling about it, let me tell you. Sir Edmund swore he would and Harry swore he wouldn't and it ended up he didn't."

"Why wouldn't he?"

"Knew her too well, very like. Was brought up here in the household from when he was half-grown. Lady Benedicta didn't favor the marriage either, and that helped him. She maybe even warned him off it, we've thought." Sia shifted so no one looking from kitchen or bakehouse could see as she laid Joliffe's hand to her hip, her own hand over his to hold him there while she smiled into his eyes. "So Sir Edmund sold him to Master Coket of Cirencester for Master Coket's daughter, this Idonea. Master Coket is a draper there and . . ." Sia leaned nearer Joliffe to say low in his ear, one breast touching him, "It's said Sir Edmund owed him money and paid him off with Harry Wyot. Settled his debts and paid back Harry for refusing a knight's daughter by sticking him with a merchant's girl instead. Harry goes down and Idonea Coket comes up. They're even still living with her family because he's not of age yet."

Despite Sia straightened away from him as she finished, Joliffe found he was having trouble keeping his mind to his questions but asked, "Harry Wyot didn't object?"

Sia frowned, not at Joliffe's hand now feeling at her hip but with thought. "He didn't. It was more like he was glad of it. Of marrying her. And maybe of being away from here."

"He's back now, though."

"That's because he's turned friends with this Amyas Breche in Cirencester. He's here to keep him company."

"I heard there was try at another marriage not so long ago."

"Oh, now that was sad, it was." Sia looked truly distressed. "That John Harcourt was as comely a young man as you could want. And mannerly." For a moment, a dream of how things could be softened Sia's voice with something besides lust, while Joliffe realized this was the first time he had heard the man's name. Sia was gazing past him into the distance of some place she would never go and said softly, "It was something to see them together. Him all gallant and Mariena all loveliness."

Another maidservant came out from the kitchen and started across the kitchen-yard toward them and Sia snapped back from her dreaming. "And then he died," she said abruptly.

"Sia!" the other maid called in a hushed, urgent voice. "You're missed. You'd best come back."

Sia gave a put-upon sigh, leaned briefly into Joliffe's hand on her hip, smiled into his face, and asked, "Later?"

"Later," he promised. She started away. He held onto her skirt, stopping her. "The water?" he said.

With an impatient click of her tongue, she turned to take the bucket with her. The other maid reached them, saying, "Sia . . ."

"I know," Sia said back and hurried away, sloshing water as she went.

The other maid lingered. Like Sia, she had a pretty enough face but was more full of body—someone easy to take hold on in bed, as the saying went. Before Joliffe could decide what her look of speculation at him meant, she asked, "That other player, the dark one, is he married to that woman with you?"

"Ellis? No, he's not married."

The maid gleamed a wide smile. "Tell him I'm not either but . . ."

"Avice!" Sia hissed loudly over her shoulder.

"Coming!" Avice shouted, then dropped her voice again to finish her message. ". . . but I like a warm bed, tell him."

"A warm bed and a merry one?" Joliffe asked.

Avice's smile widened. "A very merry one. You tell him."

"I will. Mind if I remember it myself?"

Avice laughed and said merrily as she went away, "I wouldn't mind, like, but Sia would."

Chapter 7

As Joliffe left the kitchen yard, saddled horses were being led past the tower toward the long building beyond it, where Sir Edmund was coming down the stairs from the open upper gallery, graciously leading his wife by one hand, her other hand gathering her skirts away from her feet, with Master Breche behind them, then Amyas leading Mariena, followed by the Wyots, with Will coming last.

Off to their hawking, Joliffe supposed, and lingered in the kitchen-yard gateway to watch them. Knowing more about them than he had made that watching the more interesting. Sir Edmund lifted his wife up to her side-saddle and they spoke briefly, unsmiling but courteous enough. If Sia had it right and Lady Benedicta *had* opposed him over marrying their daughter to Harry Wyot, it meant Lady Benedicta had a mind of her own and used it, not necessarily to her husband's good. That was something to hold in mind. That, and the fact they kept at least outward courtesy to each other.

Then there were Mariena and Amyas. Given they were all but betrothed, Joliffe had half-thought she would ride pillion behind him, an allowable familiarity; but Amyas was lifting her to her own saddle, while a stablehand waited with another horse for him. Whose choice was it that they ride apart, Joliffe wondered. Not Amyas', certainly. His hands lingered on Mariena's slender waist under her cloak once she was in the saddle. Her head was bare, her dark hair loosely braided, with soft tendrils already straying loose around her face. Even across the yard, her loveliness was a pleasure to gaze upon. Joliffe did not wonder that Amyas' hands lingered as she leaned forward, her face briefly above and temptingly near his.

Then she straightened and he stepped back and turned hastily to his own horse, to mount and bring it close beside hers. Whoever's choice it was that they ride apart, Joliffe doubted it was theirs. He guessed, too, not having heard otherwise, that she had accepted quietly her father's several choices of husband for her: so despite her insistence on another wedding dress, Mariena must be biddable in most matters. About that new bridal gown, there was no way to know whether Amyas or Will was right—whether she was tender-hearted maiden or greedy girl—since neither a love-blinded youth nor a jealous little brother were likely to be a good judge. Watching her gather up her reins and turn her horse to follow her parents toward the gateway, Joliffe was willing to accept she was merely a soon-to-be-married young woman with presently very little choice about her life and therefore insisting on one of the few things she might most reasonably insist on—a new gown for her wedding. That Sia disliked her meant little. Given the difference between their lives, how could Sia not dislike her?

But why had Harry Wyot refused to marry her? That had cost him trouble and money; refusing an offered

marriage always cost a ward a hearty fine to whoever held
his marriage right. Nor could Wyot have known that instead of whatever comfortable marriage portion would
come with a wealthy knight's daughter, he would end up
with a wealthy merchant's daughter instead and no worse
off, save that his wife was nowhere near the beauty
Mariena was. Even so, there seemed to be affection there,
Joliffe thought. Mistress Wyot was the one woman riding
pillion, seated sideways behind her husband on a solid grey
gelding, her arm around his waist and laughing at something Wyot, smiling, was saying over his shoulder to her.

The riders rode away, out the gateway and across the
drawbridge, and Joliffe went onward toward the cartshed,
taking his thoughts with him. Whatever quarrel there had
been between Sir Edmund and Harry Wyot must be over
now, forgiven and forgotten, since Harry was here and had
not warned his friend against a marriage he had refused for
himself. Or had he warned his friend, only to find Amyas
was brave enough to dare what he had not? Brave—or else
too foolish to take the warning?

Either way, that was by the way. It was about John Harcourt's death they needed to know more, to see if there
looked to be any threat to Amyas Breche that same way.
For that, there was need to fall into talk with other folk
here at leisurely length, to learn what else he could about
everyone and everything. And surely talk more with Sia,
who was so willing to it. Nor did he mind that talk with her
would likely lead to something more than talk. No, indeed,
he did not mind that at all.

In the meanwhile, he should keep in mind one other
thing he had learned from her: Sir Edmund had been
enough in debt to need Harry Wyot's marriage to pay off
what he owed. What bearing that might have on anything,
Joliffe didn't know. It was simply something to keep along
with the accompanying question of whether Sir Edmund

might be in debt again and in need of another prosperous marriage. Had the proposed Harcourt marriage been as rich a one as this Breche one? Could Sir Edmund have found out the Harcourt one was not as rich as he needed it to be but too late for any way out from it but the bridegroom's death?

Joliffe would have answers to none of those questions from Sia, that was sure, but what of Father Morice? It was maybe time for Basset to find reason to talk with him again. Not that direct answers could be had, since direct questions could not be asked, but Basset might learn something around the edges, as it were.

Joliffe's thoughts and legs had him back to the cartshed by then, and for next while of the day he worked at writing, and Basset worked with Gil's speaking, and Ellis and Piers oiled Tisbe's harness, and Rose mended one of Piers' hosen, refusing to admit it was out-grown and would only rip again next time he wore it. The carpenter was not at work today, and with all the other manor-sounds muted beyond the buildings and Tisbe slumbering with one twitching ear in the cart-yard's sunlight, it was as peaceful as their lives ever were. Nearly, Joliffe could have dozed along with Tisbe.

The peace was jarred to an end by the thudding clatter of horses crossing the drawbridge over the moat. Ellis, pausing over a bridle strap, said, "If that's the hunters, they're back soon."

"Maybe it's some guests come for the betrothal?" Joliffe suggested.

"I'll see," said Piers, dropping the rein he was oiling and leaping to his feet.

"Just you stay here," Ellis ordered. "Don't . . ." But Piers was already away and Ellis muttered darkly about what he'd do when the whelp came back; but when Piers did, after not very long, Ellis only asked impatiently, "Well? Guests or what?"

"It was Will," Piers said. "And everybody else. Will took a fall. They had to bring him back."

"He's badly hurt?" Basset demanded.

"I'd guess not," Piers said lightly. "He was on his own feet, anyway, when the women rushed him up the stairs. He was dripping, though, like he'd fallen in water or on boggy ground. But not hurt, no."

"You will be if you don't get on with that rein," Ellis threatened.

"Rein, rein, gives me a sprain," Piers mocked; but he sat to the work again and something of quiet came back. For a while there were voices and horse-sounds from the nearby stable as the hunters' mounts were groomed and stalled, but that settled and time passed. The fit of sunshine that had graced the early afternoon was replaced with grey clouds, Ellis and Piers finished with the harness, and Joliffe was come out of the corner to watch Basset lessoning Gil when a house-servant came into the cart-yard, so evidently on an errand that Basset made to stand up from the cushion pile, to receive whatever message the man brought.

Rose's medicine had eased all but the worst of his arthritic pains but the effort cost him, and when the servant said, "My Lady Benedicta would have you come to her in her chamber to talk about what you've planned to play these next days," Joliffe inwardly winced for Basset's sake. Lady Benedicta's chamber was surely up one set of steep stairs or another, and when Basset's arthritics were flaring like today, stairs were a torment and difficulty. But Basset was equal to the trouble. He gave a single bow of his head in gracious acceptance of the message and said, "It would be my pleasure if I were fit for it. Being somewhat unwell, though, I'll spare her my presence and send Master Ripon in my stead. He knows my mind in all of it as well as I do."

Joliffe stepped forward.

The servant shrugged. "It's all one to me. Just so some-one comes."

While Joliffe straightened his tunic and pulled up his hose to smoothness, Rose made a quick brush down his back, reminded him with "Rump" to brush off where he'd been sitting, gave him a hard look from feet to hair, and nodded he was presentable. He made her a low bow of thanks and gestured to the servant to lead onward. He had no objection at all to seeing closer the heart of the Deneby household and was the more pleased when the man led him across the yard to the stairs up to the round tower.

Stone-built and squat, ungraceful but thick-walled for defense, the tower had probably been there since the earliest days of the manor, its arrow-slit windows showing it was meant to face dangers not likely now in these far more set-tled days. What had to be the original door—thick oak planks studded with broad-headed nails—stood open at the stair-head. Inside, a single chamber took up the tower at that level. From the brief sight of it he had, Joliffe judged it to be a solar and council chamber, sparely but comfortably fur-nished, with what had been an arrow-slit in the far wall widened into a fair-sized window, giving the chamber day-light it would otherwise have lacked. Below, in the tower's windowless lowest level, would be storage. Above would be Sir Edmund's and Lady Benedicta's more private chamber, Joliffe guessed as he turned to follow his guide through a narrow, stone-framed doorway and up a long curve of stairs built into the thickness of the tower's wall. Narrow and dark save where a little daylight fell through an arrow-slit, they were somewhat worn with the several hundred years of use they had probably had and Joliffe went careful-footed, ready for the usual one step made higher than the others to betray an attacker into a stumble, making him easier victim for whoever might be fighting up the stairs in retreat.

The step came and he did not stumble, and at another
stone-framed doorway his guide turned into a chamber like
the one below, save here was clearly more a woman's
world. Close-woven reed matting covered most of the floor
for warmth and comfort, and a window twice larger than in
the lower chamber had been cut through the south curve of
the tower's wall. The wide stone windowseat under it was
softened with bright cushions, while the ceiling beams
were painted a gay yellow and the walls were a deep au-
tumnal red with a hunting scene of galloping riders and
leaping stags drawn in white outline all around. Set against
one wall was a broad, tall bed hung with blue curtains em-
broidered in a red chevron pattern, with coverlet that
matched. A wooden chest nearly as wide as the bed itself
sat at the bedfoot, the Deneby arms deeply carved and
brightly painted on its front, a woman's needlework basket
and a folded heap of richly blue cloth sitting on its flat top.
Other women's things were here and there around the
room, too, not untidily but giving the sense of a room well-
lived-in as well as presently over-crowded, with not only
Lady Benedicta there, seated on the bed's edge, and
Mariena standing at the window, but Mistress Wyot, too,
perched uneasily on a curve-backed chair with sewing in
her hands, and several maidservants bustling, and Will sitting gloomily near the fireplace on a low stool, wrapped to
his ears in a fur-collared cloak far too large to be his own.

The fireplace was the least expected thing about the
chamber. At some time, the stone around one ancient narrow window had been chipped away to make a hearth and
the gap then stone-hooded to chimney the smoke out the
window-slit. Though still early in the autumn for a hearth-
fire, one was blazing high there just now, surely for Will's
sake, because close by was a high-sided metal tub with
soap-scummed bath-water still in it but two maidservants—
one of them Sia—beginning to empty it.

Best, of course, would have been sturdy men to carry the tub down the stairs and out to dump it all at once but there was no question of carrying anything the tub's size and full of water down the tower's stairs. The water had come up bucketful by bucketful, probably hot from the washhouse and re-warmed beside the fire, and now it would go bucketful by bucketful out the window, with Sia scooping water out with a bucket to pour into another bucket for the other maidservant to carry across the chamber to empty out the window while Sia filled a third bucket to have ready when she returned. Since the tub was large and the buckets, for the sake of not spilling, could not be filled, this was going to take some while.

Will's fall must have been disastrously wet and muddy to warrant this much trouble, but as Piers had reported, he seemed unhurt, except perhaps in his dignity. He assuredly did not look to be enjoying himself here.

"One of the players, my lady," Joliffe's guide said with a bow to Lady Benedicta.

Joliffe bowed, too, but found Lady Benedicta somewhat frowning at him when he straightened.

"It wasn't you who spoke in the hall yesterday," she said while making a small beckon at the servant that he should leave. "You're not the head of your company, are you?"

"No, my lady," Joliffe said with another, slighter bow. "But Master Basset is somewhat unwell today—a passing rheum—and sent me in his stead. I'm bid to ask your pardon and tell you that I know his mind in the matter—what he intends for your household's and guests' pleasure this week."

Lady Benedicta accepted that with a small bow of her head and, "Tell him I send my regret for his discomfort. Does he have anything to ease it?"

"He does, my lady. My thanks, though, for your asking."

"Of course. Now draw over that stool. We'll talk."

With another small movement of one hand, she showed him a joint stool not far from where Will was sitting. Joliffe fetched it, thinking that Lady Benedicta, with her small movements and short words, was not a giving sort of woman. Her courtesy in letting him sit while they talked was something, though, and Joliffe smiled at Will as he picked up the joint stool. Will gave back an unhappy grimace, then slid around to face his mother and ask, "Can I get dressed and go now?"

"You may not. If you know no better than to fall into mud and water, we must all suffer the consequences."

"My saddle slipped!" Will sounded as if he had already protested that more than once. "It slid right around and dumped me. It wasn't my fault!"

"You will learn," his mother said coldly, "to check your own saddle girth, not trust it to servants."

"Can't Sia take him to the kitchen?" said Mariena from the window. Her voice—this first time Joliffe had heard it—was pleasant and a little laughing at her brother. "He'd keep even warmer there and be out of the way."

"He'll stay—" Lady Benedicta began.

"I am warm!" Will said.

"—until I'm satisfied he's taken no harm," Lady Benedicta finished.

"He's not hurt. Hear how he keeps whining," Mariena said. "Send him to whine somewhere else."

Will threw an angry look at her and opened his mouth to answer, but Lady Benedicta said, "You're whining more than he is, Mariena. Set to your sewing and be quiet."

"I'm tired of sewing."

Mariena did sound truly tired, as if worn with hours of it, but Lady Benedicta answered with asperity, "It was you who wanted this second wedding dress. There's no reason the rest of us have to suffer for it *without you do, too*." She slightly turned her head toward Mistress Wyot and said, "Idonea, cease sewing, please."

Seen nearer, Mistress Wyot was somewhat more pleasing than she had appeared at a distance. Although perhaps a little older than her husband and certainly older than Mariena, she was still very young, with youth's bright color in her plump cheeks. Or maybe the color was embarrassment as her hands went idle on the sewing in them and her glance flicked unhappily, uneasily, back and forth between Lady Benedicta and Mariena.

Joliffe watched them all with his face correctly blank of thought or feeling. He was here as hardly better than a servant and a servant's place was to serve, not to hear or see what his betters did among themselves. Servants did see, though, and everything he was seeing told him something of how things were in the heart of the Deneby household, Mistress Wyot looking ill at ease, Will crouched and sullen in the enveloping cloak, Mariena stiff with offense and glaring at her mother, Lady Benedicta sitting straight-backed on the edge of the bed as on a throne, regarding her daughter coldly, waiting for Mariena to choose what she would do.

They were all waiting, even Sia and the other maid, standing unmoving now beside the bath, until finally Mariena, after a long moment of an angry look locked with her mother's, suddenly shrugged, sat down on the end of the window bench, and took up the sewing waiting there. With that, Mistress Wyot began hers again, Will scooted around on his seat to face the fire, putting his back to everyone, and Joliffe returned his look from Mariena to Lady Benedicta, to find her watching him.

He thought he hid how much that disconcerted him, while she said, "My daughter is lovely, yes."

Joliffe held back from saying, "Lovely is as lovely does." Settled for silently bowing.

And that should have been the end of it, but Lady Benedicta went on coldly, "Unfortunately, she is not entirely happy at marrying someone who gives her no title. She had counted on being a lady, like her mother. But it's somewhat too late for that."

Before Joliffe quite sorted out whether Lady Benedicta meant both of the possible meanings to the last part of that, she went on, "So. What does Master Basset purpose for our pleasure?"

He gave himself over to business. Lady Benedicta heard him out, then questioned him more closely about what the players intended for this evening. "It will not go to ribaldry?" she asked.

"Nothing beyond the most mild, my lady," Joliffe assured her, silently setting himself to warn Basset and Ellis. "Master Basset was wondering about the wedding feast, though."

"I want to laugh," Mariena said from the windowseat.

"I'm certain you will," her mother returned without looking at her.

It not being his place to hear such things, Joliffe seemed not to and went on, "Master Basset had thought *Griselda the Patient* might serve."

"I know the story, but tell me how you play it," Lady Benedicta directed.

"Might I say it quietly?" Joliffe asked. "Rather than give all away to everyone?"

Barely lifting her hand from her lap, Lady Benedicta made a beckon for him to come nearer. Leaving the joint stool, Joliffe did and knelt on one knee beside her, not minded to stand bent over while he talked low-voiced to her. Thus far he judged her a stiff, ungenerous woman, curt of words and doing her duty toward her son without show of particular affection. He half-expected her to give him trouble for trouble's sake over what he told her, but she did not and her few questions were well-made and to the point. Only at the end did she raise her voice to say, just loudly enough to carry across the chamber, "*Griselda the Patient* sounds satisfactory indeed. Though there are some who won't agree."

She did not look toward Mariena as she said it, but Joliffe and probably no one else in the chamber had doubt where the words were aimed. Mariena jerked her head up from her sewing as if about to answer sharply, but Lady Benedicta forestalled her, saying in the same raised voice to Sia and the other maid, just finishing with emptying the tub, "Thank you. You may go. Tell Fulk and Gefri to come when they can to take it away."

Mariena threw aside her sewing, stood up, and without asking her mother's leave, went out of the chamber while the maids were curtsying to Lady Benedicta, who ignored her daughter, only saying to Joliffe while the maids gathered up the buckets and towels and left, "Please tell Master Basset I'm well-content with what you've told me. If there's aught that your company needs, either toward the plays or your comfort, let me hear of it."

Joliffe rose to his feet and bowed his thanks, was about to assure they were well-content when he saw Will looking sad-eyed at him over the furred edge of the vast cloak, and said before he thought better of it, "One thing, my lady. Your son has taken interest in what we do. May he have leave to keep us company sometimes while we're here?" And added in inspired after-thought, "With his tutor, if that would make it better."

Lady Benedicta looked from him to Will sitting suddenly straighter and brighter-eyed, and for the first time the possibility of a smile lightened her own face. It did not quite happen but she was near to it and said, "Father Morice might enjoy the respite after the work we've put him to of late. Yes. Will may spend time with you if he wishes."

Will shot to his feet, exclaiming gladly, "Mother!"

"Sit down. You'll let a draught under the cloak and take a chill," she ordered at him. He sat, still beaming, and she said to Joliffe, "It will be for Master Basset to say whether Will is in the way or not, and for him to send Will away when he wishes." She looked at Will. "Understood?" He nodded eagerly. She returned her look to Joliffe, who noted for the first time her fine eyes, deep-set and dark, before she dismissed him with a nod of her own. He bowed again and withdrew, hearing her say behind him as he started down the stairs, "Idonea, how goes the sleeve?"

He was on the curve of the stairs beyond sight of anyone at their head or foot when he met Mariena coming up. In the stone-walled narrowness he stepped as much aside as he could, flattening his back to the wall to let her pass. Though she had to turn sideways, too, there was room for her to pass without touching him but she did—and more than touched. She brushed her body, her breasts, and hips across his, for a moment paused with her fine-boned, beautiful face upturned to his, her lips slightly parted, inviting a kiss he might have given except he was so startled he only stared at her in the instant before her gaze fell and she went on, with the slightest of smiles at the corner of her mouth and a sidelong look back at him from under her lowered lids before the curve of the stairs took her from sight.

Swallowing thickly, shaken by how easily she had raised him, he went uncomfortably downward, only to meet Sia on the last curve of the stairs. He would rather not have dealt with her just then and would have gone past when she stepped aside, out of his way, but she put out her arm, barring him from going down, and said, "She was waiting for you, you know."

"And so were you," Joliffe said lightly; and because Sia was almost as near to him as Mariena had been and her face was turned up to him the same way, he kissed her. The kiss turned into more than he had meant it to be, with Sia's arms coming around his waist and her body leaning into his, pressing him back against the wall.

He was the first to break it off, but Sia, still leaning against him, smiled up into his face with a sigh of satisfaction. "There now," she said. "That's better."

Joliffe took her by the shoulders and set her back from him as much as the stairs allowed. "I have to go."

Sia continued to lean into his hands so that he could not let her go lest she fall against him again. Mellow with pleasure, she said, "It's no matter, you know. We're used to getting her leavings, the other girls and me."

"Leavings?" Joliffe asked.

Sia twitched her head the way Mariena had gone, up the stairs. "Hers. She does like she did with you. For the sport of it. Heats men to where they don't know whether they're coming or going. Never satisfies them, just heats them. They're easy to have then." Sia wiggled a little, wanting to be close again. Because he couldn't be sure he'd hear anyone coming, Joliffe kept her where she was and she went on, "These past few years, while she's had suitors here now and again, some of us have gathered a pretty lot of coins helping them ease their longings. If you know what I mean."

He'd have to be both gelded and stupid not to know what she meant and he said, smiling, "I'm no wealthy suitor come to woo. I've no coins to give you."

"You're fair-bodied enough with a face I don't mind kissing"—Sia slipped free of his hands, came close, and kissed him again to prove it—"that I'll have you for my own pleasure and no need for coins."

Enough was enough—and he'd not nearly had enough. "Where?" he asked. "And when?" Since here and now surely did not suit.

"Tonight after supper. There's a loft above the cow byre. Behind the stables. Can you find it?"

"I'll find it."

"Here." She pulled a square of red cloth from inside the front of her gown. "If you go now and leave this on the ladder, it means the loft is bespoke for tonight. Then we'll be sure of it."

She gave him the cloth, warm from her body, and another kiss to go with it, then was gone down the stairs, leaving him with the thought that lust seemed very well served here.

Chapter 8

Joliffe took his time going the rest of the way down the stairs, tucking the red cloth out of sight up his sleeve as he went. Outside the tower's doorway, he paused at the stairhead and saw Sia well away along the open gallery running outside the wing of rooms beyond the tower before he went the other way, down the stairs to the yard and in search of the cow byre, although his thoughts were mostly busy elsewhere than with Sia.

Until now, he had vaguely considered Sir Edmund's willingness to marry his daughter lower than he might have as simply a matter of money. Merchants tended to be wealthier than lords these days, and though lords and the Church might find that against the right way of things, they could not change it and so made what use of it they could to their own ends, the way Sir Edmund had used Harry Wyot. But an only daughter—and a beautiful one, at that—was another matter. Sir Edmund's first choice for her had been a knight's son, and surely there were other marriages as good as that to be had. Joliffe had somewhat wondered why this haste toward a merchant-marriage. Now he had to wonder if it was because of a need for haste. There had been no maiden moderation in Mariena's encounter with him on the stairs. Had she lost what women were supposed to prize the most?

He'd sometimes wondered why men were not supposed to prize their virginity as highly, but that was a question beside the present point and he set it aside. And after all, Mariena's lust did not necessarily mean her virginity was gone. Joliffe had met with lustful virgins before now. But the very fact she showed her lust so openly cast a different light on her. And on her mother's coldness to her. And maybe on her father's readiness to make her a husband's problem instead of his. Supposing they knew about her game. They might not.

Joliffe would willingly wager that if Mariena were up to mischief, her father would be the last to know, and it was perfectly possible Lady Benedicta's irk at her today was nothing more than impatience over the bother of the new gown. To judge by Sia's words, though, the servants knew about her; but Joliffe was very sure that if he were a servant here, he'd not be the one to tell Sir Edmund or Lady Benedicta about their daughter. Indeed, he would not. It might be wrong to "kill the messenger," but it happened anyway.

But if Mariena's lusting was unknown, why this haste to marry her to Amyas Breche? Was it for other reasons altogether, with lust having nothing to do with it?

Remembering Mariena's body pressed against his as she passed him, Joliffe was willing to warrant that lust came into it somewhere.

Had she gone beyond bounds with John Harcourt in expectation of their marriage and now must be married as best as she could be, rather than as well as she might have been? That would somewhat account for Sir Edmund's haste and her mother's unhappiness.

Or had John Harcourt found out more about her than was good to know and been about to refuse the marriage? The disgrace that would have followed that might have given someone reason to murder him. If he had been murdered. Which he might not have been.

Either way, it did not explain Master Wyot's unwillingness to marry her. The Harcourt betrothal and purposed marriage had come after his refusal. Had he refused Mariena because he knew too much about her? But if that were so, wouldn't he have warned the Breches against her? Or, if there were a secret worth murder, wouldn't Wyot have been dead before John Harcourt?

He must have refused the marriage for another reason or reasons and knew nothing about Mariena's lust. And most likely John Harcourt's death had been simply one of life's mischances. And Amyas Breche was going to get more with his wife than he bargained for.

And that, Joliffe concluded, left it all no business of his.

His thinking had seen him across the manor-yard to the far end of the stables from the cart-yard. Just as bakehouse and dairy, granary and flour-store were gathered near the kitchen, and the carpentry and other craftsmen's sheds clustered together, so byre and stable and hay-store had their own part of the yard and he found the cow byre easily enough—a long shed enclosed above but open below along most of one side. This time of year the milch cows would be grazing in the harvested fields through the day, only brought in for evening milking and the night, too, with the weather so wet, so the byre was presently bare of cows and the packed-earth floor was cleared and clean, but its use was given away by the line of stanchions with chains and rings along the rear wall for tethering the cows, each with a hayrack into which hay from the loft could be dropped though long gaps in the loft's floor.

Set near the gate but behind other buildings, the byre could be approached from several ways unseen, which might be among the things that recommended it. Joliffe doubted that much mattered, though, given the loft's use must be an open secret. The ladder was there, as Sia had said. Joliffe pulled the red cloth from his sleeve and draped it over one of the upper rungs, thinking as he turned away that there must be honor among the lustful if that was sufficient to secure the place for a night.

He was only slightly discomfited to find a stableman leaning on a pitchfork at the far end of the byre, grinning big-toothed at him.

Joliffe grinned back.

"Sia, is it?" the man said with a nod toward the ladder.

Since the man didn't sound or look about to fly into a jealous rage, Joliffe admitted, "Sia. Yes. Did she leave her name on me?" He touched his cheek questioningly as if feeling for a mark.

The man chuckled. "Easier than that. The red is hers. Avice uses blue. Tabby has green, see."

"What about you?"

The man grinned wider. "Us stable-fellows have our own loft, don't we?"

Joliffe had traveled much these past few years and been a good many places, but he had never known any manor so easily, openly libidinous. Did Sir Edmund have any thought of what went on? The steward must, if he were worth anything, but he must be gathering no leyrwite—the fine for lechery, owed to the lord of a manor as his right—in the manor-court, because then Father Morice would know of it, too, and surely make more trouble than there was any sign of being. And Sir Edmund must not know, because Joliffe had yet to meet or hear of a lord who knowingly forwent anything owed to him. Yet judging by Sia and this man's easiness about it, it must be open, and therefore Master Hanney the steward must know and accept it. For a bribe? For a share in it? Surely his place as a knight's steward was worth more than that?

With the uneasy certainty that he was gathering pieces he did not know how to use, Joliffe said, matching the man's lightness, "There's enough for everyone then, and good times all around?"

"I'd not say there's ever enough, like." The man gave a leering wink. "Never is, is there? That Sia, for one. If she did it as much as she talks about it, she'd never have time for her right work here."

Joliffe straightened in pretended dismay. "She's leading me on?"

"Nah," the man scoffed. "She'll have you. She likes fresh meat. Her and that Avice toss a coin, they do, to see who goes after a new man here. Must be she won you, eh?"

The man laughed and Joliffe laughed with him and leaned a shoulder against a post, to show he was ready to talk. Being won on a coin toss was not quite how he had seen things between Sia and himself, but he said easily, to keep the man talking, "Not that I'd be the loser either way, Sia or Avice?"

"That you'd not."

"So, Master Henney turns a blind eye to all of this?"

"Must do. Never asked him," the man said, then chuckled at what he must assume was his own wit.

"Sir Edmund ever take his share?"

The man guffawed. "Not him. He keeps a narrow line, he does. Takes his due in the marriage bed and let's it go at that. For all the good that does him."

The sideways swipe at Lady Benedicta took Joliffe by surprise. The little he had seen her and Sir Edmund together, they had seemed courteous enough with each other. Deliberately, he drew the man on with, "She's not all she might be for him?"

"It's not what she is but what she's been that maybe keeps him wondering. If you take my meaning."

Joliffe did not and shook his head to say so.

The man shifted happily, settling to tell a good story to someone who hadn't heard it. "It was years back and I was a boy then, but there's some as might best know who say she had her day of swiving where she shouldn't. Not married all that long, she took on with a man that was friend to her husband. Not so good a friend as he might have been, seems. The thing is"—the man grinned, all his teeth showing—"this 'friend' was father of that same John Harcourt as was going to marry Sir Edmund's daughter this summer past. Nobody knows how far it went with my lady, but it must have gone somewhere because it cooled things between her and Sir Edmund right enough, not to say between him and his 'friend,' too. It was years between the girl being born and young Master Will, with no babies between."

"That happens," Joliffe said easily.

"Oh, aye, it does, but talk is that there was no bedding between Sir Edmund and Lady Benedicta in all that time as would make those babies."

A thing servants would know almost as well as the couple themselves, Joliffe thought. "And now?" he asked.

The man shrugged. "They made up, seems like. First there was the boy, then a string of dead-borns. Been a few years since even the last of those, though, so likely they've given over trying for another son. Pity, that is, now it looks like it'll be a wonder they keep Master Will, the way things've been going."

"Why?" Joliffe asked as if alarm wasn't suddenly prickling inside him. "He doesn't look to be sickly."

"Not so much sickly as ill-fortuned. A fall on the stairs last spring. Sick on his food twice this summer. That tumble today." The fellow shook his head. "He's not going to last, the way things are going."

The man's regrets looked to be no deeper than a flea-bite, but they kept him talking, and Joliffe said with feigned lightness, "Today was a loose girth. That happens."

"It does, and Bert's been talked to about it, never fear."

"He swears he made it tight enough, though, doesn't he?" Joliffe said, making a jest of it.

"Course he does," the other man agreed with a laugh. He shifted the pitchfork from one hand to the other. "I'd best be back to work or I'll be the next one talked to."

"Ah, well," Joliffe said, more lightly than he felt, "a fall on boggy ground never hurt anybody much, so no harm done in the long run."

"Would have been harm done if he'd fallen ten feet sooner. There was rocks there, Matt from the mews says."

The man had started to leave. Joliffe joined him. "Rocks? He nearly fell on rocks?"

"The hunt ranged upstream to where's there's rough ground. Rocks cropping out and such like. They were just riding off it when Master William went down. Like I said, could have been bad. Here. I'll show a short way back to the cart-yard."

He led Joliffe behind the haystack beside the cow byre and into the dung-yard beyond it. A dung cart was standing there, its rear toward the heap, and the fellow must have been shifting the heaped dung and straw from stable and byres into it when he saw Joliffe go past. It was the time of year for spreading dung over the fields ready for the autumn plowing and planting, if only the rain stopped long enough for there to be an autumn plowing and planting. The man pointed to a gap between the back of the stable and the manor's wall behind it. "That'll take you."

He was so willing with talk that Joliffe would have liked to lead him on to something more about Sir Edmund—what sort of master he was, how he was with his neighbors, how had he taken John Harcourt's death—but could think of no unobvious way to do it, so simply thanked him and made to go.

But the man asked, "You fellows doing something to-night will make us laugh like last night?" and Joliffe paused long enough to answer, "We're going to try," then—because the man looked so hopeful for laughter—made him a flourished bow, so low and over-done that the man burst into laughter. Joliffe backed away, making another, lesser bow, turned, and with a skip and quick-step left him still laughing.

Which was the way Basset said was the best way to leave, because, "If nothing else, folk don't tend to throw things when they're laughing. Except maybe coins, and that's all right."

The way behind the stable was narrow, well-used enough the dirt was packed hard-down and—overhung by the stable's eaves—not so muddy as it might have been. It would be bastard-dark there after nightfall, but if he brought the small lantern with him . . .

He would rather have thought about tonight, but Will intruded on that pleasantness. Did the boy's troubles these past few months—two falls and two bouts of sickness—mean anything besides a run of ill-fortune? That happened, Joliffe knew. Though things were supposed to run in threes and now there had been four. Unless Will was starting on a second set of three, which seemed unfair of Fate.

When had John Harcourt died? Sometime this year and not long ago. Before or after Will's "accidents" had begun?

Joliffe caught himself on the wry twist he had given to

"accidents." Was he turning too readily suspicious of things he could leave alone? But Lord Lovell had sent him here to be suspicious. Lord Lovell had felt there was something wrong about John Harcourt's death, and now Will's accidents felt wrong to Joliffe. If he could find *why* they felt wrong, he would feel far better, he thought.

He wondered how much talk he could get from Sia tonight, before or else after their pleasure together.

All was peaceful in the cartshed. Basset was still seated on the piled cushions, but leaning back against the cartwheel, dozing. Piers and Gil were sitting on the shafts of another cart farther along the shed, Piers holding what looked to be a script and Gil apparently learning lines. Rose was gone somewhere, and Ellis was sitting on his heels beside the firepit, nursing sticks into a small fire under a kettle of water on a long-legged trivet.

Joliffe squatted down beside him and said, low enough not to wake Basset, "I'm to pass word on to you that there's a wench here is taken with your looks."

Ellis cast a quick look around to be sure Rose wasn't somehow behind him and asked with open interest, "Is there?"

"Avice. She'll be looking for a chance to wiggle her hips come-hither at you."

Ellis's eyes narrowed with suspicion. "How do you know that?"

"Because her friend wiggled her hips come-hither at me, and when I hithered, she told me as much." Watching Ellis's face, he added for pure—or not so pure—mischief, "They tossed a coin to see which of them would get which of us. Avice lost."

"I'd say she won," Ellis shot back, then caught up to the rest of that and protested, "They never tossed a coin."

"If the stableman was saying true, the two take turns on

who tries for likely men around here. They tossed a coin for us, seems like."

Ellis frowned. "I don't know I like that."

"The question is," Joliffe said, "whether you like what's offered. If you do, I doubt you'll mind the rest." And added with a wide smile, "Either way, just keep in mind the cow byre is bespoke for tonight."

Leaving Ellis swearing under his breath, Joliffe stood up and left him. He had seen Basset open one eye while he talked with Ellis. It was closed again, but when Joliffe sat down beside him, Basset said, eyes still closed, "Now that you're done corrupting Ellis, what did Lady Benedicta say to our purposed plays?"

"Your ears are working well. How are your aches and pains?"

"Better. I'm just being lazy now. Lady Benedicta?"

While Joliffe told him she had approved of everything but wanted no lewdness, Ellis shoved a clutch of sticks on the fire, stood up, and left the cart-yard.

Basset opened his eyes to watch him go, then said, "Rose won't thank you for leading him into evil ways."

"I've more likely kept him out of them. I doubt he likes being chosen on a coin toss. He wants to be loved for himself, does Ellis."

"And you don't?" Basset asked dryly.

"The likelihood of being loved for myself is so slight that I content myself with what I can get instead."

"Idiot," Basset said, friendliwise; and then, serious, "Learn anything else we might want to know?"

Serious, too, Joliffe told him everything he had seen and heard and guessed in Lady Benedicta's chamber, then what had happened with Mariena on the stairs afterwards, and then with Sia, to explain how he came to be at the cow byre, finishing with what the stablehand had told him about Lady Benedicta and about Will's several mishaps.

Having heard him to the end, Basset considered a while, then said, "There's nothing out of the ordinary about it all. Boys have mishaps and sometimes are ill. Wives can be unfaithful. Daughters can be like mothers. And never a mention of John Harcourt's death in it all." He cocked an eyebrow at Joliffe. "And yet?"

Glad to say it aloud, Joliffe said, "And yet there's something doesn't feel right."

"Which puts us no further ahead than when Lord Lovell set us to this."

"Except there seems no reason to be worried for Amyas Breche's safety. No one's objecting to the marriage."

"Did anyone object to the Harcourt marriage?"

Joliffe frowned. "Not that I've heard."

"We've heard altogether too little about it, seems to me. You're going to meet this Sia of yours tonight? See what you can find out from her."

"Yes, that's likely. 'I'm passionately joyed to be with you. What about John Harcourt's death?' "

Matching his dryness, Basset suggested, "Try for somewhat more subtle than that, if you can. Meanwhile, think about what you've found out so far, on the chance you've found out more than you know."

Joliffe made a face.

Basset made one back at him and pointed out, "It's your thinking got us into this business, so don't stop now."

"What I think is that there's nothing to be found out."

"That's what you *think*. But you *feel* differently. Just as my Lord Lovell does."

"What about you? What do you think? Or feel?"

Basset settled back against the wheel and folded his hands over his stomach, closed his eyes, and said, "I think I feel glad to be an old man too stiff in his joints for climbing into the loft of cow byres even if I was asked."

Joliffe snorted in derision and went to fetch his writing

box from the cart. There was maybe just time before supper to work a while on *Dux Moraud*. So much of the play
depended on the mindless, conscienceless drive of lust that
surely after this afternoon he could find some new sight
into the duke's sins.

Chapter 9

Ellis and Rose returned to the cartshed together, looking happy in each other's company. Ellis was carrying a basket of wet clothing that showed Rose had been to the manor's laundry, taking the chance of laundry tubs and plentiful hot water to do more than scrub and rinse the company's clothes in a large bucket or a clean stream; and while Ellis strung a rope from the cart to a peg in the shed wall, she put up the low frame near the fire to begin the tedious business of drying everything.

"Hear any useful talk?" Basset asked.

"I saw the doublet and hosen and cloak young Will was wearing when he fell," she said. "They were so dirty, he must have rolled as well as fallen. Must have been galloping hard, too, to fall that hard. The women were saying they hadn't heard he was hurt, though. Joliffe?"

She leaned to look under the cart at him in his corner, and he answered, "Not enough to matter. He was lucky it was sog-wet ground."

Rose straightened back to her work, saying, "It was that, right enough."

"He's had other accidents of late, I heard," Joliffe offered.

"The women were saying that, too. Well, one accident. A skinned knee and bruised hand from a fall on the tower stairs. Worse has been he's twice been badly sick to his stomach this past summer. There's worry he's turning sickly."

"He looked well enough to me," Basset said. "Father Morice didn't seem worried that way about him."

"Oh, him," Rose said dismissively. She shook out a shirt and draped it over the drying frame. "You should have heard the women about *him*."

Joliffe began putting away his work. This was talk too valuable to let pass and he asked, "Troubles the women, does he?"

"Not the way *you* mean," Rose said back tartly. "What it was, they were laughing over how fast this marriage-talk went, compared to last time. Last time he questioned every point as it came up, dragging things out and out."

"That's as it should be, isn't it?" Basset said. "Sir Edmund would want him to find the points that could make trouble later and straighten them out now."

"Seems even Sir Edmund was impatient at him before it was done. And Mariena swore she'd throttle him if he kept it up."

"She threatened a priest?" Ellis said, laughing.

"Not for him to hear," Rose said. "But some of the servants did."

Putting his work back into the cart, Joliffe said, "She wanted the marriage, then?"

"Seems so." Rose held up the long leg of half a pair of hosen she was about to hang over the drying frame, checking to see if it needed mending. Their best garb was kept only for playing. Otherwise, they each had a single change

of clothing—one to wear while one was being washed—
and their traveling took heavy toll. "Everyone did. The intended bridegroom was well-liked all around. Good to look
on and well-mannered. A knight's son, too, and come into
his lands not so many years ago."

Taking a shirt from the basket and making to hang it
over the rope now Ellis had it firmly up, Joliffe asked, "His
father is dead?"

"Three years past or so, I gather."

"What about the present bridegroom? What do they say
about him?"

"The women think it's shame Mariena is being married
no higher than a merchant's son, but they've naught to say
against Amyas himself."

"Merchants tend to be richer than knights these days,"
Ellis said. He was dipping a finger in the water on the fire,
testing its warmth. "Richer than some lords, even. Probably Sir Edmund needs what the marriage will bring in the
way of money."

"I wonder if he's gone into debt again since selling
Harry Wyot's marriage," Joliffe said. He wondered, too,
how long ago that had been. Long enough for Sir Edmund
to be badly in debt again? Or was Sir Edmund the sort who
didn't take long to be in debt?

"Where'd you pick that up?" Ellis asked.

Making much of hanging another shirt straight over the
line, Joliffe shrugged off the question. "You know. Just
around. People talk. Rose, what do they say about Mariena
and this marriage? Does she want it?"

Rose went on hanging other hosen over the drying
frame while answering, "No one said she doesn't. What I
gathered was that they're ready for her to be married and
away from here, she's such a trouble."

"A trouble?" Joliffe asked.

"You know. Quarrels with her mother. Fights with her brother. Demands too much from the servants." Finished with the hosen, Rose took Piers' shirt from the basket. "All the usual things from a girl who's almost done with being only a daughter but isn't yet a wife. That being caught betwixt and between, it wears on a person."

Joliffe gave a quick look from her to Ellis and back again, wondering if they saw themselves mirrored in what she had just said, caught as they were between Rose's vanished husband and their own desire for each other. But Rose was simply shaking out Piers' shirt and Ellis was pushing more sticks into the fire, and Joliffe said, to lead the talk onward, "She's maybe still mourning her other betrothed."

"Now that's odd," Rose said. Odd enough that she paused, still holding Piers' shirt. "From what the women were saying, she took her first betrothed's death . . . What was his name?"

"John Harcourt," Joliffe supplied.

"Well, she took his death hard, it seems. Wept and did all the expected moaning and so on, and I gather she's been in this ill-humour ever since, despite she's sweet enough to this Amyas and willing to this marriage, too."

"Likely, she just wants to be married," Basset said.

"Still, given she's had so little time to be over her last betrothed," Rose said, "they're fortunate she's so willing to this Amyas."

"Out of sight, out of mind," Ellis said. "And a man can't be more out of sight than in his grave."

"Ellis," Rose said quellingly.

Followed by Gil, Piers ambled over, rolling the script-scroll closed as they came, asking, "Is it time to eat yet?"

"It is," said Basset. "Which means time for you and Gil to go to the kitchen to fetch it."

"Wash your hands and faces first," Rose said, nodding at the kettle.

They did, Piers' necessary grumbling increasing when Ellis held him by the collar long enough to wash the often-missed back of his ears. Then he and Gil went, and it was time to begin readying for tonight's playing. Together, Ellis and Joliffe lifted out of the cart the hamper that held their older, more worn properties, used for such knock-about playing as *The Fox and the Grapes,* when the battered properties—bent sword, tattered garments, straggling wigs—added to the laughter.

While Ellis fetched from the cart the box of masks used in some of their plays, Joliffe asked Rose, "So, in your laundry talk, was there aught said about Lady Benedicta?"

"Just that things are never good between her and her daughter and are worse of late."

"Nothing else?"

"You saw her this afternoon," Basset said. "What did you think of her?"

Joliffe considered before he answered. What *did* he think of her? Finding himself uncertain, he answered slowly, "She wasn't happy with her daughter, that's sure. Nor was Mariena happy with her, come to that and just as Rose said. But she was likewise angry at Will . . ."

"For what?" Rose asked.

"For falling? For spoiling the hawking? For making more work for everybody?" Joliffe ventured, finding—now that he thought about it—that he really did not know. "Or maybe . . ." He paused, considering a new thought before going on, slowly, "I'm not certain but what she's always angry, one way or another."

"At Will?" Rose persisted.

"At everybody, for all I know," Joliffe said with a shrug. "Why not?" Even a lost love of long ago could shadow a life, he supposed. If the love had been strong enough. And then to lose that love and afterwards bear children to an unloved husband and lose most of those children at their births—for a woman who would not accept it, that could all be enough to break her or else to harden her into unceasing anger at her life and everyone in it. But he kept those thoughts to himself and only said, "She dealt fairly enough with me, though, so I'll not complain against her."

Piers and Gil came back with supper. They all ate, then Basset, Ellis, Joliffe, and Piers made ready to go, Basset, moving better than he had been this morning, putting on his sober best robe—"The one I'll wear when I'm summoned to dine with the king"—that would mark him as the story-teller, not part of the story, while Ellis and Joliffe dressed more boldly in their parti-colored hosen and short doublets and Piers put on the blue tabard Gil had used the other day.

"He's grown again," Rose said in despair, pulling at its hem. "Look. And his tunic is nothing to hope for, either."

"Never mind," her father said cheerfully. "Next market town we come to, we'll buy cloth for another tunic. Ribbons for Tisbe and a tunic for Piers."

"Or the other way around," said Joliffe.

Everyone ignored him.

Gil was coming with them but would only watch from the screens passage. Rose was staying at the shed, to keep the fire going and turn the laundry so it would dry the sooner. As he and Ellis picked up the hamper to carry between them, the mask-box a-top it, Joliffe said jestingly to her, "You shall sit in quiet and peace, contemplating the joy of doing nothing."

"I shall contemplate," Rose said back at him, "the joy of having no men around."

They were somewhat early to the hall. They were to perform at supper's end, but the meal was not yet over and they waited in the screens passage, Piers sitting on the hamper, the rest of them standing. Basset was telling Gil in a low voice what he should be learning by watching them tonight; Joliffe and Ellis were leaning against the wall, arms crossed, able to hear the cluttered sounds of tableware and talk in the hall while the servants waiting on the tables tonight gathered in the passage, waiting to clear. Sia wasn't among them, but Avice was and she sidled close to Ellis and cast her eyes up at him, her hips making a small, suggestive sway his way. Ellis looked instantly willing to answer her suggestion with one of his own, but before he could, Joliffe said cheerfully, "Avice. We met at the well this morning, remember?"

She gave him a quick look that entirely dismissed him, but Ellis, reminded he was only prey to her, lost interest. Joliffe pretended to be interested elsewhere while she tried to get it back until she had to go with the rest of the servants into the hall.

"If you're done playing coy with the servants," Basset said, "shall we ready to play in earnest?"

Pretending that wasn't a jibe, Ellis poked Piers to get him off the hamper. The noise from the great hall changed to the clatter of tableware being cleared, then servants bearing filled trays and used serving dishes came out, headed back to the kitchen, while several others went in with tall pitchers of wine or ale to refill goblets and cups. With the sudden sharpening of heed to the moment at hand that almost always came in the moments before a performance, Joliffe reached for the hamper at the same moment Ellis did, picking it up between them again as Basset took up the mask-box and Master Henney asked if they were ready. At Basset's assurance that they were, the man went into the hall and declared them.

As he finished, Piers leaped from the shadows of the screens passage into the bright hall, posed for an instant— both to be seen and to be sure the way was clear—then spun around and backflipped his way down the hall between the tables to just short of the hearth, where he stood up, arms out, to be acclaimed. But Joliffe and Ellis were directly behind him, running with the hamper between them, giving him a bare instant of glory before he pitched forward as if flattened by the hamper and afterwards scrambled to his feet and scurried after Joliffe and Ellis now setting the hamper down in front of the high table. Amid laughter, they all bowed to Sir Edmund and the others there, Will among them, looking well-scrubbed, then to the tables along the sides of the hall. By then, Basset, proceeding with more dignity, had joined them. After setting the mask-box on the hamper again and making his own bows, he declared in a full voice rolling with dignity, "Tonight for your pleasure, we purpose to perform *The Fox and the Grapes,* my fellows to enact it while I tell the tale."

With that, Ellis threw open the box of masks and he and Joliffe both made play of grabbing among the masks as if in quarrel over who had which one, until Ellis "won," seizing up the pointed-nosed mask of a fox. Piers instantly grabbed the mask-box and set it aside, leaving Joliffe, feigning sullen disgust, to throw open the hamper and make show of rummaging through it until finally he held up a picture of grapes painted on a thin board and proceeded to pretend he was a grapevine with an outward ill-grace that kept the already-started laughter going.

The Fox and the Grapes in itself was hardly a long enough fable to entertain a household for an evening, but with Basset's telling, it turned to include a Knight, a Giant, and a Damsel in Distress, keeping Ellis and Joliffe in lively change, first from Fox and Gravevine to Knight and Giant, sorting with frantic haste through the hamper for sword and helmet and Giant's club and to find an ugly mask in the mask-box to turn Joliffe into the Giant. Given that he was somewhat less tall than Ellis, he made an unlikely Giant, which added to the sport. Then when the Damsel was

required, he dragged a gown and wig out of the hamper but
was left standing helplessly still wearing the Giant's mask,
the Damsel's gown and a bedraggled yellow wig in one
hand and the Giant's club in the other, until in apparent
desperation, he dropped gown, wig, and club, grabbed
Piers—who had spent the while flirting at the ladies along
the tables with all the charm his ten years and golden curls
gave him but "happened" to be in reach at the necessary
moment—swung him onto the top of the closed hamper,
plopped the Giant's mask over his head, and thrust the club
into his hand, making him into the Giant and leaving Joliffe free to pull on the gown, drape the wig randomly over
his head, and become the Damsel.

All the while of that Basset went on with the story,
steady-paced and solemn, as if unaware of the chaos
around him. The Knight became a Hermit with whom the
Damsel took sanctuary, the Giant came in search of her,
the Knight appeared to fight the Giant and rescued her, and
finally, with Piers sprawled in pretended death across the
top of the hamper and the Damsel safe in the Knight's
arms, Basset said, "So the Fox, who had watched all this
from the vineyard . . ." setting off a seemingly desperate
scramble by Ellis and Joliffe to rid themselves of their
Knightly and Damsel gear, find the discarded Fox mask
and painted grapes, and return to their first roles as Basset
finished, ". . . at last took heart from the Knight's bravery
and leaped higher than ever before, to seize the bunch of
grapes"—Ellis snatched the pictured grapes from Joliffe
before Joliffe could even lift it up—"and lived happily forever more." Pause. "Until the Knight, on quest again . . ."

Ellis started to grab for the helmet but Joliffe grabbed
for Basset instead, silencing him with a hold on his head
and hand over his mouth. Basset, taking in the glares at
him from Joliffe, Ellis, and Piers, gave a nod. Joliffe released him and he announced loudly, "The End."

They all took swift bows to satisfying clapping and laughter. Ellis and Joliffe did not wait for it to stop but threw their properties back into the hamper while Piers had the masks back into their box, the three of them then running with their gear from the hall, leaving Basset to make dignified departure behind them.

Outside, as they crossed the yard's darkness by the light of a lantern one of the servants had had waiting for them, Basset said, "That was well done. Gil, what did you learn from what you saw?"

Listening to Gil and Basset trade answers and questions the rest of the way back to the cartshed, Joliffe was the more sure the boy had a true instinct for their craft. There were some men who—no matter the time and training spent on them—never seemed to grasp there was more to playing than the pleasure of showing off themselves. Others could be taught, if only eventually, otherwise; and then there were some like Gil, who seemed to understand in their bones the need to take on the seeming of whom they were playing, rather than turning every person they played into himself. Gil still needed to build the necessary skills of voice and body, but he increasingly looked to be worth the training.

The cart-yard and -shed were deep in shadow save for the low red glow of their own fire to welcome them back. Rose had their beds laid out and ready and welcomed them back with a hug for Piers and questions how the playing had gone. While Basset told her, Joliffe and Ellis set the hamper near the cart, to be put away tomorrow, and Piers put the mask-box a-top it. Asking her father how he felt, Rose started to ready Piers for bed, stripping his player's garb from him. The rest of them were likewise undressing, stripping to undergarments to go to bed, except for Joliffe who, after seeing his garb safely folded and laid on the hamper, pulled on his own hosen and doublet. Ellis at least knew why but none of the others asked him what he was doing. Only when he picked up the still-lighted lantern and started out of the shed did Ellis ask mockingly, "Where are you away to?"

Mockingly back at him, Joliffe said, "Just a walk."

Ellis snorted and Piers laughed. Rose shushed them both, but Basset called cheerily, "*Walk* carefully!"

Joliffe waved one hand over his shoulder without looking back and kept going. The rain had softly started up again, but under the eave of the narrow way behind the stable he was dry enough and crossing the dung-yard hardly dampened him. The cow-shed was lined with cows now, their munching of hay and cud-chewing loud in the night-stillness. The lantern-light disturbed them. Hind-quarters shifted and heads lifted, throwing shadows far more giant than anything the players had managed in the hall. Joliffe made soft, cow-hushing noises at them, reassuring them he wasn't come to attack them, and then climbed the ladder awkwardly one-handed with the lantern. Not that a lighted lantern was the best of things to have in a hayloft full of dry hay but—as he had rather expected—that problem was forethought: the hay was cleared away from the ladder's end of the loft and there was a peg in one of the beams to hang the lantern.

No one was there. Joliffe hung the lantern, checked its candle, judged it would last to see him back to the cartshed, and took a long look around. Not that too long a look was needed. It was a hayloft, with bare roof-beams and bare wooden floorboards, where they weren't covered by the piled hay, and that was all. What surprised him was that there was nothing else.

"The way Sia and Avice are said to go on, you'd think they'd have themselves a bed here," Joliffe told the shadows.

Besides that, he had always found hay made for prickly lying. But he'd also found that if the prick of the body's desire was strong enough, the hay's prick hardly mattered,
and hay was better for lying on than bare boards or ground,
that was certain. The hay was new enough, too, that it still
smelled sweetly of summer and sun. There were worse
places for lusting, and Joliffe sat himself down on the floor,
his back against the wall, content to wait.

Unfortunately, his mind was not content. For prefer-
ence, he would have kept himself happily occupied with
thoughts of pleasures to come, but what came instead was
thought of why he was here at Deneby at all. Sorting through
what he had found out so far, there seemed little to go with
Lord Lovell's vague doubts and worry. John Harcourt had
fallen ill and then been dead. That was common enough,
with little to be made of it. It didn't mean the same couldn't
happen to Amyas, but neither did it mean that it would.
But what of Will? He'd had a fall on stairs lately, a thing
that could happen to anyone, but today's fall would have
been far worse than it had been if it had come a few yards
sooner. And lately he'd twice been ill. That was much mis-
fortune for one boy in a short time.

Still, such things happened, just like John Harcourt's
sudden death.

But if they weren't happenstance, who might have reason to want Will dead?

Amyas Breche for one. With Will dead, Mariena would
be her father's sole heir.

Or Amyas' uncle could want it on his nephew's behalf.
A wealthy, landed nephew could be of use to a merchant.

But could either of them have had anything to do with
John Harcourt's death? From what he'd heard, Joliffe
didn't think they'd even known of Mariena then. They
might have, though, by way of Harry Wyot, and found

some way to bribe someone here to poison Harcourt . . .
The likelihood of that seemed thin. They couldn't have
been certain Sir Edmund would turn to Amyas for
Mariena's next betrothed, and there were surely other valuable marriages to be had for far less trouble. Nor did
Amyas seem so besotted with Mariena that he'd kill for the
chance to have her. And while it would be to Amyas' profit
to have Will dead and Mariena sole heir of Deneby, why
start trying to have him dead before being certain of
Mariena?

There was still Harry Wyot to consider. He'd gain nothing by Will's death, any more than he was going to gain by
Mariena's marriage, and Joliffe couldn't make it likely that
he'd do it for Amyas' gain, however good friends they
were. Revenge against Sir Edmund was possible, of
course. There must have been quarrel between them when
Harry Wyot refused Mariena. Had it been bad enough—or
was his present marriage bad enough—that he wanted revenge on Sir Edmund, even if it meant bettering Mariena,
whom he must not like or he would have married her?

But Will's fall today had been by way of a loosened
girth. If it wasn't the stableman's fault, then someone had
pulled the buckle loose while riding and hoped for Will's
fall on the rocks. But today Harry Wyot and his wife had
been riding together. If he had loosened that girth, she had
to know of it and their marriage would have to be a sound one
if he trusted her with a secret about him like that, and that
took away revenge for a bad marriage as reason to harm
Will. Damn.

Who else was there to consider? Mariena for one, Joliffe supposed. Head tilted back against the post, he
frowned up at the underside of the thatch-covered roof.
She would gain by her brother's death, most assuredly, and
have better chances at hurting him than Amyas or Harry

Wyot did. But murder? Lust was one thing, murder was another. He might as well consider Lady Benedicta while he was at it. And why not? Her affection for Will seemed thin. Even though she was presently out of humour with her daughter, she might prefer Mariena's betterment to that of a son favored by a husband for whom she didn't care, if the servant-talk was right—and servant-talk was usually right about things like that. Forced into one childing after another by a husband wanting more sons, she might be seeking now to hurt that husband in one of the few ways left to her—by taking his one son away from him.

But surely she could find better ways than falls on stairs and loosened saddle-girths, and other times than now, with so many people around. Mariena would benefit whenever Will died. Later would do as well as now.

It was Harry Wyot who couldn't count on having other chances at the boy.

Except Joliffe didn't see that he had a reason to want Will dead.

Come to that, Joliffe couldn't see any sufficient reason for anyone to take the risk to have Will dead. Being caught at murder and risking danger of damning one's soul to Hell were large chances to take for *any* reason, whether for revenge or gain, and he couldn't see there was that much to gain here. Not set against the risk involved.

So there was no reason anyone would want John Harcourt dead and no one was trying to kill Will and he was wasting his time trying to find answers to pointless questions, he thought disgustedly. If he was going to go making twists and turns, why not take up the possibility that a whole array of people, unbeknownst to each other, wanted Will dead for a whole array of different reasons, and one after another were trying for him. That worked as well as anything else he had come up with. No. The simplest way to see things was that John Harcourt had died of a sickness and that Will was having a run of bad fortune. There. No more problems. Everything settled and taken care of. No more need to think about the matter anymore at all. Or of anything else except of Sia now softly calling up the ladder, asking if he were there. About her, he was very ready and more than willing to think.

Chapter 10

Knowing what was expected of him as well as what he expected, Joliffe stood up and went to meet her as she came up the ladder. With her skirts to hold, the climbing was not easy, and he took her arm to help her the last way, steadying her as she stepped from the ladder. Her smile rewarded him for that as she slid a folded blanket off her shoulder, where she had been carrying it, saying as she handed it to him, "I brought this to make us the more comfortable."

"Wise as well as lovely," Joliffe said, bending to take a quick kiss from her ready lips. She stretched toward him, plainly willing for others, but those would come. He was never in favor of hurrying these things if it could be helped, and he turned his back on her, leaving her wanting more as much as he did while he made show of shaking out the blanket and throwing it across the low-mounded hay nearest to them. As he bent to pull it more even, Sia came close behind him, stroked her hands down his sides to his hips, and then pulled him against her. As he straightened up, she pushed her breasts against his back and slid her hands around him and upward, under his doublet's lower edge.

Her boldness was enough to raise any man's . . . lust, and Joliffe's very certainly rose. He turned, took her in his arms, and gave the long kiss they both wanted. When they had to pause for breath, Sia began to unfasten his doublet. While she did, he explored her body with his hands, until she had finished and he drew back a little from her, gazing into her flushed face, ready for her lips again but holding back while he shrugged out of his doublet. Then, with it off and tossed aside, he took his turn, beginning to unlace the long opening down the front of her gown to come at her breasts. Sia's hands in return slid under his shirt and up, warm over his bare flesh.

With her gown undone enough for him to come at the drawstring of her undergown, he loosened that and pulled her gown open and her undergown down, baring one of her breasts. Cupping it with his hand, he bent to kiss it. Sia moaned with pleasure, her head bending back, opening her throat to more kisses. Her legs giving way, she began to sink down. He caught her and lowered her onto the blanket and himself on top of her. But one part of his mind was still detached from what they were doing and he slid aside, onto his side beside her. She made a wordless sound of protest and rolled onto her side, too, holding on to him. He did not resist. His own hands were too busy pulling up her skirts. But he asked, forcing the question past his lust, hard though the words came, "Have you done aught against childing?" Because whatever his other desires, he had no desire to leave bastard children behind him.

Sia gasped, somewhere between her passion and unexpected laughter, and pulled back from him, not away but only enough to look into his face. "There's none ever asked me that before."

"And doesn't the unexpected add to pleasure," Joliffe said. He had no fear of losing what they were doing, enjoyed prolonging their sport. Finding her bare thigh under her skirts, he stroked his hand along it. Sia sighed, her eyes closing, her hips moving with the pleasure of his touch. "You haven't answered," he whispered.

She whispered back, "There's no fear. We all know what to do. Ummm. That's good. Don't stop."

He stopped. "You do what?"

Sia twisted in protest and opened her eyes. "What?"

"What do you do?"

On the edge of laughter, she said, "We've pennyroyal and rue and one thing and another, not to fear." She stretched, wiggled a little to settle herself deeper into the hay, and—not by chance, Joliffe was sure—let her gown fall more away from her breasts, which she lifted toward him with an arching of her back while she added, "The trouble is keeping enough for us, what with my lady wanting so much for herself."

Even as he leaned forward to take the invitation of her breasts, Joliffe wished she had not said that. He kissed where she wanted him to, but his mind was going somewhere else, and regretting his curiosity even as he gave way to it, he began to work his way up her throat with more kisses, asking between them, "Does . . . Sir Edmund . . . know . . . she . . . wants . . . no more . . . children?"

Sia bent her head back to take his kisses as she breathed, "Who knows what Sir Edmund knows."

"He doesn't take his pleasures elsewhere?" Joliffe whispered back, making it plain with his hand under her skirts where he meant to take his own pleasure.

Sia writhed, and answered on a gasp, "He doesn't." She found her hand's way into Joliffe's short braies. It was his turn to gasp as she whispered, "More's the pity for Lady Benedicta."

Holding to a last shred of curiosity, Joliffe forced out, "There's no love lost between them, then?"

"None . . ." Sia's hand was making use of all it was discovering and Joliffe groaned. ". . . that I've ever noted." Without warning, she pulled her hand out of his braies, instead slid it up under his shirt again, making a small torture of pausing his pleasure even as she moved against him, urging him onward to her own. He caught her hand and tried to force it back where he wanted it to be. She brought his hand, instead, to where she wanted it, saying into his ear, her breath cool over his heated flesh, "I won't get with child if you have me. I promise. With all the men whose longings I've eased and no child yet . . ." Satisfied as Joliffe began to pull her skirts altogether up, out of his way, she began to work at loosening the drawstring of his braies, finishing, ". . . I do know what to do."

He had no doubt she knew what to do, in several senses. She was too excellent at her chosen sport for him to doubt that, and he asked, to add to their sport along with his pressing need to have their clothing out of his way, "How many men has it been? So I know who I have to rival to keep your favor."

"You don't want to hear about my other men."

"Believe me, it won't cool my desire in the least." He began to kiss his way from her throat to between her breasts to prove it. She writhed most satisfactorily, her back arching with pleasure even as she made wordless moan, demanding more. Returning the small torment she'd given him, he withheld that more while he asked, "Is Master Amyas someone whose 'longings' you've eased?"

Hand behind his head, drawing him toward her, Sia said, "No. He's Avice's." And went on, between kisses set hard on Joliffe's lips, "Except . . . he hasn't . . . been . . . interested . . . in her."

Joliffe drove his own kiss against her mouth, pressing

her down into the hay; but when he finally relinquished her
lips and drew back, leaving her gasping for breath, he had
another question, come from his not-quite-extinguished
curiosity. "What about Mariena's other betrothed? The one
who died?"

Sia moaned, whether with memory or with pleasure
at what Joliffe's hand was presently doing to her, he couldn't
tell, but he went on doing it, asking in her ear, "What
about him?"

"Him," Sia gasped. "Yes. He was . . . so . . . ready . . .
we shared him . . . Avice and I . . ."

A drawn-out moan and a great writhe of pleasure took
her body. She twisted, first toward him, then away, and at
last with a long, satisfied sigh went slack, eyes closed, lips
parted, one arm thrown out to the side, her other hand
holding to Joliffe's shoulder as if to make sure he was still
in her reach.

Joliffe's need was far from slacked or satisfied, but
knowing it would take time to bring her back so he could
go on, he curbed his need, settled himself as best he could
beside her, began to stroke her thigh, and said softly, "So.
About Mariena's late betrothed. Did she know what he was
doing?"

Sia giggled—at him as much as at the question, he
thought. Not opening her eyes, her voice still slow with satisfaction, she said, "She couldn't have or we'd have heard
about it. Or he would have, surely. What's hers is hers and
nobody else better try to have it, too."

Joliffe slipped his hand to a warmer place than Sia's
thigh. She was quickening to his touch already, her hips beginning to move in response to his touch, proving she was
fully a wanton in the most delightful sense of the word.
Her hand on his manhood was returning the favor, almost
distracting him from asking, "She wanted him, then?"

"Or wanted him to want her, anyway. Always touching

his hand and leaning herself toward him so he could see a little down her dress to what he'd be getting." Sia shifted her own breasts, letting Joliffe know they were still on offer. As he obligingly began to kiss them, she murmured, "She likes being desired, does Mariena."

And so did Sia. She slid her hand from his shoulder to take hold on his hair and pull his head gently up so they were face to face. Softly she asked, "Did you come here only to talk?"

Joliffe widened his eyes in wholly feigned innocence. "Could I dare hope for more?"

Sia laughed at him, slipped her hand around to the back of his hips, rolled onto her side, and pulled him toward her. "There's no dare about a certainty."

And certainly no more wish for words by either of them. Taking her mouth in another long kiss, Joliffe pushed her to her back again and himself on top of her. But only for half of a completely insufficient moment, before someone called up the ladder with a desperate need different than their own, "Sia! You're wanted! You have to come!"

They both went still. Then Sia went limp under him and called back with irk and disappointment, "Avice, go away!"

"You have to come! Mariena is sick and vomiting and we're needed!"

Joliffe tried to say something about Sia being needed here, too, but she was already wiggling to be out from underneath him and he rolled off her. She sat up, muttering against Mariena and saying there'd be another time between them, not to worry.

"Sia!" Avice called again, impatiently.

"I have to lace my gown again, don't I?" Sia yelled back. "I'm coming up."

"You're not! I'm coming down."

Sia bid him farewell with a quick kiss that landed

vaguely near his mouth. He kept his hands to himself and let her go, much though he wanted to seize her and finish the business. Going down the ladder, she waved once and blew a kiss at him. He waved back, then she was gone, and when her voice and Avice's had faded as they hurried from the cow byre, he rolled over and buried his face in the blanket, his sorry certainty of loss made the worse by knowing his own curiosity had helped to spoil it. If he hadn't taken time with question-asking . . .

Mariena had seemed well enough at supper. How did she come to be suddenly so sick?

Another question without likelihood of any easy answer.

Thwarted of body and curiosity both, he gathered himself up, dressed again, hung the blanket on the peg when he'd taken the lantern in hand, and went down the ladder, to return through the wet dark to the cartshed.

There, he was grateful to find no one awake to make jibes or question him and that Rose had left his blanket hanging over the frame beside the fire, to go warm to his bed with him. It wasn't so warm as Sia would have been but it was better than no comfort at all, he told himself, uncomforted.

Chapter 11

In the morning, once Basset had been helped up and some of the stiffness rubbed from his joints, he and Ellis were ready with the jibes there had not been last night, the two of them taking turns asking if Joliffe had had enough "sleep" last night, had he slept "warm" enough, had he . . .

Joliffe cut them off by telling of Mariena's sickness.

In the instant pall thrown by that, Basset explained to Gil, "There's never need for players at a funeral." He pointed at the water buckets and added, "You and Piers fetch those full and see what you can hear from any servants at the well."

Both boys went, and with them out of hearing, Basset asked of Joliffe, "Did you learn aught else?"

Joliffe paused over his answer, considering what he had learned. Other than about Sia. Slowly he answered, "There's either layers of secrets here or else there's none."

"Thank you," Basset said dryly. "But if you think I'm looking for a scholastic debate about the nature of Truth, you're wrong. Certainties, my fellow, certainties."

"I'm thinking," Joliffe protested.

"Don't. Just report," Basset said.

Obeying, but aware that Ellis and Rose were watching them strangely, Joliffe said, "Lady Benedicta is seeing to it she bears no more children. It's uncertain Sir Edmund knows that or if he thinks he still has chance at more sons. The servants say there's no love lost between him and his wife but that he doesn't take his pleasure elsewhere, so far as they know."

"And they would," Basset said.

"Probably," Joliffe hedged. "Lady Benedicta *has* taken her pleasure elsewhere, but it was a long time ago and the man is dead."

"How?" Basset asked.

Joliffe had wondered that, too. "It's something to be found out. I think it's said to have been only a few years ago, though. The thing is that he was John Harcourt's father."

Basset said something curt and crude.

"Yes," Joliffe agreed. "So about him I'd like to find out more, but no one has said there was anything suspicious about his death."

"Any more than anyone here seems suspicious about John Harcourt's death," Basset said. "Nor that anyone was openly objecting to him marrying Mariena."

"She at least was willing to it. Very willing, from what Sia said." Or maybe Mariena was just very willing generally, he added to himself.

Like echo to that thought, Basset said, "It hasn't stopped her being willing to this one, too. What about Harcourt? Was he willing?"

"I've not heard otherwise. In truth, the only thing I've heard about him for certain is that while waiting for his marriage he was heartily availing himself of what else is on offer here."

"What else . . ." Basset started, then caught Joliffe's meaning and lightly mocked, "Your Sia isn't only your own?"

"And wasn't I taken aback to find that out," Joliffe said dryly back at him, then took a tragic tone and added, "Alas, no, she has been other men's, nor was she Harcourt's only swiving-partner here."

"Not the daughter," Basset said, firmly ready to disbelieve that.

"No." With an eye sideways on Ellis, he added, "Just with every servant girl who offered herself, I gather. And there's several of them that offer themselves readily."

Ellis knew that jibe was meant for him and took it with a glare since Rose had her back to him, collecting the dried hosen from the drying frame so he didn't have to pretend he didn't know what Joliffe meant.

Basset held to the point. "What about this Amyas Breche? Does he take his pleasure among the servant wenches, too?"

"No."

"So there's a difference there between them," Basset said, considering.

"That, and that there's been no talk linking Lady Benedicta to any of his relatives."

Rose turned from the drying frame, her hands full of hosen, and demanded, "What are you two talking about?"

Basset refuged instantly in earnest simpleness. "Just talk, my dear. To pass the time until we go to break our fast."

"Just talk," Rose mocked back at him. "I hardly think so. What's this about?"

Joliffe and Basset traded looks, and Joliffe lifted his shoulders slightly, giving the problem over to Basset, who sighed and said, "Lord Lovell has doubts about the man

Harcourt's death and is somewhat uneasy about this Breche marriage. Since we were going to be here anyway, he asked us to learn what we could."

"It's because Joliffe was too sharp-witted last summer. That's the root of it, isn't it?" Ellis said, hot with accusation. "Lord Lovell wants him to find out trouble the way he did then, doesn't he?"

"He wants me to find out there's *not* trouble," Joliffe defended.

"That's no more than word-play," Ellis scoffed.

"It's not as if I had choice, is it? Not once he 'asked' it of me."

"You had choice last summer, before you put your nose in where it didn't belong," Ellis snapped.

"Joliffe did what needed doing," Rose said with her rare sharpness. "It was probably even *because* of it Lord Lovell took note of us." She looked at her father, who shrugged and somewhat grimaced, acknowledging the likelihood of that; and she finished at Ellis, "So it better suits us to help than make trouble over what can't be changed."

Her glare defied Ellis to disagree and he did not, although his, "I can see that, yes," was given grudgingly, his truer feeling about it showing through the unwilling acceptance.

"We're none of us happy about it," Basset said, to soothe. "But it's as Rose says. We've little choice, do we?"

"When did you mean to tell us what was a-foot?" Ellis asked, an edge of his anger still showing.

"We'd hoped never to have to tell you," Basset answered. "We hoped to see the thing through to a quiet end and no one else troubled about it."

Rose, the hosen set aside, came to Ellis' side and slipped her arm through his and smiled up at him. "They didn't do it simply to anger you, you know," she said gently.

As always to her slightest sign of affection to him, Ellis eased back from his anger. He made a small, accepting gesture at Basset with his free hand and said, "I know." He pointed at Joliffe and added, only half-jesting, "But I still think *he* did it just to cross me."

Joliffe raised his shoulders in a high shrug. "There has to be *some* benefit to it."

"Children, children," Basset said. "Let us not quarrel. All we're truly doing is hearing what we can and making of it what can be made, and when Lord Lovell comes for the wedding, we'll pass everything on to him. There's hardly trouble in that."

Probably even Ellis would have granted that, but they were interrupted by Piers' approaching voice, loud and happy beyond the carpenter's shed, and Basset said, "We'll keep it from Piers and Gil, though, I think."

"If we can," Ellis muttered as they all turned to be doing something else than talking when the boys came into the yard, Will with them.

He looked surprisingly cheerful for someone whose sister had been deathly ill last night, and Basset greeted him with, "Master William, we've been grieved to hear about Mariena. She's better?"

"She's all well," Will said with disgust. "My father says it was all trouble over nothing."

"She was very bad, though, wasn't she?" Joliffe said, determined his trouble and the alarm weren't going to have been for nothing.

"She was vomiting and everything," Will said. He had a small boy's delight at that. "The servants were kept scurrying most of the night with it. She was so bad for a while that Father Morice had to come to confess her. But she wouldn't!" Will seemed as enthused for his sister's defiance of the priest as for her being ill in the first place. "She said she wasn't going to die and she wasn't going to confess. So now Father Morice is upset about that, and Mother is angry at her, and Father went to see Mariena this morning, now the vomiting and all has stopped, and he takes her side—he always does—and says Mother made much out of nothing and he's angry at *her* for it, and he's told Father Morice to read the banns today, just as planned, and don't make fluster where there doesn't need to be."

Will was forced to pause to take a deep breath, which he let out with a sharp sigh of satisfaction at having said all that.

"Amyas must have been as sick with worry that Mariena was that ill," Joliffe ventured.

"It was something she ate," Will said cheerfully. "Or ate too much of, Mother says. Amyas wore himself out with pacing back and forth along the gallery outside Mariena's chamber until he was told she was better. Then he went to bed. Harry was there, too, but he didn't pace; he just leaned on the railing, looking glum and keeping him company. Amyas told him to go back to bed. He said no point, what with his wife gone to help with Mariena—"

"How are you this morning?" Rose interrupted.

"Me?" Will sounded surprised at the question, as if yesterday's fall had never happened. "I'm well. I didn't eat whatever she did." He turned his heed to Basset, Ellis, and Joliffe. "I almost fell on the floor laughing at you all last night! May I watch you practice today? Are you going to practice today? What are you doing tonight? I want to laugh like that some more."

"Tonight will be something more in keeping with the marriage banns being first read," Basset said. "Something"—he tipped a wink toward Will's open disappointment—"only almost as much to be laughed at. And, yes, we'll practice today, but as for watching us, won't you be at lessons again, now Father Morice is no longer needed to clerk the marriage talks?"

"He's going to be busy fair-copying the agreement out several times over. He has the best hand on the manor, my father says," Will said. "With that and going to the village

to say the banns, he'll be too busy for me most of the day."
Will's face fell. "You don't want me to watch you, do you?"

That leap to expected disappointment seemed to come
from nowhere, and Basset laid a hand on his shoulder, saying, smiling, "After we've broken our fast, you may watch
us rehearse all morning if you want."

Will stared at him, so openly uncertain whether Basset
meant that or not that Joliffe wondered who lied to him so
often he expected it. Basset must have seen Will's uncertainty, too, because he said, "I mean it. You can watch for
as long as you want, or until someone comes to fetch you."
Because, as he had otherwise said, there was never a bad
time to encourage a love of plays in those who had—or, in
Will's case, would someday have—the money to pay for
the playing. "It may not much benefit us here and now," he
had told Joliffe in his early days with the company, "but it
may serve other player-folk when they come this way, and
hopefully they're doing likewise for us wherever they are."

"But," Basset said now to Will, raising a warning finger,
"you must keep our secrets and not give away aforetime
what you see us do here."

"I won't," Will promised readily, happily. "I'm good at
keeping secrets."

"Such as?" Joliffe asked.

Will opened his mouth to answer, then broke into laughter. "I'm not going to tell you!"

They laughed with him, except for Ellis, who settled for
shoving Joliffe hard on the arm, rocking him to the side.
Joliffe, for more laughter, turned that into a wild-armed
tottering before he windmilled himself back onto the balance he had never lost. That made Piers, Gil, and Will
laugh more as they all started away to breakfast, walking
slowly because of Basset's stiffness.

Joliffe let himself wonder what they would do if this
arthritic flare didn't ease before it was time to move on

again. Basset would have to ride in the cart and that would slow Tisbe and that would slow all of them, lengthening the times between when they could play. Still, that was not so desperate a matter as it might have been, not with Lord Lovell's gold coin for comfort against lean times.

The trouble with once having that comfort was that the thought of losing it was the harder to face. They had been cast adrift as lordless players before this, when they lost their last patron's favor. It wasn't something Joliffe wanted to happen again, but what if he failed in the task Lord Lovell had set him and Basset? It was a vague enough task at best—determine if something had or hadn't been wrong about a death, and whether there was or wasn't something to be worried over about the present marriage plans. Maybe Lord Lovell would be satisfied with a vague answer at the end of it all?

Probably. He did not seem an unfair man.

But neither did he seem a man who would take less than he paid for. If their vague answer at the end included another death, how less than satisfied was he likely to be?

In a poor attempt to lighten his own dissatisfied thoughts as he trailed behind the other players across the wide yard toward the hall, Joliffe decided that would probably depend on who was dead.

Of course, if Harcourt's death *had* been murder, why was the pattern changed? Last time the bridegroom-to-be had died. This time it was Mariena who had fallen so ill that the priest was called. And yet, despite of that, she had been so certain she would not die that she had refused his help.

Had that been merely from the blind refusal of mortality too many people had, or did it mean something else?

And were Will's accidents only accidents, or were *they* something more than they seemed, too?

Had an attempt at murder been made against Will yesterday and another against Mariena last night?

John Harcourt's death had disappointed Sir Edmund's plans of a profitable alliance. Mariena's death would make an end of any other plans forever and at all. And Will's death would disappoint Sir Edmund's hope of a male heir. But if someone was that set against Sir Edmund, why not just straight-forwardly kill *him* instead? Because there was more satisfaction in destroying him piecemeal? Or because someone was simply against the whole family?

The first person who came to mind that way was Harry Wyot.

What if he indeed had a deep-running resentment against Sir Edmund for his disparaging marriage to this Idonea Coket? It could be he liked his wife and still resented Sir Edmund. Sia might be able to tell him if that were likely, Joliffe hoped, and on his own he'd assuredly be taking more careful look at them together when he had the chance.

Chance didn't come in the hall this morning, though, either to watch the Wyots or to talk to Sia. Neither she nor Avice were to be seen and there was no sign of their betters, but from the general talk and tired faces, Joliffe easily gathered everyone's night must have been long and as fully unpleasant as Will's telling had made it seem.

When Basset reasonably asked after the family's health, the clerk Duffeld told him, "They're all having their breakfasts in their chambers this morning. With all the toing and froing last night there was hardly sleep for anyone until nearly dawn." Including him, by the look of him.

"You're likely glad, then, that Father Morice is to copy out the marriage agreement, rather than you," Joliffe said. Ellis looked at him sharply, instantly knowing what he was about.

Duffeld, probably bored with watching other people eat, huffed agreement with that. "I am, and he's welcome to it. With all the 'and ifs' and 'shoulds' he and Sir Edmund and Master Breche argued into it, the thing goes on forever."

"Worse than the one for the Harcourt marriage?" Joliffe asked. Ellis turned his back to him.

"That one," Duffeld said with open dislike and disgust. "That one I thought would never be finished. This one is nothing to that. With the Harcourt one, every point was looked at from fifty ways and then looked at again. And then for him to die before ever . . ." The clerk broke off, shaking of his head.

"I've heard good of him," Joliffe lied. "That he was well-liked and all."

"Have you?" Duffeld seemed surprised by that but discretion held sway; he only said, "Yes, well, my lady Mariena favored him, assuredly. She was nigh ill with grief and anger after his death."

"Anger?" Joliffe prodded lightly.

"That he could be dead. Grief takes some people that way, you know."

Joliffe had to grant that it did. "Who was his heir?" he asked, making it sound like no more than shallow curiosity.

"A cousin of some sort. No one we ever saw."

The other players had moved away, but there were still folk around the table, keeping the clerk in watch on them. Seeing no reason not to make use of the chance to ask him everything possible, Joliffe asked, "Sir Edmund could have pursued a marriage for Mariena with the cousin, couldn't he? Or is the man married?"

"I'd not heard he was married, no, but Sir Edmund never seemed to think of another marriage that way. A month on, Amyas Breche began to be talked of."

"That was Master Wyot's doing, wasn't it?" Joliffe said, · deliberately wrong.

"Master Wyot's?" The clerk seemed to find that both improbable and laughable. "I doubt that very much. No, assuredly not. He'd never . . ." Duffeld stopped short, abruptly disapproving, maybe of himself, and said repressively,

"Master Wyot is here only as Amyas Breche's friend. He has nothing to do with the marriage."

Unrepressed, Joliffe asked cheerfully, as if simply making talk and not much interested in the question or any answer, "He was supposed to marry Mariena himself, wasn't he?"

"There was brief talk of it." The clerk was beyond repressive to curt. "It was decided otherwise."

"Hard on Master Wyot," Joliffe said with a sad shake of his head.

"He didn't mind," the clerk said coldly and walked away.

Keeping unconcern all over his face, Joliffe took a long drink from the cup he held, sorting what he had learned. Besides making clear his disapproval of the whole subject, Duffeld had confirmed that it had been Master Wyot who did not want the marriage. About the proposed Harcourt marriage he had talked freely enough, though, and what he had had to say there had been as interesting, in its way, as his not wanting to talk about Harry Wyot at all.

Ellis butted him with an elbow in his back. "We're going. Time to work."

In truth, the play they meant to do tonight—*The Husband Becomes the Wife*—was one they did often and at most they needed no more than an easy run through it to be sure their speeches were crisp in their heads. With Will there, though, looking vastly eager, Basset made something more of the business than he might have, telling Joliffe to wear the rough rehearsing-skirt and making show, while they walked through it, of telling Gil what to note while he watched.

The story was simply the old one of the husband who complained his wife's life was too easy compared to his and all the misfortunes that came of him taking her place for a day. As the husband, Ellis got to swagger at first, and then fall about in hapless disasters. Joliffe as the wife got to shrill at him and flounce about, while Piers was the ill-mannered, whining child and Basset the husband's mother-in-law, with a fine time had all around, especially by the lookers-on.

At the end of their run-through, Basset said, "That was well. I think we need not go it again."

Ellis muttered for only Joliffe to hear that they need not have gone it this time so far as he could see: they could all do the old thing in their sleep.

Basset sat down with stiff care on the piled cushions against the cart's wheel. Rose had been brewing one of her herbal drinks to ease his pain and he took it from her with thanks, then asked, "Gil, what do you think?"

"Skirts," said Gil. "I need to learn more with skirts."

"Well noted," Basset said with approval. "Skirts and swords and how to walk across a stage . . ."

"Everybody knows how to walk," Will protested scornfully.

"Ah," said Basset. "That's what you think. Everyone but Will, come stand here by me. You, too, Rose. Now you, Will, go out to where we were playing and walk back and forth for us."

Will obeyed. Or tried to. It took him only a few steps to know he was being awkward, too conscious of all their eyes on him and nowhere else. He couldn't make his walk go easily; it wanted to be either strut or stiff shuffle, and he couldn't stop looking sideways at all of them watching him, until he suddenly bent over in laughter and shouted, "I can't!"

They laughed, too, and Basset said, "Now you do it, Gil."

Will came to sit cross-legged beside Piers while Gil went in front of them and tried to walk. He was somewhat better but still too openly aware of being watched, his stride too stiff.

"Now Joliffe," Basset bade.

Taking Gil's place, Joliffe asked, "What sort of walk?"

"Just a man's stride," Basset said.

"What sort of man?"

"A knight."

Joliffe put hand to imaginary sword hilt and strode out as if expecting a fight.

"A clerk," Basset said.

Joliffe was immediately carrying a bundle of books in his arms and walking the small way of someone who spent much of his time at a desk.

"A young girl."

Joliffe's steps turned light and his hips had a sway not there before.

"An old woman."

Joliffe's shoulders curved forward and he shuffled, helping himself along with a stick that was not there.

"Me," Basset said.

Joliffe straightened and asked, "With or without the arthritic hobble?"

Piers and Will laughed. Basset told Joliffe he was a rude boy and could have done. Ellis muttered, "He's not done; he's half-baked," and got up to do something else. So did Rose, but Gil sat looking deeply thoughtful and that was to the good, Joliffe thought. Like Will, too many people saw play-acting as only a matter of learning the words and walking around with people to look at you. To Joliffe and Basset and anyone else in earnest about the work, playing was a craft whose skills had to be learned like the skills of any craft; and as with every craft, some folk were better at it than others were. Ellis was good within his limits. Joliffe was better, able to play far more sorts of parts, though no one in the company—including himself—ever said as much aloud. Basset, as befitted a company-master, was good at many parts and best at seeing a play as a whole and setting them all to what they had to do. What Gil would be able to do remained to be seen but that he sat there now, thinking, promised well.

A manservant whom Joliffe recognized from the hall came around the corner of the carpentry shed, and Will stood immediately up, saying, "I'm wanted."

"Your lady mother was asking for you, yes, Master William," the man said with a bow. "You're to ride with the company to hear the first banns read at the church."

"Now?" Will's disgust at the thought showed openly.

"Now," the man said.

With all the shine gone from him, William thanked Basset and then the others and went away, sullen-faced, with the servant. When they were beyond hearing, Basset said, "Not looking forward to losing his sister, do you think?"

"Not looking forward to riding after his fall yesterday," said Ellis. He was settling to oil some more leather. "Is Tisbe going out to graze today or not?"

"It's going to rain again," Piers protested, then added, "It *is* raining," as a few drops pattered down in the yard.

"We'll wait until there's no rain before we feed you," Ellis said. "See how you like that."

"I think," said Basset in a considering voice, "it looks like clearing by this afternoon. Tisbe can wait until then. Only do your duty now." He nodded toward the shovel. "Nor I doubt we'll be grudged half an armful of hay if we ask. Piers, shovel. Gil, hay. And then the both of you can go with Joliffe to the village to add some festive cheer to this bann-reading."

"Go to the village?" Piers moaned. "Walk, you mean?"

"It's how we get most places," Basset pointed out.

Piers shoveled up Tisbe's dung and went away with it while Gil went for the hay and Basset said to Joliffe, "This will be chance to see Sir Edmund and them all together other than in the hall and afterwards to hear among the village folk what they think of this marriage and all."

Aware of Rose watching them both with worry and of Ellis deliberately very busy with a piece of harness, Joliffe said easily, making little of it, "Well thought. And if I send Father Morice to give you comfort in your affliction, maybe you can have more from him, too. See if he'll tell you about this present marriage agreement, for one thing. I'd not mind knowing why it's been easier done than the Harcourt one, since it seems he was the one who made the difficulties there."

Rose turned away in a way that said she was unhappy with them both, and Ellis' head went lower over his work, but Basset nodded agreement and said, "Have him come, yes, if he will. I'll even be somewhat more afflicted than I am and"—he slumped and his voice went feeble—"and in need of talk to distract and cheer me."

Chapter 12

As it happened, it was Sir Edmund, Will, the Breches, and Harry Wyot who rode into the village to hear the first banns read. Whether for the rain—still pattering down in fits and starts—or other reason, neither Lady Benedicta, Mariena, nor Idonea Wyot went with them, but a good gathering of villagers drew to the church, it being near to mid-day and folk in from the fields to their dinners. Joliffe watched with Piers and Gil from under the eaves of a house across the lane from the churchyard while Father Morice, in full priestly vestments, stood in the church doorway to read out to the riders and gathered villagers the first banns, declaring that a marriage was intended and telling between whom, his voice not trained for the strain of being heard any distance in the open air. Not that it much mattered; he was heard enough for the betrothal between Amyas and Mariena to be now publicly known, with no way to break it off or stop their marriage without expensive legalities and troubles from the church.

Or death, thought Joliffe.

Finished, Father Morice came away from the church door to Sir Edmund, who leaned from his saddle to say something to him, smiling. The other men were already turning their horses away, but Will stayed at his father's side and the villagers still lingered. With good reason, Joliffe saw, as Sir Edmund finished with Father Morice, gathered up his reins, and while turning his horse away, said something to Will. It must have been an order for something already arranged between them, because Will nodded, fumbled in the leather pouch at his belt, and brought out and threw a handful of pennies across the hard earth of the lane outside the churchyard gateway as Sir Edmund and the other men rode away. Children and a few women darted forward to snatch up the coins almost before they were on the ground. One man bent to take one that fell at his feet but otherwise the men left the scurrying to their children and wives, doing their own part by raising a brief cheer of thanks to the backs of the departing men and Will before crowding into little family groups to count their gains. Father Morice, Joliffe saw, had gone back into the church to take off his vestments.

Joliffe nudged Piers. "Now's the time." And to Gil, "Watch."

Piers, ever ready to be noticed, cried a glad, "Hah-ha!" to draw people's eyes to him and, stepping forward into the street, set five bright balls immediately fountaining from his hands to a little above his head and down and up again, around and around. People turned, first to look at him, then to gather around to watch, making a horseshoe that left Joliffe and Gil standing alone with their backs still to the house where they had sheltered.

Piers made a fair show, varying how many balls he had in the air at once and keeping them going, but it was simple juggling, such as could be seen from any common juggler anytime, and Joliffe began to shake his head, looking dissatisfied with what he was seeing. Then he stepped forward to Piers' side. Piers glanced aside as best he could without losing track of the balls and went on juggling, turning to put his back to Joliffe. Joliffe moved to his other side, to force Piers to notice him. Piers turned away again. This time Joliffe pushed his shoulder from behind. Piers gave him a glare but kept on juggling. Joliffe gave him another shove, hard enough to stagger him forward a step. Seemingly off-balance, Piers grabbed wildly and caught all the falling balls save a red one that hit the hard-trodden mud and rolled away to the nearest feet among the lookers-on. Piers scurried after it, people laughing at him as people did at others' troubles. Behind him, left alone, Joliffe reached into the breast of his doublet, brought out three juggling balls of his own and strutted in a circle, holding them up for everyone to see. Then, ignoring Piers' glare at him, he set to his own juggling, throwing the balls awkwardly one after another high above his head.

They came plummeting down as out of rhythm as he had thrown them. He grabbed at them frantically, caught one, missed the other two. They landed with flat plops in front of him. The lead weights inside of them and slight lack of stuffing ensured they would. To more laughter, this time at him, he snatched them up and tried again, to no better avail. He was making his third desperate attempt when Piers—having started his own juggling again—came forward and grabbed first one and then another of Joliffe's ill-fated balls from the air, adding them to his own. Left with only one ball, Joliffe tried to make show of tossing it straight up in the air and catching it as it came down. On his second time of that, Piers scornfully grabbed it, too, and sent all eight balls in a merry fountain of color high over his head and back, around and around, while everyone laughed and Joliffe took awkward, inadequate bows that brought more laughter, until Piers collapsed his fountain, caught all the balls one after the other into his arms, and made his own deep, graceful bow to thorough clapping all around. But when one woman started forward with a coin, Joliffe held up a hand and said, smiling, "For the lady Mariena's betrothal. Sir Edmund gives pennies. We give laughter. For each, the best that he can do."

That brought more clapping, to which Piers gladly bowed some more, until Joliffe collared him and hauled him away along the lane, leaving more laughter behind them. The alehouse was hardly a dozen yards along; they went in. Today there was no warmth of crowded bodies and candlelight, only wet, grey daylight through the open doorway and the glassless gap of the window, and sitting at a battered table a lone young man with a bandaged foot resting on a stool and two old men, one of whom raised an ale-filled bowl to the players and said, "Saw most of that from the doorway. Sir Edmund put on a good show, but yours was the better."

Piers started to bow again. Joliffe feigned booting his backside, steered him to a bench near the table and sat him down, gave a coin to Gil, and said, "Get small ale for all of us. I have to see Father Morice, but it won't take long. I'll be directly back."

He turned from the bench to find the alewife had come in behind him, a woman in middle years, her kerchief over her hair somewhat askew and her apron as clean as much scrubbing could make it. Both she and the small child she had by the hand were smiling as she told Joliffe in passing, "The first drink is free to you fellows. For the laughter, thank you."

"Thank *you*," Joliffe said and gave her a bow more flourished than he would have bestowed on the queen, leaving her in a smiling blush as he went out the door, to find that his luck was in—Father Morice was just setting off along the now-deserted street toward the manor. Stretching out his stride, Joliffe overtook him, saying as he caught him up, "Sir, a favor, please."

Joliffe had made no effort to hide his footfall, but soft-soled shoes made little sound and the priest must have been deep in thoughts of his own and heard nothing. He turned, unready, toward Joliffe, his face showing a naked, stark unhappiness in the instant before he shifted it into surprised welcome and said, "Well met! What do you here?"

Pretending he had seen nothing amiss, Joliffe said, "Some of us came to juggle a little for the villagers after the banns were said. Our own celebration for the betrothal."

He said that last deliberately to see if the priest's trouble lay that way; and if the flinching at the corners of Father Morice's eyes was sign, it did; but the priest only said, "That was good of you. The villagers need all the celebrating there can be after this year's poor harvest again."

"Too true," Joliffe agreed. "But I've a good to ask of you, sir, if I may."

"Ask."

Joliffe told him of Basset's arthritics and the comfort it would be if Father Morice went to talk with him. The priest assured him it would be his own pleasure to do so, and they parted company—Father Morice on toward the manor, Joliffe back to the alehouse, where he found Piers giving Gil and the alewife's little boy a juggling lesson and the alewife setting bowls of vegetable pottage on the table for the three village men. Aware he and Piers and Gil were going to miss their dinner at the hall, Joliffe asked for some for them, too.

"If there's enough?"

"There is," she said. "The turnips in the upper field did not so badly as everything else this year, and with all the rain the grass has the cows giving plenty of milk for the while."

"Not but what we're getting tired of your milk-and-turnip pottage," one of the old men muttered between spoonfuls.

"You'd get more tired of being hungry," the woman said as she went back toward her kitchen. "Be thankful we have what we have."

Piers, Gil, and the little boy were crawling about among the floor-rushes, collecting fallen balls. Joliffe sat down on a bench near the table, making a show of being somewhat stiff, although he was not, to give him an opening with the men, and said, "This weather gets into the bones, doesn't it?"

"Not into theirs," the injured man said, nodding at the three boys. He sounded both disgruntled and envious.

Joliffe nodded at his bandaged foot. "Gout?"

That surprised one of the old men into a hoot of laughter. The other snorted into his ale bowl, and the hurt man said, "A dropped pitchfork. Right through it."

Joliffe made a pained noise of fellow-feeling.

"Good it was a cleaned fork," one of the old men jibed, "or you'd not be sitting here to complain of it."

"Better if I'd not done it at all," the other man said sharply back. "You fellows," he said at Joliffe, "you've the life. No pitchforks for you. All words and the women looking at you. If you don't like it here"—he made a wide swing of his arm, endangering the ale in the bowl he held—"you go on there. Free as birds, you fellows are."

He had downed too much ale. Even a brew as weak as this one would finally be too much if someone drank enough and he had probably been at it all morning, adding it to the mix of pity and the pain he was probably in. So Joliffe, forbearing to point out that birds were "free" to be cold in hedges and hunted by anyone who felt like it, only said easily, "The trouble is that, even if we happen to like wherever we are, we still have to move on to somewhere else, like it or not."

"I wouldn't mind moving on to somewhere else," the man grumbled into his ale.

"It's as good here as anywhere," one of the old men said. "They're all the same, most places."

Less philosophically, his companion in age and drink said, "Everywhere had as ill an harvest as we did, from what's said. There's no point going somewhere else." He gave Joliffe a nod. "'Less you have to, 'course."

"I'd still like to go," the hurt man grumbled. "I'd still like to *do* something else than this."

"What?" one of the old men said. "Something else than sit dry and drink the livelong day? Don't be addle-witted. I'll tell you I worked a lifetime to be able to do this."

"'Til your daughter decides you've had enough and hails you home to chores," the other old man chuckled.

"Aye, and the more reason to enjoy what I have while I have it." He poked the younger man's arm. "You heed me, boy. Be glad you've got what you've got." Raising his bowl, he mumbled just before burying his nose in it, "It's not like you've choice in it, anyway."

The other old man raised his own bowl to that and drank, too. The younger man simply drank, staring broodingly at the wall while he did. Joliffe, watching him over the rim of his own bowl, felt for his discontent. In his own life there were other things he could have been besides a player—several other things he *had* been besides a player—but at least he had had choices and made them. He doubted this fellow had ever seen anything else to be but what he was. Or else he had refused other choices if they ever came. But staying with what you were born to was a choice, too, and the one that most people made—a choice that Joliffe could have made, too, upon a time, but had not and of that he was still glad. However cold the hedge sometimes was.

But this was not getting him what he wanted. The three
boys were sitting on the floor at the far end of the room,
each with a bowl of pottage the woman had just handed
down from a tray. As she came along the room with another bowl for Joliffe, he harked back to the bad harvest,
saying, "Going to be a lean year all around, no matter
where you are. Will Sir Edmund scant the wedding feast,
do you think?"

"Nah, not him," one of the old men said. "There'll be
plenty. And even if it's no more than plenty of turnip pottage, it'll taste the better with what his cook does with it."

Joliffe smiled his thanks to the woman as she handed
him the bowl, a wooden spoon ready in it.

"Spices and like," the other old man offered. "Brings
'em in from London-town." A far-off, foreign place they
would never see. "Those nutmeg-savored cakes, remember
them?" he asked his fellow, who smacked his lips in answer and said, "Could do with more of those."

Joliffe had tasted the present pottage by then and said,
unfeignedly approving, to the woman still standing there,
"London spices or not, you've given this savor. It's very
good."

She smiled at him. "There's herbs to be had here that do
well enough for those as know what to do with them."

"Basil?" Joliffe guessed at hazard.

Her smile warmed. "Yes. And a touch of sage."

He had another spoonful, letting her see how much he
enjoyed it, while one of the old men granted somewhat
grudgingly, "Aye, girl, you do well. But you'll eat as hearty
of the wedding feast as any of us, come the time."

"I never said I wouldn't, and I'll remember it afterwards
with as many sighs as you do. Sir Edmund does what's
right by folk, I'll give him that."

Something in the way she said that, though, made Joliffe ask, "But?"

She moved her shoulders uneasily and shifted her tray from one hip to the other. "It's *how* he does things."

"Ah, you've gone on about that before," one of the old men said. "You've got a flea on your brain about it."

But hers was the first thing near to a complaint of Sir Edmund that Joliffe had heard and he asked, "How do you mean?" The question was too open. He saw her start to close off from saying more and added quickly, "If we don't please him well enough—the boys"—he gestured to Piers and Gil now making her son laugh as they started his juggling lessons again—"and me and the rest of the company—he might ill-speak us to Lord Lovell. Is there a way we're likely to put a foot wrong?"

Appealed to that way, the woman opened up again, re-assuring him, "No, you'll likely please him without much trouble. He'll do right by you, too, but . . ."

She paused, trying to find what she wanted to say. The hurt man grunted, brooding into his ale bowl. "All 'buts' and 'ifs.' Everything is all 'buts' and 'ifs.'" Without lifting his head, he thrust the ale bowl toward her. "More."

She took it. "It's that there's no heart to him," she said. "In Sir Edmund, I mean. No heart in what he does, no matter who he does it for."

"You've a flea on your brain," the old man said again. "What's heart got to do with it, so long as he gives us our rights, takes no more than his own, and leaves us alone the rest of the time?"

"And feasts us at harvest and Christmas, remember," his fellow added.

The woman shook her head, impatient with them but lacking words for more answer.

Joliffe offered, "Without his heart is in it, it's hollow, what he does."

"That's it," the woman said, pleased. "He's hollow."

"Doesn't matter he's hollow so long as—" the old man started.

"It does matter," the woman interrupted. With Joliffe to back her, she was suddenly fierce. "It's like saying it doesn't matter if . . . if . . ."

She cast around for way to say what she wanted to say, and Joliffe put in, "It's like saying it doesn't matter if the two sides of a roof stay up if you lean them together without any rafters. It does matter, because without the rafters, you can't be sure how long it will stay before it falls on you."

"Like that, yes!" she said, pleased to have it said for her. "Or those puffball mushrooms you find, all big and looking solid, but you step on them and they turn to nothing, being all hollow inside."

"More ale," the hurt man said sullenly.

"Only because your wife will thank me for keeping you quiet," the alewife snapped and went away.

Left to see what else he could have from the old men, Joliffe harked back to, "At least there'll be fine feasting at the wedding."

"Aye," one of the old men said and the other agreed, "That there'll be. Fool woman."

"You must have thought you'd lost your chance at it for this year when . . . What was his name? The other one the girl was going to marry. The fellow who died?"

"Harcourt. John Harcourt," one of the men obliged.

"That was it. How near was it to the wedding when it happened? He died here, didn't he?"

"He did," one of the old men said, and the other went on, "The cart carrying his body home to bury passed right through the village, it did. All draped in black and him coffined and all."

"No funeral feast, though, because they took him away to bury."

The alewife was back with a filled bowl for the hurt man. He took it without thanks or shifting his stare from the wall in front of him; nor did she give him more heed than to be sure his grip on the bowl was firm before she rejoined the talk with, "He'd ridden through here on his way to the manor four days before, and a fine sight he was. Dressed in green and yellow and sitting his horse like the fine knight he was going to be. It was said Sir Edmund would knight him at the wedding, belike."

"He was come then for the wedding itself?" Joliffe asked.

"Not then," she said. "It was a month maybe to the wedding yet, but he couldn't stay away from Mariena, like. He lived only a day's ride away, so it was no great matter."

"Less than a day, if you hurry it, I hear," one of the old men said.

The other one chuckled deep in his throat. "Which Lady Benedicta did upon a time. And more than once."

"Half a day if they met in the middle, and half a day's ride back," his fellow said.

"Don't start in with that old story," the alewife said. "It was all long ago, if it ever happened at all."

"It happened," one of the men said.

"Long summer days when it doesn't get dark until late," his fellow went on, "there'd be time to meet in the middle and do what they'd do and her be home again before dark."

"As if she could be gone that long without Sir Edmund wondering," the alewife scoffed.

"He wasn't home that summer, was he?" one of the men said, sharp at being contradicted. "Gone off to London about some trouble needing lawyers."

"Westminster," his fellow said. "He was gone to Westminster and the courts there."

"All the same. He was far off and not to know what his wife was doing."

"Do you think," the alewife said, sharp, too, and impatient, though this was likely something they had all gone around more than once before now, "that Sir Edmund would set to marry his daughter to the man . . ."

"Always supposing she is his daughter." The old man nudged his fellow in the ribs. His fellow nudged him back. They were both taking ribald pleasure in sins—or supposed sins—long past. But then their own sins that way were probably long past, too, and in memory other people's would do as well as their own.

"She's his daughter," the alewife said, more impatient and at them both. "She was born a good more than nine months after he came back, wasn't she? And if he doubted she was," the woman added triumphantly, "do you think he'd set to marrying her to the son of the man who'd cuckolded him?"

She had them there and they knew it, but one of them made a fighting retreat, saying, "Aye, right. But something went on that summer someways. Things was never warm between Lady Benedicta and Sir Edmund since then."

"Things weren't probably warm between them before then," the alewife shot back. "I've said—"

"Aye, aye, we all know what you've said."

"And whatever happened or didn't," she went on, "the man is long since dead anyway." Remembering Joliffe was a stranger and probably unknowing about all this, she added to him, "It's all old talk and nothing to do with anything now."

Joliffe nodded as if she had enlightened him on some great matter and tried, to keep the talk going the interesting way it had been, "If that's the only talk there's ever been against Lady Benedicta, seems there can't be much in it."

The alewife willingly took him up on that. "She's as good a lady as could be asked for," she said firmly, then pointed an accusing finger at one of the old men. "And you know it, Rafe. She sent that syrup for your grandson that stopped his cough last winter when it was like to have driven him into his grave. So mind your tongues, all of you, in this house anyway."

Probably minding more that she was the alewife who let them sit about her place not drinking much, one of the old men said, "You're in the right, goodwife. You're in the right about her. There's been no other talk about her in all these years since."

"Learned her lesson that time," his fellow said into his ale, low enough the alewife ignored him.

"And Sir Edmund has never strayed?" Joliffe tried, to keep the talk going.

"Not so it matters," the other old man said. "Not that we know of."

The alewife came back at him, "Meaning it doesn't matter what one of you men do, so long as we don't know about it? That it isn't wrong unless it's found out and we jaw about it forever? Is that what you're saying?"

"Nah, nah," he hurriedly denied. "That's not what I'm saying. Wrong is wrong. But—"

"Something's wrong somewhere here, though," the young man said broodingly at the wall. The links between his mind and his mouth and the world around him were slurring away with drink and he said the words with the deliberate care of someone having to work at them. "Something's wrong somewhere, that's sure. Bad harvests two years in a row. Another hunger-winter coming. God's against us. Something has set God against us. We—"

"He's against more than us, if that's the way of it, and I doubt Father Morice will thank you for saying so," the alewife snapped. She turned to Joliffe. "You folk get around. It's no better anywhere else, is it? Weather and harvest and all, they've been bad everywhere, haven't they?"

"It's no better anywhere else, that I've heard or seen," Joliffe said. "Not for anyone."

Thought of the bad harvest and the famine-winter to come settled into a dark quiet on them all. Across the room, Piers and Gil were encouraging the alewife's son at his juggling—he had two balls behaving well for him—and their merriment was sharp against their elders' sudden silence. The alewife said suddenly, "Well, there's *some* has work to do." She held out her hand to Joliffe. He had the coins ready, gave her two pennies, and asked, "Enough?"

She gave him a wide smile. "Town prices for village fare."

"Well worth it, it being fare better than I've had in many a town."

"You'll be welcome here again," she said warmly, gave the other men a look to tell them their welcome was less likely, and went away through the rear doorway, calling her son to her as she went.

Figuring he had likely learned all he was going to here, Joliffe stood up, too, called Piers and Gil to him, made farewell to the men, and left, satisfied in belly if not in mind. He'd heard much and learned little, but at least the story against Lady Benedicta had been repeated, so he knew it wasn't just one man making up tales. He'd like to know if the syrup she'd sent to the ill grandson had been of her own making. Was she skilled at healing with herbs? Because the skill could be set the other way—to kill. Or to make ill. The way Mariena had been suddenly ill last night.

But why her own daughter?

Answer to that would be hard to have. Nor did it go with Will's fall yesterday. If that had been more than accident and Mariena's illness more than chance, someone was against both of them, and Joliffe had trouble forcing his mind around the possibility it was their own mother.

But if she was . . . then why? Or rather, why now?

He'd probably do better to consider who else it might be. Who had reason? And what reason?

But those would be answers equally hard to come by. Maybe better to consider *how* the attempts against Will and Mariena had been done.

Always supposing there had truly been attempts against them and not simply mischances.

Either way, *how* at least was an outward thing and more likely to be found out than the inward workings of someone's mind. More likely—but not *very* likely, Joliffe regretfully admitted to himself.

Chapter 13

Joliffe's thoughts had seen him a good way back to the manor, forgetful of Piers and Gil walking and talking together behind him, but as they neared the drawbridge, Piers came beside him and pushed at his elbow, saying, "Gil has a question."

Ready to think about something other than the Denebys, Joliffe said grandly, "Ask, and from my wisdom I shall answer."

"It won't be much of an answer then," Piers said.

Joliffe gave him a shove that threatened to topple him into the water-flowing ditch beside the road without putting him in any danger of really doing so; Rose would skin them both if they came back muddier than need be. Joliffe looked to Gil, now walking on his other side, and asked, kindly, "What is it?"

"Your juggling. Piers says you're really as bad as you pretended to be there in the village." Gil sounded doubtful that could be possible.

Joliffe shook his head in sad, mostly false, regret. "He, alas, speaks true. Mind you, it takes some skill to juggle badly in exactly the right way, as I did then . . ." Piers snorted but was carefully beyond reach and Joliffe went on, "It's true, though. I can't juggle. Basset can juggle. Ellis and Piers can juggle. Rose can juggle when she chooses. I can't juggle. But even skillessness can be put to use, and so we use mine for what it's worth. In balance against it, I somewhat play the lute and I sing . . ."

"Somewhat," Piers put in crushingly.

". . . and Ellis can't do either," Joliffe continued smoothly. "And mind you," he added thoughtfully, "for *his* lack of skill we've yet to find any use at all, while mine is good for something."

"If not much," Piers said.

He had come in reach again and Joliffe gave him a solid shove on the shoulder, saying, "If I want to be insulted, I'll ask Ellis. He does well enough at it without you help him out."

"But it's so—"

"If you say 'easy,' I *will* shove you in the ditch and take what comes."

Darting ahead and out of reach, Piers cried, ". . . easy!" and set off at a run for the drawbridge.

Joliffe gave Gil a friendly nod. "Go on with him, if you want."

Gil shook his head, looking as if he was gone suddenly shy, and it came to Joliffe that after all Gil was about half the way from Piers to him in age and very probably would prefer other company than a small boy's. Piers was old for his years in many ways but still a small boy in most, and Joliffe was not so far from being Gil's age that he couldn't remember the urge to be even farther away from childhood. So he smiled friendliwise and asked, "How goes it with you? Still want to be a player?"

"I do," Gil said instantly. "The more I learn, the better it is."

St. Genesius help the boy, Joliffe prayed silently and said aloud, "This isn't much the way it mostly goes. Mostly we're from place to place one day after another, not lying about like this."

Gil bobbed his head in ready understanding. "I know. This has just been good chance for me, giving me time to learn more before we move on. But the moving on is part of the good part of being a player, isn't it? The always being somewhere different?"

"That's part of the good, yes," Joliffe granted—and didn't add that sometimes that was a very small good against the weariness there could be in forever being somewhere else. Gil's pleasure in the traveling would wax and wane like everyone's. Or else just wane completely and he'd find something else to do with his life. For now, though, he thought he wanted to be a player, and Joliffe asked, "What are you finding hardest to learn of Basset's lessons thus far?"

"How to be a girl," Gil said so quickly and from the heart that Joliffe had to hold back a laugh.

Waiting until sure his voice would be sober enough, he agreed, "That can be hard, yes. Skirts and voice and gestures and all. You're doing well from what I've seen."

"Not good enough, though."

"It will come. You have to start feeling you're a girl, and that takes a time."

"How can I feel like a girl? I'm not."

That was a fair question and a good one and Joliffe paused over his answer, then said, "It isn't true just of playing a girl. It's what you have to do when playing anyone. None of us have ever really been most of what we play, a multitude of saints be thanked for that. We're not likely ever to be a hero or a tragic lover or a saint and certainly never the Devil or God. We play the seeming of a great many people we'll never be, without ever becoming them. In truth—and if Basset hasn't told you this, he will—for us to think ourselves into fully being whatever we play would be the worst thing we could do to our playing. Has Basset told you about the layers of your mind you need when playing?"

"No."

"He will," Joliffe said with deep feeling. It was one of Basset's best lessons and he had said more than once, to set it firmly in mind. "That's not to be you out there for the audience to see. Nobody is likely to pay coins to look at you, my fellow. Or any of us, come to that. But if *you* ever forget it's you out there playing the part, I'll whip you black and blue afterwards." Which he would not have done; that was only to show how deeply he meant what he was saying as he went on, "When you're playing, there should be three layers all happening together in your mind. Outwardly, for the world to see, everything you say and do are the words and gestures of whoever you're playing. You should even be thinking as whoever you're playing. But only with the outermost layer of your mind. Behind that outward seeming, there's you yourself—the craftsman never losing judgment over his work, never losing heed of the play. That will be the layer of your mind that saves you if anything goes wrong, the part that makes sure the play doesn't take over so strongly that it's running you instead of the other way on. Behind that, there'll be the back part of your mind that has better things to do altogether and will be wondering if the ale is good in the nearest tavern and why is that woman talking to the woman next to her among the lookers-on instead of watching you and if there'll be roast beef for dinner or only porridge."

Since Basset would be saying all that when the time came for it, Joliffe chose not to burden Gil with it just yet and settled for saying, "What will maybe help you best now is to remember that you're not learning to *be* a girl. You're learning to *seem* a girl. Just as you're learning the skills that will help you seem to be a saint and a tragic lover and everything else you'll ever play. You'll find no better master for teaching you that than Basset." Easily, careful not to come too heavy-handed about it, he added, "But if you aren't willing to seem to be anything and everything, you've no business being a player at all."

He hoped it was a good thing that Gil made no answer to that, merely looked deeply thoughtful the rest of the way back to the cartshed. There, despite Basset looked to be right about a drier afternoon—the clouds were thinning, streaks of blue beginning to appear among them—Piers wailed when Basset, still seated on the piled cushions but looking somewhat less ill-eased, said he and Gil were still to take Tisbe out to her grazing this afternoon.

"We've just been walking our legs off," he protested. "You want us to walk more?"

"You can ride Tisbe out and Gil can ride her back if you're feeling feeble," his grandfather said.

"She's bony! Her spine cuts right into me!"

"Then you can walk," Basset said pleasantly. "Your choice. Just get on with it."

"It's Joliffe's turn to take her!"

"I need to talk with Joliffe."

"Gil needs more lessons."

"Gil will have them, but not just now." Basset pointed firmly away. "Go."

Gil already had Tisbe untied and was waiting, the mare nuzzling and nibbling at his shoulder to show she was ready if no one else was. Piers tried one more time, pitiful now. "I didn't have much dinner, you know."

"Good," his grandfather said. "You're getting soft. This will toughen you up for the road we'll be on again in a few days."

Scuffling and put upon, Piers joined Gil and Tisbe and they went. For a moment Basset waited, probably half-expecting Piers would pop back with one last try. The carpenter was at work; the tap-tap-tap of wooden pegs being gently hammered into holes suggested he was joining something. It was a small, friendly sound, as sounds went, and when it was plain that Piers was not coming back, Basset said, as if one of them had commented on the tapping, "That isn't bad. He was sawing ere dinner. That wears worse on the ear. Mariena was at dinner, by the way. She looked much recovered. Amyas hovered most attentively."

"How was everyone else?" Joliffe asked.

"I would say tired."

"Did you learn aught from Father Morice?"

"If he didn't, it wasn't by lack of trying," Ellis grumbled from where he stood on the other side of the firepit.

"We had a pleasant talk," Basset said. "Thank you, too, for asking how I do."

"You're doing far better," Joliffe said, "or you wouldn't have so much enjoyed thwarting Piers. *Did* you learn aught from Father Morice?"

"He's not a happy man. I think he's not very good at priesting."

"He wouldn't be the first," said Ellis.

"Hush," said Rose. She was sitting near him, sewing in her lap. She reached out and tugged gently at the hem of his tunic. "Sit down here with me. They're only doing what they have to do."

"It's going to get us into trouble," Ellis complained.

"We're players," said Basset smoothly. "We're always in trouble, one way or another. The thing with this trouble is that we have Lord Lovell behind us and I don't doubt we'll be in worse trouble if we don't please him."

Ellis made a wordless mutter in answer to that and gave way to Rose's pull, sitting down beside her and taking up a stick to poke angrily into the fire. Rose leaned over and kissed his cheek, then drew him sideways to lean his head on her shoulder. There he eased, shutting his eyes with a sigh, and she returned to her sewing.

Not to disturb the peace more than need be, Basset said quietly, "He's not very good at being a priest and unhappily he knows it. I'd judge he would have been happier as someone's clerk, but somebody was probably ambitious for him and here he is."

"I thought there was more unhappiness in him than that," Rose said quietly, still stitching. "When you made talk about Mariena's marriage, he should have been happier that it's all but done with."

"Why should he be happy or unhappy about it?" Joliffe asked lightly. "It's not his marriage."

Without opening his eyes or shifting from Rose's shoulder, Ellis said, "What he sounded about it was relieved."

Joliffe wordlessly asked Basset with raised eyebrows if that was true.

Basset slowly nodded that it was.

"Maybe relieved, yes," Rose said. "But unhappy about something else, then."

"There was naught seemed wrong about him when you first met him in the village, was there?" Joliffe asked Basset.

"We were two strangers talking about plays. I didn't note anything in particular." Basset thought a moment. "He drank quickly and deeply and drank some more after that as soon as he sat down. That could have mellowed him."

"By St. Thomas the Doubter," Ellis said impatiently, "you two *want* to find trouble." He started to lift his head from Rose's shoulder, but she left off her sewing to curve her hand around the side of his face and hold him there, whispering something in his ear that quieted him again.

Lowering his voice as if that would be enough not to rouse Ellis despite he could still hear everything, Joliffe said, "So he's relieved about this marriage but unhappy about something. Were you able to find out why the Harcourt marriage-talks were so much harder than these seem to have been?"

"When I made comment that I'd heard they had been, all he said was, yes, they had been, and went very glum, I thought. I didn't see how to have more out of him."

"He probably didn't like that marriage because he's heard Lady Benedicta is supposed to have affaired with this John Harcourt's father years ago. A marriage that way maybe seemed not right."

"If Sir Edmund could countenance it, what was it to him?" Basset said.

"Maybe Sir Edmund hasn't heard about his wife."

Basset grunted disbelief of that.

"Or," Joliffe tried, "maybe he doesn't believe it. Or he doesn't care."

"Any of that's possible," Basset granted. "The thing is, he wanted the marriage."

Rose had gone back to sewing. Without looking up from her stitching, she asked, "When did Lady Benedicta 'affair' with this man? Could Father Morice have feared Mariena and this boy were half-brother and -sister?"

"That's been thought of," Joliffe said, "but the alewife says Mariena was born well more than nine months afterward."

"She knows so unerringly when matters ended between Lady Benedicta and this man?" Basset asked.

"It had to do with Sir Edmund being gone to Westminster and then coming home. So far as the village thinks, everything happened between then and no talk of anything more between them."

"How much afterward was Mariena born?" Rose asked.

"I don't know," Joliffe said.

"You might try to find that out. There is such a thing as a nine-and-a-half-months child."

Both Joliffe and Basset paused on that thought. Then Joliffe said slowly, "That would mean Sir Edmund didn't know of the affair, had no suspicion the girl might not be his own."

"But Lady Benedicta would have known," Basset pointed out.

"But we've not heard she ever protested against the Harcourt marriage, have we?" Joliffe asked.

"None," Basset confirmed. "Nor could Father Morice have suspected aught was wrong or he would have protested it."

"If he only suspected it, he might have kept quiet," Joliffe said. "If he only suspected, he might have . . ." He broke off, considering what he had been about to say.

Basset finished for him. "He might have made as many difficulties about the marriage as possible."

"Which we know he did," Joliffe said.

"Though that doesn't mean Mariena isn't Sir Edmund's daughter," Rose put in.

"You were just saying . . ." Ellis started to protest without lifting his head or opening his eyes.

"I was just saying Joliffe should find out something, that's all. She could well be Sir Edmund's daughter and not half-sister to this John Harcourt, and Father Morice still feel uneasy about them marrying after what maybe—only *maybe*, mind you—passed between Lady Benedicta and this John Harcourt's father."

To Joliffe, that Lady Benedicta had not resisted the Harcourt marriage was strong sign she had seen no problem with it. If indeed she had affaired with John Harcourt's father, however briefly, she perhaps still had strong enough feelings about him that she had welcomed her daughter marrying his son as a fulfilling of . . . what? A lost love? A lost lust?

"Heed," said Basset quietly as Will came around the corner of the carpenter shed.

Will was smiling, but his hurry slowed and his smile faded as his quick look took in that neither Piers nor Gil were there. Understanding his look, Basset said, "They've taken our mare out to graze while the rain holds off. They'll be sorry to have missed you. Will you pardon me not standing up?"

Ellis, Rose, and Joliffe had already risen to their feet, Ellis and Joliffe bowing, Rose making a curtsy. Will waved an easy acknowledgment that excused Basset doing the same while he said, "You're not practicing anything today?"

"Done this morning, I fear," said Basset.

"Oh." Will sighed his disappointment. "You'd have to stop anyway, I suppose. My mother sent me to ask if someone of you could come to sing or play music or something for her and the others while they're sewing Mariena's new gown."

Joliffe gave him deep bow. "That will be me, and most assuredly I'll come and with pleasure. Give me but leave to fetch my lute and then you may show me the way."

Joliffe's excess of manners brought back Will's smile. "They're where they were yesterday. You can find them well enough. I'm going to go find Piers and Gil."

"Before anybody catches you to run more errands?" Basset asked, conspirator to escaping prisoner.

"Before anybody catches me for anything," Will said.

"Would you like," Basset offered, "to stay here and I'll tell you all the stories my grandson is tired of hearing but I'm not tired of telling?"

Already started to turn away, Will missed the sharp looks Joliffe, Rose, and Ellis all gave Basset; and by the time Will turned back, asking, "Stories?," their faces were as bland as Basset's, and Joliffe was going to the cart for his lute.

"Stories," Basset assured him. "Come sit here beside me. Take Joliffe's cushion."

Basset was well away into a tale of King Arthur as Joliffe left the cartshed, his lute hung around his shoulder and easier in mind than he would have been if Will was not there safe with Basset and the others instead of gone off alone in search of Piers and Gil. Unhappily, that ease of mind told him how deeply his suspicion was set that all was not as right as it might be here at the manor of Deneby.

Chapter 14

For those who were only minstrels, with no need to be aught else, their trade truly was to sing for their suppers. Players crossed a wider range of skills, it serving a company well to have as many skills as possible among its people, to meet whatever an occasion brought. Joliffe, going up the curve of the tower stairs toward Lady Benedicta's chamber, was wondering what this occasion would bring.

If nothing else, it would give him another chance to see how things went among the womenfolk here and how better Mariena was or was not.

The door to the chamber stood open, but as Joliffe neared it, the silence from the chamber beyond was so complete that he wondered briefly if the women had left, had maybe gone up to take the air on the tower's top or some such thing, and he would have to follow them. As he reached the doorway, though, he saw Lady Benedicta and Idonea Wyot were on the window bench, where the weakling sunlight fell most strongly, while Mariena sat on a chair nearby, to Joliffe's eyes seeming none the worse for her night's illness. They were all of them stitching at the rich blue cloth of Mariena's new gown, and at his light knock they all looked toward him—Idonea Wyot with what seemed hopeful relief; Mariena eagerly, probably glad for any diversion; Lady Benedicta with the same cold nothing as yesterday. But she remembered his name, saying, "Joliffe, is it not? Come in. We're in need of something to pass this sewing time for us less tediously. You sing, I take it?"

Joliffe made her a respectful bow. "You will be the judge of that, my lady."

With the narrowest of smiles, she nodded agreement and gestured for him to sit on the chest at the bedfoot. That put him at an angle to them rather than fully facing, which did not matter since it was his singing they wanted, not his face, while by looking sidewise from his lowered eyes he could see them all well enough. Bent over his lute while bringing it into tune, he said, watching them, "We were all sorry to hear of my lady's trouble in the night. I hope she's well-recovered?"

Mariena opened her mouth to reply, but Lady Benedicta said first, coldly, "It was a passing indigestion, nothing more, with too much made of it."

Mariena closed her mouth into a tight line and said nothing.

Stroking the lute's strings, finding they were ready, Joliffe said mildly, "Something she ate then."

Lady Benedicta gave him a sharp look, followed by an equally sharp glance at her daughter, who met her look darkly, not hiding her anger. At what?

Idonea Wyot merely huddled further over her sewing, shoulders curved forward and head down as if readying for a storm, while Joliffe went on easily, "Is there aught you'd care to hear first, my ladies?"

Again, Mariena made to answer. Again Lady Benedicta cut her off, saying, "I leave it to you."

Again Mariena's mouth tightened over in-held words. Was she subdued by her night's ordeal? Or was she for some reason become wary of her mother? She had certainly not been wary of her before. If she was now, why was she? John Harcourt had fallen ill and died here. Now Mariena had been ill. She hadn't died, though. And why would her mother want her dead anyway, however much dislike there seemed to be between them? Why even want her ill, for that matter, given the trouble it had surely caused for most of the night? But then, come to it, why would Lady Benedicta have wanted John Harcourt dead?

He had yet to find *why* John Harcourt might have been murdered, let alone by whom. But he noted that "yet" in his thought, even as he started to sing a song he thought matched the women's grey and lowering humour, that seeming the better way to go, rather than against them. His voice low and sad to match the words as he sang, "Alone walking, in thought 'plaining, sore sighing, death wishing both early and late . . ."

There were a good many verses, useful for those times when one was particularly ready to feel miserable, but watching the women, Joliffe judged by the sixth one that they were ready for a change and let the song fade away into a quietness of plucked strings before suddenly thrumming forward into the merry, "Of a rose, a lovely rose, of a rose I sing a song. Listen, hearken, both old and young, how the rose even now hath sprung . . ."

Words and music skipped quick as sunlight over rippling water, and the women were caught by surprise. Idonea Wyot raised her head, looking on the edge of laughter. Mariena dropped her sewing and clapped her hands with delight. Lady Benedicta, who had been paused at her sewing, looking away out the window, turned back to the room, almost smiling. But a moment later Mariena shoved her sewing to the floor and sprang to her feet and into a dance, arms out-stretched as she twirled to the wide middle of the room, her long skirts and dark hair flaring out around her. Her suddenness so immediately matched the music that Joliffe forgot he meant to seem seeing nothing and lifted his head, watching her and smiling as he sang.

But Lady Benedicta said, "Mariena."

Only the word and not loudly, but it was an order that stopped Mariena where she was, arms and skirts falling straight, her hair swirled partly forward over one shoulder. Momentarily mother and daughter stared at one another, no liking in either of their looks. Then Mariena threw up her head and defiantly spun around one more time, back to the chair, where she flung herself down and glared at her mother, her arms folded and her hair partly over her face.

Coldly, Lady Benedicta said, "Put back your hair and take up your sewing."

Mariena shoved back her hair from her face with both hands, then folded her arms again, defying the rest of her mother's order. Lady Benedicta with gaze fixed on her said evenly, "Idonea, put down your sewing," putting down her own on her lap with a finality that said she would not take it up again until she was obeyed. "If we have to sew on this gown of yours," she said at Mariena, "you will sew, too. If you do not, no one does."

The stare between mother and daughter held a long while this time with Idonea Wyot and Joliffe frozen in wary watching of them before Mariena gave way with a toss of her shoulders and grabbed her sewing from the floor. Without comment, Lady Benedicta took up her own and Idonea followed and Joliffe carefully began to set quiet, light notes into the taut silence, only gradually weaving his way back toward a song while thinking how much more alike to each other Lady Benedicta and Mariena were than he had heretofore thought. Lady Benedicta's will was the stronger, but that only came from more years of practice at it, Joliffe suspected. Beyond that, both she and Mariena were passionate in their different ways—Mariena's passion still raw and open while Lady Benedicta's passion was . . . Joliffe watched his fingers on the lute's strings rather than the women while he considered Lady Benedicta. Her passion must have run hot once upon a time, but if passion could be said to run cold, he suspected hers still ran, no longer with fire but with the force of ice.

Against the hotness of young life in Mariena, perhaps? Very possibly. Reason enough to want the girl married and away from here.

He eased his way into a gentle song, trying now for no more than soothing over all the raw edges in the room, including Idonea Wyot's, out of place here and ill at ease as she surely was, with seemingly no one trying to make her feel otherwise. All stayed quiet among the women, and in a while he moved on to more lightly playful songs, trying to raise smiles if nothing else; and when finally the song of the lady wakened by the crowing cock that nightly perched in her chamber brought even Lady Benedicta to laugh softly and shake her head, he dared try a love-song. After all, he was not supposed to know there was anything here but joy for the coming marriage, so a song of love was reasonable; but he sang the one he chose—"When the nightingale sings, the woods wax green"—in such a melting, over-lovestruck voice that by the time he reached, "I have so loved all this year that I may love no more," first Idonea Wyot's shoulders and then Lady Benedicta's twitched with silent laughter that broke out aloud as he finished in the most mournful of voices, "I shall moan my song for my love it is for, until my heart doth fall on floor." Which was not the end to it he had learned but the one he used when it suited him.

Putting their sewing on their laps, the two women clapped, still laughing. Mariena did, too, but not with such open pleasure; and when the women took up their sewing again, she demanded at him, "Now sing one as if you meant it."

"Mariena," her mother said in the tone of someone reminding a small child of its manners.

Tight-voiced, her words at Joliffe but her glare for her mother, Mariena said, "I pray you, sing one from the heart."

Since Lady Benedicta said nothing against that, Joliffe began, "Nights when I turn and wake—by which I am waxed pale—Lady, all for thy sake is longing come on me," obeying Mariena, singing as if such love-longing came from deep inside himself. It didn't. All he had was the wish he might some time truly feel such love-longing for someone—and better yet, that that beloved someone would feel the same and equally for him. Since it had yet to happen, he made use of his skill as a player to show feelings he did not have, off-setting that, to his mind, his singing and his skill on the lute were no more than ordinary.

He pleased Mariena well enough, anyway. At the end, she sighed like someone satisfied and said, "There. That was good. Another one, please?"

If that wooing voice, as honey-smooth as her fair skin, was the one she used to her suitors, there was small wonder John Harcourt had come back well before their wedding to be with her, or that Amyas Breche had been doting on her the times Joliffe had seen them together. He found himself smiling warmly without meaning to as he answered, "If you will, my lady."

But before he could begin, there was sound of someone on the stairs and Sir Edmund entered. Joliffe stood up and bowed to him. Mariena and Mistress Wyot rose and curtsied. In strict courtesy, Lady Benedicta might have done the same, but she stayed seated. With an easy gesture for

Mariena and Idonea to sit again, Sir Edmund crossed to his wife and kissed her cheek.

She accepted it, nothing more; made no sign of welcome or willingness, nor did she give greeting of her own, merely looked at him, her gaze flat and shallow, as he stepped back from her. Seeming to expect nothing more than that, he turned and said easily to Idonea, "They're keeping you busy. A guest shouldn't be put to so much to work."

"It's my pleasure, sir," she answered, which was only politeness; but she added, "I enjoy sewing, and this is lovely cloth."

"From Flanders," Sir Edmund said. He lifted a thick fold of cloth from Mariena's lap. Guessing from the quantity of cloth there, she was sewing a seam in the gown's skirt, the least demanding but most tedious part of the task because it went on, unchanging, for so many stitches. "A gift from Master Breche on his nephew's behalf." He smiled on Idonea. "But you knew that." He laid the cloth down again, absently patted Mariena's shoulder, and said, still to Idonea, "I hope you'll be my daughter's friend when she's gone to live in Cirencester."

"I will, sir. Gladly."

He turned his smile to Mariena. "It will be all new to her and she'll be missed. It will help to know she's not gone completely among strangers." He laid a hand on Mariena's shoulder again. "Won't it, sweetling?"

Mariena looked up at him, meeting his smile. "It will," she agreed. "Though I'll miss you." Said with the faintest weight on "you" and a bitter sidewise glance at her mother, who made no more response to her daughter's jibe than she had to her husband's kiss, simply watching all with that same flat gaze.

Sir Edmund made a small laugh, satisfied by his daughter's answer, it seemed, and said, "We're going riding, the Breches and Harry and I. And Will, if we can find him.

I only came to be sure you still did well, Mariena. Amyas will be pleased to know."

"I'm more than well enough," Mariena said eagerly. "Let me come with you." She made as if to rise, ready to go on the instant.

Before Sir Edmund could answer, her mother said, cold as ice over dark waters, "Not if you want this gown done for your wedding."

Mariena sank back with disgust. Her father patted her shoulder again, smiling with fellow-feeling. "Tomorrow you can ride in with me to hear the banns read," he promised. "I'll see you at supper, my ladies." He gave his wife another kiss that was no more welcomed than the other had been, exchanged bows of the head with Idonea, and left, having not once so much as looked at Joliffe, still standing because he had not been given leave to sit.

"Joliffe," Lady Benedicta said when her husband was gone, "sing us something bright."

Joliffe sat and set immediately and light-voiced into the shining, "I have a new garden that new is begun. Such another garden know I not under sun," because he felt, with her, the need for something bright against whatever had come into the chamber with Sir Edmund.

Yet Sir Edmund had done nothing beyond the ordinary and common. He had given greetings, made polite talk, said courteous farewell. Even Mariena seemed the better for her father's visit. Whatever the ill-feelings and lack of trust between her and her mother, things looked to be well enough between her and her father. That might be simply because he did not have to spend hours in her company, Joliffe thought dryly. Still, it left him certain Mariena did not resent the marriage being made for her. If she did, she would likely have shown her anger against her father as readily as she showed it against her mother. What surprised him was his pity for Lady Benedicta, because even as he wondered at her coldness toward her husband's open willingness to affection toward her, he was wondering, too, if Sir Edmund was not only aware she did not want his attentions but gave them deliberately in a place and way where she had to accept them with some outward grace.

If that were the way of it, Joliffe thought, he did not want to know how matters went between them when they were alone, with no need of good manners between them.

He then wondered which servants shared their bedchamber at night, and if there was any way he could make chance to talk with them.

He finished the song. Before he could ask what Lady Benedicta would like now, Mariena flung her sewing aside and stood up, stretching her arms and back in show of how stiff she was become, saying, "Please, may I have rest for a while?" To which her mother, more quietly setting down her own sewing, answered, "We should all rest a while. Idonea, may I trouble you to find out a servant and ask that wine and something slight to eat be brought us? For our player, too, say."

With a willingness that might have been flight, Idonea said, " Most certainly, my lady," put aside her sewing, rose to her feet, curtsied, and went out. Lady Benedicta shifted on the windowseat to look out. Mariena crossed to Joliffe, sat down beside him, and said, smiling, "You play so well. I have a lute, but I don't play nearly so well. I'd ask you to show me how to play, but it's in my chamber."

She was not touching him but was so near she might as well have been, her face turned up to his, eyes welcomingly bright, lips invitingly red.

Not doubting that Lady Benedicta could hear them and need only slightly turn her head their way to see them, too, Joliffe said in a carefully bland voice, "Good playing is a matter of much practicing, my lady."

"I do practice, but surely lessons would help, too," she

said in her warm-honey voice, which was enticement as definite as her body pressed against him on the stairs had been.

Steadfastedly refusing the bait, Joliffe said, "Surely. Beyond doubt there will be someone in Cirencester skilled enough to teach you when the time comes you're there."

"But what of lessons from you here?" she asked and slid her hand, where her mother could not see it, along his thigh and down between his legs.

Joliffe came to his feet and away from her before he had thought of what he would do once he was on his feet. Once up, he had to do something that seemed casual and so strolled toward Lady Benedicta at the window. She looked around. He had the instant certainty that she was not in the least doubt about what had happened; but her hard look went to her daughter, rather than at him, as he said, desperate for something to say, "Would you have me lesson your daughter, my lady?"

That came out with more possibilities of meaning than he had intended, too late for him to take it back. Lady Benedicta's sudden, bitter smile told she saw the possibilities as well as he did, but she surprised him by saying evenly, "I think my daughter has lessons enough, nor do I doubt you have enough to do without taking on more."

"Indeed, I do, my lady."

Dropping her voice too low for Mariena to hear, she surprised him more by asking, "With Sia, was it not?"

His wits now caught up to his tongue, and with a mental gulp as he swallowed that, Joliffe said, matching her quietness, "That came to nothing, my lady."

"Did it? You surprise me."

"As you do me, my lady."

He had wondered if any of her smiles ever reached her eyes. Now as her eyes warmed suddenly with in-held laughter, Joliffe was as suddenly, however unreasonably, on her side, whatever that side was, because—given she was beset with a husband she gave no sign of loving and a daughter who gave every sign of hating her—that silent laughter was a gallant thing. It was even still there as she asked him, looking past him to Mariena, now on her feet and moving restlessly around the chamber, "Will you feel hard done by if I give you leave to go ere the wine comes?"

"Not in the least, my lady."

"Then you have my leave." To get away from her daughter, she did not say aloud.

Joliffe bowed very low, more truly respectful of her than he had been, and made for the door. Mariena did not cross his way but caught his eye with a taunting smile that dared him to change his mind and come to her. Only barely he kept his slight bow to her plain rather than mocking in return before he escaped out the door and down the stairs.

This time it was Idonea he met on the stairs, returning from her errand. He turned sideways and pressed his back against the wall for her to pass but she paused a step below him and asked with a nod up the stairs, "How is it in there now?"

It was such a simple, worried question, and her plain face so pleasant after Mariena's heated interest in him, that Joliffe answered straight-forwardly, "No worse than it was."

She sighed, "That's bad enough," and went on, past him and up the stairs.

Joliffe, going down the stairs two at a time and glad to be away, silently agreed with her.

Chapter 15

Will was gone and Piers and Gil not yet back with Tisbe when Joliffe returned to the cart-shed. Basset and Ellis were sitting in low-voiced talk beside the cart. Rose was lying down on her bed, blanket-covered and apparently sleeping, and as Joliffe joined the men, Ellis tipped his head toward her, saying in a half-whisper, "She's resting," adding in answer to Joliffe's immediately worried look, "She's well. Just resting." Not something they had chance at most days. Joliffe thought he might try it himself sometime.

"How went it?" Basset asked.

"Well enough." Joliffe heard the uncertainty under his words and amended, "Well enough with me. It was watching mother and daughter dislike each other that was strange. Sir Edmund found Will?"

"That Deykus came for him. Said he was to go riding with the men," Basset said. "He should be safe enough there."

"He wasn't yesterday," said Joliffe. He looked at Ellis,

waiting, then asked, "You're not going to protest that yesterday's fall was only an accident?"

"How much good would it do if I did? Besides," Ellis went on grudgingly, "he's frightened. Not happy either. Something has him worried and scared."

Basset nodded agreement to that, and Joliffe asked, "Could you tell of what? Or, better, of whom?"

"He said nothing sure," Basset said. "He wouldn't, would he? Not to us. It's more in how he was than anything he said. You could all but see the knots in him loosen while he sat here listening to me tell him stories."

"That would be because he was being dulled to sleep," Ellis muttered.

It was a half-hearted scoff and Basset and Joliffe both ignored it, Basset going on, "You could see him forgetting to be worried or afraid or whatever he is. Then you could see every knot all tighten up again when Deykus came for him."

"Frightened of his father?" Joliffe asked.

"He seemed to ease a little when he heard it was his father wanted him."

"Frightened of his mother then?" Joliffe wondered.

"Or just worried Father Morice was after him," Ellis said, "Only, no, it was more than that. For all his boldness and talk, he's not a happy boy."

"Whatever the reason," Basset agreed.

"Did you learn anything of use from Father Morice?" Joliffe asked. "About Will or anything else?"

"I don't know how much of use it is, and it's more what was behind what he said than in his words."

"Does he think everyone is as pleased about this marriage as they seem to be?"

"I gather so. In truth, if I were asked, I'd say there was a general eagerness to have Mariena married and out of here."

"No sign that Mariena doesn't want this marriage?" Joliffe asked.

"By what Father Morice says, she's very willing to be married and away."

"And Lady Benedicta has no objection to it?" Though Joliffe would be very surprised if she did, given the irk between her and her daughter.

"I asked that directly of Father Morice, under seeming concern that we not rub folk the wrong way with over-playing the joys of marriage to someone who might not be so happy about it. 'Is her mother, for one, quite resigned to losing her daughter?' I asked."

"And he said?"

"He said with somewhat staggering bluntness that Lady Benedicta just wants to have her married and gone. More than that, I had the feeling that so does Father Morice."

And yet Lady Benedicta had been unwilling for Harry Wyot to marry her, which would have got her out of here far sooner. Thinking on that, Joliffe said slowly, "From what I've seen, Lady Benedicta and Mariena don't get on, true, but I can't tell if that's merely for the present or something more."

"That's something long-set between them," Basset answered with firm certainty. "Given the chance, Father Morice does like to talk. I said something slight about mothers and daughters going through a difficult time, and he said from all he's heard, it's a time they've been going through since Mariena was small. She likes to have her own say about everything—final say, mind you—and goes angry if she doesn't get it. That sets her at cross-purposes with Lady Benedicta, who's not minded to give over being mistress of the household to her."

"So it stands that the sooner Mariena is married and gone to a household of her own, the happier they'll both be," Joliffe said.

"Them and everyone else, I'd say," said Basset.

"You know," said Ellis, "it could be no more than all the

dislike going on around him that's troubling Will. It would keep me ready to duck, that's sure."

"It could account, too," Basset said thoughtfully, "for Sir Edmund going after the Breche marriage instead of waiting for better, if the difference was made up by having a happy home in its stead."

"Were there other offers for her?" Joliffe asked quickly.

"What Father Morice said was that when the Breche offer for her came, Sir Edmund took it on the leap. Mind you, it's a rich marriage and no disparagement to the girl."

"Is Sir Edmund badly enough in debt to need a quick, rich marriage?"

"Or is maybe his daughter in need of a quick marriage, rich or otherwise, for another reason," Ellis said meaningfully. "She had a betrothed she expected to marry."

"She'd be showing by now if she'd done anything beyond bounds with Harcourt," Basset said. "Nor is she likely to have had chance with anyone since then."

Joliffe kept to himself what he knew about her that way, partly because he thought that Mariena probably valued her place in the marriage market too highly to give herself freely to anyone, however much she took delight in stirring a man to lust. In truth, part of her delight in that might come from never satisfying a man once she had roused him.

Only with that thought did he face how much he had come to dislike her.

"Altogether," Basset said, "I'd say we've learned nothing except this is an unhappy family and may be the happier once Mariena is married and gone."

"Not if the trouble runs deeper," Joliffe said. "Not if matters have never been mended between Sir Edmund and his wife since she strayed. And don't tell me they've had two children since then and still share a bed," he added at Ellis, "because none of that means anything is mended at all."

Ellis, who had started to open his mouth, shut it again, looking darkly at Joliffe, who gave him no heed him and asked Basset, "Did you learn anything about Sir Edmund that we didn't know?"

Basset brooded on his answer before finally saying, "I'm trying to think whether Father Morice deliberately avoided talk of him, or if it only seems that way. I know I made openings he could have talked into, if he'd wanted."

"You did that," Ellis said. "You did everything but ask him openly to tell you what he knew about Sir Edmund."

Basset made a frowning, agreeing nod to that. "I did," he granted. "And he never took the chance. He talked enough about Lady Benedicta and Mariena, but not about Sir Edmund at all. I wonder why."

"Discretion," Ellis said. "He's the man's priest after all."

"He's priest to everyone here," Basset pointed out.

"Fear?" asked Joliffe, keeping to the question.

"Of what?" Basset asked.

"Of the same thing Will is afraid of?" suggested Joliffe.

"Which is?" Basset returned.

They all fell silent, no answer among them, until Basset folded his hands across his belly, leaned back against the cart wheel, and said, "I'm going to nap on it a while," and shut his eyes. Ellis stood up and went out. Joliffe sat a few moments more, then went to get his writing from the cart and sat down in his corner to work a while more at the problem of Dux Moraud's repentence of his terrible sins. As the play went now, when confronted with the dire consequence of his greatest sin, the duke was supposed to cry out, "Jesu have mercy on my corrupted soul," fall prone before the altar, and lie there while an avenging angel spoke at length unto him, until finally the duke was allowed to say how badly he felt about the whole business and promise to do better hereafter.

Given the line of corpses his sin left through the course of the play, that finish struck Joliffe as altogether too easy, both for the duke and for the player playing him. Ellis wouldn't thank him for making the part more difficult, but then Ellis never thanked him for anything, so that made no difference, Joliffe thought with a wide smile to himself. He briefly tickled himself under his chin with the feathered end of his quill, considering, then began to write.

Ellis returned. Rose and Basset both awoke, and while Basset moved around—loosening his sorry joints, he said—Piers, Gil, and Tisbe returned, bringing firewood. Ellis complained that not much of it was dry. Piers said he was welcome to go hunt for dry wood in the wet woods himself if he thought he could do better. Rose said it was time for someone to fetch their supper from the kitchen, and since Ellis and Piers seemed to have so much strength to spare, why didn't they? They left, still wording happily at each other, and Joliffe put away his writing, ready to turn his mind to this evening's work and give over thinking about both Dux Moraud and everything there might—or might not—be wrong here at Deneby.

In the hall, with all the work of settling the marriage agreement done and the first banns read, everyone seemed in a festive humour, ready for the fall-about sport of *The Husband Becomes the Wife*. While the players waited in the screens passage, Basset had time to judge the level of general merriment and said, "I think we should do it 'with them' tonight."

Joliffe, Ellis, and Piers all made muted groan together. It was one thing to do the play as it was, but "with them" meant they drew the audience into it as well, and while that made much more sport for the audience, it made much more work for them.

Giving their groans no heed, Basset went on, "Piers, you and Will can be twins. I think we should best leave Mariena and Lady Benedicta out of it?" He looked at Joliffe, who nodded ready agreement with that. "But Sir Edmund may join in if Will does, and that would be good. Maybe Amyas or Harry Wyot for the table . . ."

He went on quickly laying out his plan, and then it was time to begin, far too late, Joliffe thought, to smother Basset, hide his body in the hamper of properties, and escape into the night. Instead, perforce, they sallied forth and set to being merry. For this play, he and Ellis switched their usual parts, with Joliffe the husband and Ellis the wife, looking unlikely in a deliberately ill-fitted gown and overlarge apron that overwhelmed Joliffe when given over to him along with the housekeeping.

It quickly became clear that Basset had read the hall a-right. Whether from plain high spirits or a plenitude of wine, everyone Basset gathered from behind the tables into the playing area came readily and with laughter. Will came eagerly to be Piers' "twin," their business being to lie on their backs and at the most awkward moments pretend to be wailing babies. Amyas became a table, down on all fours in the square laid out for the unhappy couple's cottage, his laughter a constant threat to the plate and bowl set on his back. Harry Wyot was willingly the hearth, sitting cross-legged and waving his arms over his head to be rising smoke, although when the Husband laid sticks across his lap and set a kettle there, he laughed so hard along with everyone else that he nearly fell over.

With Joliffe confined to the "cottage" as the husband making a desperate mess of everything he tried to do, Basset and Ellis kept busy pulling one person and another from behind the tables to play "neighbors" come to call, including Father Morice (with Basset at his back to urge him on), who walked into the cottage, pretended horror at what he saw, signed a cross in the air, cried, "God's mercy on you all," and retreated; but that was enough to bring on roars of laughter from one end of the hall to the other.

It was all something the players had done uncounted times before here and all went as it usually did. Some people fell into the game eagerly, over-playing their part to everyone's delight, including their own. Some, not sure at all what they should do, gamely tried, able to rise to nothing more than stiff dignity until released back to their places. But they all tried. Only Sir Edmund did not rise to the moment when Will forsook being a baby to jump up and run to help Basset bring him into the game. Pulled by his son, Sir Edmund came, and when Will had flung himself down beside Piers on the blanket that was their "cradle" and begun to wail and kick again, Sir Edmund let Basset guide him through the cottage doorway and even said, as Basset had directed but very stiffly, "Ho, good neighbor, aren't we going fishing today?"

Joliffe, pretending a particularly frantic moment of trying to quiet the wailing "babies" by dandling over them a bright cloth ball on the end of a stick, turned with a despairing, "Here. Quiet these brats if you can," thrusting the bauble toward him. Always before, whoever was there had taken the stick—out of surprise if nothing else—and dandled it over the babies, who immediately fell to quiet cooing. Sir Edmund did nothing. Neither took the stick, nor moved. Only stood there, rigid, blank-faced, staring at Joliffe. For a perilous moment the whole headlong forward rush of the play was in danger of stumbling. But Ellis, probably reading Sir Edmund's back, entered sooner than "she" might have, coming into the cottage declaring loudly, "What is this wailing, these cries of grief? What have you done to my darlings dear? Have you been deeply into the ale, that even the children you can't calm?" With bustle and busyness, "she" hurried Sir Edmund out of the cottage, for Basset to return to the high table while "she" snatched the bauble from Joliffe and quieted the children and set the play on to its roaring finish and a loud beating of goblets and spoons on tabletops by all the lookers-on, even Sir Edmund as if nothing awry had happened.

Despite they were tired to their bones, the players made their way back to the cartshed satisfied with the evening. After a little talk and a little ale around the fire and general agreement that they could put everything away in the morning, they made for their beds. It being Joliffe's turn to bank the fire once their blankets were warmed, he was the last to lie down. By then Gil was slackly asleep with his mouth a little open, Basset was gently snoring, and Ellis was tucking a blanket higher around Piers' neck with a tenderness that told Piers was soundly asleep already, too. All his angelic look was on him, his lashes soft on his rounded cheeks, a small smile curving his lips, everything belying what he was when awake. Ellis, turning, finding Joliffe's look on Piers, scowled, maybe angry at being caught in such open tenderness, but Joliffe said quietly, to disturb no one else, "He's better off than Will is, our Piers."

Ellis cast a scornful glance around them. "I don't see it." But then added grudgingly, "Aye, he's not frightened, for one thing. And he's loved and wanted." His look sharpened on Joliffe. "Though I'd break my own neck before telling him as much."

Joliffe held up his hands in silent assurance that he'd keep Ellis' secret. But Ellis was looking past him, eyes a little widening, and Joliffe looked over his own shoulder to see Rose was pulling Ellis' mattress from its place beside the fire to beside her own bedding.

Turning back to Ellis, he asked, low-voiced, "No token on the cowshed for you tonight?"

"Shut up," Ellis muttered, equally low, starting past him toward Rose.

"Poor Avice," Joliffe murmured. "Thwarted of her prey."

"Poor the other one," Ellis muttered back. "She got you."

Joliffe did not disabuse him with the truth. Why hand rocks to someone who enjoyed stoning you? Instead, listening to Ellis and Rose settling together behind him, he finished settling the fire and slid into his own bed, glad that at least sleep—if nothing else—was in his reach. But as he burrowed against his thin pillow, he found himself considering what Ellis had said about Piers being loved and wanted. Wasn't Will both loved and wanted? As heir, as the son who would carry on his father's name and blood, he had to be; and yet, once asked, the question sat uneasily among Joliffe's other thoughts.

Why?

Joliffe wrapped his blanket more tightly to him and thought about it. What had he seen or heard that made him uneasy over it? Put to it, he could name nothing. If only as his only son, his heir, at least Sir Edmund must value Will. Or did Sir Edmund know something more about his wife's unfaithfulness than others did? Had there been—or did he suspect there had been—a later lover than the one so readily talked of? Did he doubt the boy was truly his?

But Sir Edmund gave no sign of resenting Will, seemed neither to neglect nor abuse him. Nor was it his father that Will feared. Basset had said Will was relieved this afternoon when told it was his father who wanted him. In truth, everything Joliffe had seen between them had looked like affection.

Looked like affection.

Seemed neither to neglect nor abuse him.

More awake than he had hoped to be by now, Joliffe held his choice of words up in his mind and studied them.

Why "seemed"? Why "looked"? What—of the little he had seen between Sir Edmund and Will—gave him this feeling of something not right? He could think of nothing he'd seen or heard to make him doubt Sir Edmund's affection for Will. So far as Joliffe had seen or heard, Sir Edmund said and did what he should both for and with Will.

Sir Edmund said and did.

Sir Edmund seemed and looked.

Sir Edmund said and did and seemed and looked but . . . There was a hollowness behind it.

Rain had begun to fall again, a quiet pattering on the cartshed's thatch and yard, perfect to accompany him into sleep, but Joliffe held awake, caught by his thoughts, wondering from where that one had come.

Then he knew.

He had told Gil that a player needed to have layers in his mind while at his playing—that whatever passions were being outwardly played, an inner layer of the mind had to keep watch and control over all. In good time Gil would learn, too, that, beyond that, a player had to regard not only the passions of the person he played but the passions of all the others on stage, the better to play off them while they played off him, weaving the play into a tight-bound whole. Without that, a play was dead even while the players spoke and moved through their parts.

When Joliffe had first joined Basset's company there had been a player in it—Serle; that had been his name—who played faultlessly in every outward seeming, yet gave nothing to anyone else on the stage with him. To play on stage with Serle had been much like playing to a wooden post. He said the words and made the gestures that went with whatever was supposedly taking place between him and anyone else, but nothing *did* take place between them. No matter what part he played or with whom he played it, all he gave was a flat front. He had given the needed words and gestures but with never a sense he *felt* any of it, and whatever another player tried to give him to bring the business alive between them had died somewhere in the air between them.

He had left Basset's company for a larger one a few months after Joliffe joined, seen away with Basset's good wishes. But afterwards Basset had said, "He'll do better there than here. They won't ask so much of him and that's what they'll get—not much of him." And had added in answer to Joliffe's questioning look, "You meet them sometimes, his sort. There are women like him, too. You can give them your heart's core and it means no more to them than a rotted apple. They're useless in life because they care for nothing but themselves and they're useless on stage for the same reason." Then Basset had pointed a sudden, fierce finger at Joliffe. "And if I ever catch you at anything so feeble as unfeeling playing, I'll stick-wallop you the next three miles we travel."

Sir Edmund reminded Joliffe of long-unthought-of Serle. Why?

Because when he had tried to thrust the fool's bauble into Sir Edmund's hand tonight, he had been looking straight into Sir Edmund's eyes at that moment, and out of all the responses Sir Edmund could have had, there had been nothing. The players had played that game enough to know the responses there could be: laughter, eagerness, confusion, uncertainty, even offense. None of them had shown on Sir Edmund's face. Looking into Sir Edmund's eyes had been like looking into emptiness.

At the time there had been no time to think about it. Joliffe had simply swung away from him, intent on not letting the play falter. Only now, thinking back on it, did he see how like to long-forgotten Serle Sir Edmund had been in that moment. That emptiness had been there. For Serle nothing had mattered beyond himself. Was it that way with Sir Edmund? Or maybe was it not so much that nothing mattered as that everything beyond himself was no more than a puppet-show, that everyone around him were no more than puppets for his use—some puppets of more use, others of less; good puppets doing easily what he wanted from them, bad puppets needing to be forced.

Or killed?

In that moment of trying to bring him into the game, Joliffe had been a "bad puppet," had been outside the part Sir Edmund allowed to him. If he had persevered, would Sir Edmund have simply, coldly crushed the sport and Joliffe with it, as he would have a fly that would not leave off troubling him? Because in his stare there had been no more regard for Joliffe than that. And for all that he had smiled when he talked with Lady Benedicta in her chamber, his eyes had been as blank on her as they had been on Joliffe. That had been what made Joliffe uneasy without he could name why. What Sir Edmund had been doing outwardly had been linked to nothing inward. There had been a hollow ring behind every seemingly true note he had struck.

How many years now had Lady Benedicta lived with that blank gaze turned on her above a smile she must have long since come to hate?

And Will and Mariena? Sir Edmund feigned "father" as well as he did "husband" and "lord of Deneby." Knowing nothing better, was it enough for them—that seeming? Or was their father's coldness corroding something in them? Were Mariena's willfulness and furious humours her shield against him? And did Will take the other way, being ready to his father's wishes in hope of keeping safely inside the circle of his father's approval, not understanding how false-based that approval was?

And John Harcourt. Had he in some way strayed too far from whatever puppet-place Sir Edmund had for him, somehow given too great offense and been killed because of it? Had he gone beyond Sir Edmund's tolerance, and Sir Edmund killed him to be done with him?

Joliffe lay for a long while in the dark, listening to the rain rustle in the thatch, trying to fit that possibility into the rest of what he knew and suspected, but there were too many questions to make a comfortable fit of it yet. It was like all the rest of life—too many questions and nearly no answers.

Only eventually, and not happily, did he find his way into sleep.

Chapter 16

At its beginning, the next day went much the way of the day before. Through the morning, while the rain made uneven effort to keep falling, the players briefly worked through *The Baker's Cake* for that night; then Basset took up teaching Gil again, still helping him find how to lighten his voice into a girl's.

"Not 'seeming' of a girl's voice," Basset told him. "If you try to 'seem' like a girl, the falseness will make farce, whether you want farce or no. Joliffe, show him. Do Constance, I think. First, as if you meant it."

From his corner beyond the cart, Joliffe paused trying to prod *Dux Moraud* into likelihood and said, "Alas, what wonder is it that I weep, that shall be sent into strange lands, far from friends that tenderly till now did keep," in the noble, saddened voice of the ill-fated queen.

"Now 'seem' to be her," Basset directed.

Joliffe promptly said the same but this time with a shrill lift to his voice.

"You hear the difference?" Basset asked. "The first was a woman's voice. The second was a man working to sound like a woman. Now try again."

By mid-day when the players crossed the yard to dinner, the rain was given way to an uncertain mix of broken sun and clouds. Through the meal Joliffe watched Sir Edmund at the high table as best he could without seeming to, hoping either to put aside his last night's thoughts or fully convince himself, by strong light of day, that he had seen what he'd seen. He failed of either, just as he had fairly failed with *Dux Moraud* this morning, and was glad to agree to take Tisbe out to graze this afternoon, leaving Gil to Basset and Piers to his mother, who was readying to sew new hosen for him and wanted the use of his legs for measuring before she cut the cloth.

"Though I'm sorry for Tisbe," Piers called as Joliffe led her away. "Spending the afternoon with you."

"Not so sorry as she is when she has to spend it with you," Joliffe said back at him.

"It's me I'm most sorry for," Ellis growled. "I have to put up with the other of you, no matter who goes."

Joliffe laughed and kept going, not bothering to sling more words. He had his writing box in a bag over his shoulder, was looking forward to time on his own, hoping to work a little further through the problem of the evil Moraud.

Sir Edmund, Mariena, and a servant were just riding over the drawbridge as he neared the gateway. Sir Edmund had kept his word then—that she could go with him to the second reading of the banns. That no one else was with them was no great surprise; today's reading would be the same as yesterday's. The surprise lay not in no one else going but in Sir Edmund's courtesy to Father Morice in going again. It gave Joliffe pause in his thoughts against the man. But only pause. Of all the virtues, courtesy might be the easiest to feign, needing only outward show of it at no great cost.

That Mariena would bother herself to go was not a surprise at all, since it gave her excuse to be away from her mother—probably to Lady Benedicta's relief as much as her own, Joliffe thought, watching them ride away toward the village while he crossed the drawbridge with Tisbe. Beyond the drawbridge he went left by a trackway that curved first along the moat, then away along the headland between two ploughed fields. A stretch of woodland lay beyond them and the track turned again, to run along the outer edge of the field, between it and a narrow band of rough pasture before the trees began. It was pasture that had been well-grazed, though, and he led Tisbe onward, supposing he would find somewhere better before he reached the village's common land.

Following the curve of the woods around the fields, he was maybe midway between manor house and village and well away from both when the woods opened away from him into a large bay of open ground and long grasses. Sometime there had been a cutting back of the woods here, almost enough to begin another field, though not lately if judged by the well-grown scrub closing in around its edges. Likely it had been an intake of land begun when there were more people at Deneby and need for more land, meaning probably eighty or so years ago, before the Great Pestilence made such a killing of people that afterwards there was more than land enough for those folk who were left. Joliffe could just remember, at the edge of childhood memory, his grandfather remembering that pestilence from the very farthest edge of his own very-long-past childhood. Only he and his mother had survived out of their family. She had married again and had more children. Joliffe's grandfather had grown up and generously done what he could to repeople England by way of three wives and ten children; and most of them had generously done what they could by having children of their own. However much he had sometimes wished it otherwise, Joliffe had never been a poor, lone orphan left to make his own hard way in the world. He had had to make especial effort to go so far astray from all his family as he had.

He had also strayed far enough just now for his present purpose. Since the forest had not closed on the clearing again, the land must be used for grazing sometimes, even if not lately. Tisbe would not make difference enough to offend anyone, and there was an up-thrust rock against which he could lean if the ground was not too wet, or else sit on to stay dry. If the rain held off, the place would suit well; and when he had hobbled Tisbe and turned her loose, he matted down the grass beside the rock, judged it sufficient between him and the ground for a while at least, and made himself comfortable, his writing box on his knees. He left the box closed, though; closed his eyes and leaned his head back against the rock, thinking—just as he had feared he would—not about Dux Moraud and his sins but back to last night's wondering.

Was everything that had happened here at Deneby of late—from John Harcourt's death to Will's accidents to Mariena's illness—no more than life's usual unshaped chances? Or was there a link between all those different things that made them part of some same thing? A thing still going dangerously on?

Dangerous to whom?

There was a good question. The last bridegroom had died and Lord Lovell was uneasy enough about that on Amyas Breche's behalf for the players to be here, but thus far there was no sign of any threat against Amyas. Will and Mariena were the two who had suffered of late. Were those maybe someone's revenge for John Harcourt's death?

Whose revenge?

Joliffe felt like a housewife trying to beat fleas out of a blanket—persistence was getting him nowhere.

What if he took it step by step from where he knew things had first, at least lately, gone awry here? Supposing he could tell when that was. Had it been when Harry Wyot refused to marry Mariena? And had he done that because Lady Benedicta indeed warned him away from her? But if she had, then why had she? The only certain thing about Wyot's refusal was that he had stood out against Sir Edmund despite what it cost him, settling for a marriage far more to Sir Edmund's advantage than to his own. Or so it was said.

Then there was John Harcourt. There had been delays in making the final agreement, and then when it was done, before the marriage could happen, he had died. Suddenly. In itself, that told nothing. Death happened—rarely conveniently and more often by chance than by someone's ill-will. But if his death had *not* been chance—if it *had* been convenient for someone—then who? And why?

Not for Lady Benedicta, who had surely been looking forward to having her daughter wed and gone. Not for Mariena, said to want the same. Sir Edmund? Had he found, too late, some reason against the marriage? Or some suddenly developed need for a richer marriage? Was the Breche marriage a richer one? Joliffe was not sure. No one had said as much. And how could Sir Edmund have been sure of a richer marriage anyway? Amyas Breche had not come into the reckoning until after Harcourt's death.

So far as Joliffe knew.

Was there some link between Amyas Breche and John Harcourt he had not heard of? It didn't seem likely. It was said to be from Harry Wyot that the Breches first heard of Mariena, and so far as Joliffe had heard, Wyot had not known Harcourt at all.

Harry Wyot.

Sir Edmund's first choice for Mariena's husband and now here again, companioning the man who would finally have her.

Joliffe's flare of excitement at that thought of Harry Wyot as the link between the things that had happened faded as quickly as it had come. He had been this path before. Harry Wyot had been married and gone from here before the Harcourt marriage was ever even talked of. Joliffe hadn't heard that he even knew John Harcourt, but even if he had, hadn't someone said he'd not been back here between his marriage and now?

Still, what if he had come to repent his refusal of Mariena? Could he have found someone here—maybe bribed a servant—to kill John Harcourt to keep the way clear for himself, in hope of another chance at her? That he was left with a wife himself might seem no great problem to him. She could always be sent the same way Harcourt had gone.

Except why would he have let the Breche dealings go this far when he could have stopped them by warning Amyas away from Mariena with some story against her? Unless he meant for Amyas to marry her, to get her into his reach at Cirencester, then kill both his wife and Amyas and then win Mariena to him . . .

That was so far a stretch Joliffe set it aside, only noting to himself to see if he could sometime make a play out of it.

But if not Harry Wyot, then who? Who else was there who might have an interest-unto-death in whom Mariena married?

Go back, he told himself. Try it all again around a different angle.

He rubbed his head, trying to find that different angle.

Harcourt's death. Set it aside for now. Look at everything else that had happened. Did they make a pattern of their own? What could be made of Will's mishaps? They

had started before Harcourt's death. They had continued
since his death. Had they all come during marriage talks
or randomly around them as well as during them? That
was something to find out, because maybe Will was in
danger, rather than Amyas. Or they both might be. Or neither of them.

At least who would gain from Will's death was plain
enough. If he died, Mariena inherited everything instead of
having only her marriage portion. That could be reason
enough for several people to want Will out of the way.
Amyas Breche for one. But he hadn't even known the
Denebys when the first accidents happened. Mariena then.
But her possible willingness to be rid of her brother
wouldn't account for Harcourt's death. *His* dying made no
difference to Mariena's inheritance, only served to keep
her trapped here at Deneby longer.

Joliffe realized he was back to considering Harcourt's
death as part of everything that had happened here. But
what of Mariena's sudden, strange illness two nights ago?
What had that to do with anything? No one had made mention of any mishaps to her before then. Had it been only
chance, too, like Harcourt's death had maybe been? Or did
it mean that someone had broadened their attacks to include her? Or that they had changed from Will to attacking
her? But why now and not before? Had something
changed, to bring on that change? What? The fact that her
marriage agreement was finally made? But the last time she
had been betrothed, it had been the bridegroom who had
fallen ill, not her. And he had died. She had not. Though
that could have been her good luck rather than someone's
intent. Even so, why would someone now prefer her dead
instead of the bridegroom? Or her instead of Will?

Always supposing that *all* of these happenings were not
merely mischance. Mischance did happen, could happen
even in quantity like this. What he needed was something

that linked these happenings one to another—something
that told why someone would do them at all.

But if someone was doing them, how had this someone
been able to strike down John Harcourt so skillfully and yet
done so poorly in the attempts against Will and Mariena?

Or what if two different people were at work here, pur-
suing different ends, working at cross-purposes and apart
from each other? Or could it be two people who were
working together? Or one person but with two different
ends in mind. Or, Joliffe thought savagely, half a dozen
people all working at malign counter-purposes all at once.
Wouldn't *that* make such a cat's cradle of everything as he
would never untangle.

No. Instead of adding tangles to tangles, what he should
do is convince himself that nothing was wrong here, that
no one was doing anything to anyone, that it was all mischance and would work its way out in the fullness of time.
That would make his life simpler all the way around and he
could start this very moment.

He shifted himself and his writing box, resting his head
on it as he lay out on his back in the long grass. If he wasn't
going to write, he could watch the broken clouds drifting
white across the sky and maybe even sleep. That would be
more useful than his thoughts, for certain.

Tisbe lifted her head, listening a moment before Joliffe
heard, too, hoof-fall and the chink of harness along the trackway, coming from the village. Several horses, Joliffe
guessed, listening. Probably ridden rather than led. Not
pulling anything anyway. He stayed flat. With any good
fortune, horses and riders would simply pass by, taking no
particular note of Tisbe or seeing him at all.

Fortune favored him. But when they had passed, Joliffe
gave way to curiosity, rolled to his side, and raised himself
enough on one elbow to see the backs of Sir Edmund,
Mariena, and their accompanying servant riding away

from him toward the manor. Taking the long way home to
give Mariena a longer ride, Joliffe supposed, and lay down
again, idly watching Tisbe's head instead of clouds as she
turned it, watching the riders away. She spent very little
time with others of her kind nor ever seemed to want their
company, but she took an interest in them nonetheless and
her head went on turning, watching.

Or . . . *listening* now, to judge by her forward-pricked
ears as her head went on turning, so that she had to be
looking toward the woods now . . .

Joliffe sat up, frowning toward the trees. The trackway
ran along the wood's edge. He and Tisbe had come along
it, coming here, and he didn't remember seeing even a
footpath into the woods there, let alone a track wide
enough to ride a horse easily. Why were they going into the
woods where there wasn't a path?

With one part of his mind very clearly telling him to
stay where he was, he got to his feet. Tisbe swung her head
to look at him. Suspecting that her look was much the one
Ellis would have given him had he been there, Joliffe patted her on the flank and went away from her toward the
curve of woods where she had last been looking. The riders
would be past there by now. He would be able to follow
them. Which would be better than meeting them.

Once through the brush along the woods' edge and
among the trees, he found he had been wrong about there
being no path through the woods there. It was narrow and a
rider would have much ducking under tree limbs, but it was
there. What was not there, he saw when he looked back to
where it must start, was any break in the brush along the
woodshore. The path began *in* the wood itself.

That would need closer looking at, but more immediately he wanted to know where Sir Edmund was going, and
he followed the path the other way, farther into the woods.
With all the rain there had been, the fallen leaves were too

softened underfoot to make a betraying rustle. He had only
to avoid cracking any sticks as he walked, and that he did.
The horses could not. He could hear them ahead of him;
and when sound of their going stopped, so did he, except
he stepped sideways off the path to lessen his chance of being seen should someone back-track the trail to be sure
they were unfollowed.

When no one did, he went carefully on, not wanting to
come on them suddenly and be seen. What he came on instead was the path's end as it met a trackway undoubtedly
far more traveled than ever the path was. The track's hard-
packed earth and the smooth-worn grooves running
equally apart from one another along it made him guess it
was used for sledges rather than wagons. For hauling firewood probably. Or maybe there was a charcoal burner's
camp somewhere near.

Whichever it was, even with the rain there had been, the
way was too firm to show certainly which way the horses
had gone. Joliffe listened, heard nothing, decided they
were more likely to have kept going away from the village
than back toward it, and turned and went that way along the
track.

That was nearly his undoing. He had gone less than
twenty yards, the track making a long, easy curve to the
right, when a sudden jink of horse-harness, as if a horse had
shaken its head, warned him he was far closer to the riders
than he had thought he was. He froze. There was no hoof-
fall. They were stopped. Waiting for him? Waiting for someone else?

He slipped sideways into the underbrush, more careful
than ever of his feet. Hidden behind a hazel bush that had not
fully lost its leaves yet and was covered over with the grey-
white haze of traveler's joy for good measure, he stood still,
listening, but heard nothing more than the same sound of a
restless horse. No voices. Nothing. He eased forward, not

back to the trackway but through the trees toward the horse. A little later in the season and he would have had no cover, but while many of the trees had begun their leaf-fall, the lower bushes and lesser trees had not; he could move from tree to tree with little chance of being seen unless he was careless. Or watched for.

He kept from being careless nor, he found, was anyone keeping watch. In truth, when he crouched low to look through a last screen of hazel bushes and more vining traveler's joy between him and a long clearing widened out to either side of the trackway, the man sitting nearby on one horse and holding the reins of two others looked to be doing nothing so much as wishing he were somewhere else. In the first few moments Joliffe watched him, he shifted his seat to one side in his saddle, then to the other, drummed impatient fingers almost silently on his saddle's pommel, then shifted his seat again. Of Sir Edmund and Mariena there was no sign, but he was Sir Edmund's man and those were Sir Edmund's horses, so unless Sir Edmund and Mariena had decided to walk for a while—which struck Joliffe as unlikely in the dripping woods—they could only be in the small woodsman's hut across the clearing.

Why? It looked to be a common enough woodsman's hut—was small, with low-eaved, roughly plastered, wattle-and-daub walls, the roof rough-thatched with bracken, and no bother about a chimney. A hole at the top of the gable wall under the point of the roof would serve to let out smoke from any fire made inside, though there was presently no smoke and so likely no fire. It was a place to warm yourself and briefly shelter from wet weather, nothing more, and Sir Edmund and Mariena had to be in there. There was nowhere else for them to be. But why? To get out of the rain would have been reasonable, except it was not raining. Nor was the day so cold they should need to shelter for warmth a while with the manor so short a ride away.

He considered creeping to better vantage but decided he had pressed Fortune's favor as far as he should. Instead, he shifted silently to a slightly easier crouch and settled down on his heels to wait. Except for the sometime drip of water from leaves and the occasional heavy-hoofed shifting of one or the other of the horses, the forest was muted around him. Even the servant provided no interest, slumped in his saddle with every appearance of trying, not too successfully, to doze. He wasn't keeping watch, that was sure. Even when he did rouse to restlessness in his saddle again, his long stares at the hut and sometimes a roving look at the woods around him were more to pass the waiting time than any watching out, and Joliffe did not worry about being seen. In his plain clothing of grey and muted browns—best for not showing the stains of travel—and motionless behind the bushes, he doubted he would be seen even if the man looked directly his way.

The man never did, and Joliffe had no doubt that, if he wanted to, he could withdraw as unseen and unheard as he'd come—very probably a better thing to do than crouch here, cramped and beginning to be chilled. But he stayed. He knew too well that curiosity was one of his failings. Even without Lord Lovell's behest to find out what he could, his curiosity would have kept him here. Although maybe this time he could forgo blaming himself for his weakness, could lay the blame on Lord Lovell. A satisfying thought. He could so rarely, fairly, blame someone else for his failings.

The woods went on dripping. He went on waiting, and at the end it was the servant who came alert first to the hut's door finally opening, had straightened in his saddle and was giving a long look all around the clearing as if in careful watch when Sir Edmund came out, head bowed to go under the low lintel. Clear of the doorway, Sir Edmund straightened, too, looked all around and then at his servant, who nodded in silent answer to whatever silent question Sir Edmund had asked. Sir Edmund turned back, held out his hand, and led Mariena from the hut and toward the horses.

The servant was dismounted by the time they reached him. Sir Edmund took his own horse's reins from the man and drew it aside for room to swing himself into his saddle, leaving the man to hold Mariena's horse for her to mount, his back to them both, so that so far as Mariena knew, there was no one to see her brush her hand along the servant's thigh as she went past him. Her hand lingered just long enough to leave no doubt she did it on purpose. From where he crouched, Joliffe saw the man's back stiffen and his head twitch toward Sir Edmund to be sure he did not see it, while Mariena, as coolly as if she had done nothing, swung up into her saddle and was settling her skirts when her father turned his horse toward her.

The servant remounted his own horse, and with no word among them, they rode away, not back the way they had come but on along the track that Joliffe supposed would finally bring them out somewhere near the manor.

He was supposing other things, too, and didn't like his suppositions. They kept him where he was until he was well assured Sir Edmund and the others were truly gone and not coming back. Only then did he stand up and even then waited a little longer, listening, before he left hiding and crossed the track and clearing to the hut. He did not expect it to be locked and it was not. A simple pull of the latch string loosed the latch and let him in, bent over as Sir Edmund had been as he stepped across the threshold, then standing up straight under the low, bare-raftered roof to look around, not able to see much in the gloom. There was a shuttered window in the rear wall, though. Making his way around the small, expected hearth in the middle of the floor, he opened it and with that and the light from the open door he could see enough.

Not that there was much to see. The walls were almost
as bare inside as out and the floor was hard-trodden dirt.
Enough dry kindling and logs to see a man through a wet
night were stacked against the wall just inside the door, and
two crudely made joint stools squatted beside the hearth.
The small pile of ashes there was cold, though, when he
put a hand over them. Sir Edmund had not bothered with a
fire nor—to judge by the unmarred dust on the box of can-
dlestubs Joliffe found beside an empty, equally dusty can-
dlestick on a shelf fastened to one side wall—had he
bothered with more light than he might have had through
the window, supposing he had opened it.

The only other things in the hut were a bed and its bedding and a pole fastened between two of the posts of the
wall beside it. The bed itself was no more than could be expected in such a place, a pegged-together wooden frame on
short legs and strung with rope to hold up the coarse-
clothed mattress thickly stuffed with probably straw. There
was a blanket thrown over it, another blanket carelessly
tossed at its foot, a thin pillow, probably straw-stuffed, too,
at its other end. That was all, but Joliffe stood looking at
the bed a somewhat long while before he went to it and
with reluctance ran his hand down the middle of the blanket covering the mattress.

He was willing to believe it was only his imagination
that said it was still faintly warm, but his movements were
slow with thought as he first ran a hand along the wall pole,
then took up the blanket from the bedfoot, shook it out,
folded it, and hung it over the pole; did the same with the
other blanket; then hung the mattress, too, and propped the
pillow beside it. That was how a woodsman who sometimes
used the hut or any sensible passer-by who sheltered there
a while would have left them. Hanging them up lessened
the next-user's chance of finding mice nesting in the mattress straw or pillow and holes eaten in the blankets. That

the wall pole had been free of dust except near its ends made him think they *had* been hanging there. He likewise thought it likely that neither Sir Edmund nor Mariena would take the trouble to put them back after making use of them.

The question he did not want to ask was why they had made use of them at all. Or for what.

Chapter 17

When Joliffe retreated from the hut, making sure of the latch as he went, nothing was changed outside. The woods still dripped but the sky was not gone back to and rain yet. He had to acknowledge darkly that the increased gloom was all inside himself. He had not much thought ahead about what he might find out by following Sir Edmund. He had only thought he might find out something. And even if he had thought ahead, he would not have thought to find out this—not if he was right in his suspicion of what use Sir Edmund and Mariena had made of the hut and its bed.

The irony that he just now should be working on *Dux Moraud*—a play about a father's ill "love" for his daughter—did not escape him.

Momentarily, he was diverted by watching his mind try to turn away from his suspicion, near though it was to certainty. Because what else would they have been doing there? Anything but that, he wanted to tell himself. It was a thought almost unthinkable and yet he was thinking it, even while trying hard to think of some other reason they had been there.

But he could not.

He gathered sticks savagely as he went back along the path and through the woods to Tisbe. He found her still grazing peacefully where he had left her, and she kept on grazing while he bundled the sticks onto her back, then gathered up his writing box. Only when he had loosed her hobbles and taken up her lead rope did she raise her head and huff a heavy sigh.

"I know," he said as he turned them around toward the trackway. "I feel the same way. Over-burdened and under-fed. Though in a different sense, mind you. Over-burdened with thought and under-fed with answers. And with better reason than you have, my girl. Those sticks weigh next to nothing and you've been grabbing grass for quite a while, so don't go huffing at me."

To show there were no hard feelings, Tisbe butted her head solidly against his shoulder.

"Yes," Joliffe agreed.

They were somewhat halfway back to the manor gateway when he looked up from watching his feet walk—he could shut off quite a bit of other thought by watching his feet walk—to find Rose and Ellis coming toward him. Because they were making no great haste, were in talk, their heads near together, he had no stir of alarm.

Neither was he surprised when Ellis lifted his head, saw him, and called, "There you are," as if Joliffe had been deliberately invisible from them until then.

"And there you are," Joliffe returned. "What I'm wondering is why."

"To find you," Ellis said, "and if ever there was a less rewarding errand . . ."

Rose poked him in the side and said, "We're here to hurry you back. The play's changed for tonight."

Joliffe had reached them by then and at Ellis' words instinctively increased his pace manorward, asking, "Changed
to what? Why?"

"There's some of the wedding guests started to arrive,"
Ellis said disgustedly. "A day early. They're somebody
who matters enough that Lady Benedicta sent to ask Basset
if we would do one of our better, longer plays tonight."

Joliffe groaned.

"So Basset has decided we'll do the *Robin and Marian*
tonight instead of tomorrow," Ellis said. "With Gil as the
Sheriff's Evil Knight."

Joliffe turned a hard stare on him. "What Evil Knight?"

"The one you're supposed to write a few lines for between
now and then."

"Is Gil ready for this?"

"Basset thinks so."

"Should we invoke St. Jude or St. Genesius, do you
think?" The patron saint of desperate causes and the patron
saint of players.

"Both," Ellis said darkly.

Rose laughed at him and stretched to kiss his cheek. Joliffe, perfectly aware she had not come for the pleasure of
his company but for the chance to be alone with Ellis a little, tugged Tisbe's halter and walked faster, letting them
fall behind him, willing to give them a while more with
each other, not least because he hoped Rose would sweeten
Ellis out of his dark humour, but also to begin his thinking
about what to write that Gil could quickly learn and hopefully not forget. Did Basset know what he was doing, pitch-
ing the boy into it like this?

Joliffe supposed they would find out before the evening
was done. To the good was that in the meanwhile he would
be kept too busy to think about what he did not want to
think about.

Rose overtook him as they reached the cart-yard and took Tisbe's lead rope from him as Basset said from beside the cart, "Good. You're here. Get to work."

Not bothering to retreat to his corner, Joliffe sat down with a token grumble and his back against a cartwheel, settling his writing box on his lap. Basset was working to better Gil's knightly stance and swagger, one of their false swords hung from his hip so he could learn to move with it. "Without hurting yourself or someone else before you've even drawn it from its sheath," Basset had said to Joliffe when teaching him the same thing. For a mercy, Gil looked to be a quick study at it—better than he was with skirts, anyway, Joliffe thought, then set to the business of adding a part for him to the straight-forward tale of Robin (Ellis) and Marian (Joliffe), happy in their Sherwood life until she goes to the village and is seized by the lustful Sheriff (Basset). A Village Boy (Piers) warns Robin, who comes to her rescue, fights the Sheriff after brave speeches by both of them, kills him, and saves fair Marian.

So where could an Evil Knight come into it? Joliffe decided the simplest way was to have the Evil Knight follow the evil Sheriff into the village and turn one of the Sheriff's lines into a question—"Is she not fair to see?"—to which the Evil Knight could reply, "Aye, she is, my lord." Then, with the Sheriff saying, as he already did, "And yet more fair to hold, I warrant you," the play was back to itself. Unfortunately, that left the Evil Knight standing there, doing nothing, so Joliffe added in that while Robin and the Sheriff fought, the Evil Knight circled around and seized Marian as if for himself. Then she would cry out, Robin would turn and run the Knight through with his sword, the Village Boy would cry warning as the Sheriff tried to kill Robin from behind, Robin would turn again and kill the Sheriff.

There. Simple.

All they need do now was learn it, practice it, teach Gil how to "die," and hope for the best. All before suppertime.

Ellis was right. Best to pray to *both* St. Jude and St. Genesius.

He showed Basset what he had done. Basset said, "Good," and they set to Gil learning it.

"Just follow me into the playing place," Basset told him. "Stand there. Say your line. Don't do anything else until Ellis and I have exchanged, say, five blows." He and Ellis mimed their fight without swords in hand. "Keep count," Basset said. "Five blows. Then circle left. Like that, yes, and come behind Joliffe and seize him around the waist with your left arm, keeping your body just enough aside to the right that Ellis can stab his sword between you and Joliffe without danger of Robin killing Marian instead of you. Ellis, don't even think it. Yes, Gil, just like that. Good. Ellis."

Ellis feigned a long sword thrust toward Gil.

"Now clutch your side and drop dead, Gil," Basset said. "No, just drop and lie still. Don't twitch and writhe. Drop and be dead. Do it again. Yes."

There was nothing like the dread of failure to urge quick learning. They ran Gil's part in the play four times with him, until Basset granted, "It goes none so bad. None so bad at all. You'll do, Gil. Just keep your head and you'll do. Now you and Piers go and fetch our supper. It must be nigh time for it."

Only when they were well gone did he ask Ellis, Joliffe, and Rose together, "What do you think? Have I courted, wooed, and won disaster with this?"

"Probably," Ellis growled.

Rose yet again poked him in the ribs and chided, "The boy was good. You know he was. Say it."

Ellis caught her hand and granted, smiling, "He was

good. Better than he has any right to be." He shook his head at Basset. "Damn my toe, but I think you may pull this off."

"Unless he goes cold when there are lookers-on," Joliffe said.

"He hasn't yet," Basset said.

"Let's hope he doesn't start tonight," Ellis grumbled.

Everyone ignored him, Basset saying, "Joliffe, did you get any further on with *Dux Moraud* this afternoon? I'm starting to look forward to starting work on it if Gil goes on shaping as he is."

That play with its incestuous duke and his daughter was close to the last thing Joliffe wanted to think about, but he said evenly, "I'm still not around the problem of his repentance at the end. It won't come believable for me."

"I remember he repents but not for certain how he comes to it," Basset said. "To conceal his sin with his daughter, he's had her kill their baby and her mother. He goes to church and is confronted and accused by a miraculous statue. He repents and tells his daughter he forswears his sin. That's the way of it, isn't it?"

"It is, as it stands now," Joliffe said. "I'm thinking to change it so he and his daughter go to church together and the saint's statue comes to life and strikes the girl horribly dead and damned. Devils drag off her shrieking soul and the duke is horrified into instant repentance, says some things, and the saint declares him saved."

"You mean," Rose said with coldly, "the girl dies and is damned but the duke is given chance to repent and saves his soul, even though he's the one who corrupted her? Why should she be damned and he be saved? Who's fault was their sinning anyway?"

Joliffe gave her a wry look. "That's something to think on, yes."

"She's damned," said Ellis, "because she's the greater

sinner. Besides the incest, she killed her mother and her baby."

"As I remember it," Rose snapped back, "it's her father who orders her to both murders. He doesn't even have the guts to do it himself. Besides the incest and corrupting his daughter's innocence, he's a coward as well."

Sounding suddenly wary of what he might have stirred up, Ellis carefully granted, "It could be seen that way." On the rare times that Rose broke into open argument over something, no one liked to be in her way.

Not only at Ellis but at all of them she said sharply, "Even setting aside his cowardice and despite what she did and he didn't, he's a man. Since you men argue that men are higher in God's creation than women . . ."

All three men threw up protesting hands at that, Basset saying quickly, "Not us. No. We've never claimed that, no. Someone else, but not us!"

Scorning his protest, Rose went on, "You men claim you're nearer to God than women, that it's all the fault of Woman that Mankind fell. So why, if women are so imperfect, is Eve more at fault that she succumbed to the Devil's wiles, when Adam simply gave way to her? If men are so much the better, his fall was the greater because he gave way under far less temptation than she did and so *his* sin is the greater and . . ."

"Yes," her father agreed hurriedly. "You're right. We can see that. I . . ."

Rose went right on, demanding at him in particular, "Then in this *Dux Moraud* play, why should the girl be seen the greater sinner when it was the duke who led her innocence into sin, corrupted her goodness into evil? Tell me that."

"Ah!" Basset said with the air of a man grasping at a straw. "You see there's God's mercy at work. The duke is in greater need of salvation and is given the chance to repent and . . ."

Able to see what was coming, Joliffe was already stepping backward in open retreat as Rose snapped with growing anger, "And the girl is damned for eternity, despite his was the greater sin. It must be because I'm a weak-headed woman that I don't quite see the fairness of that."

Basset and Ellis made haste to agree they did not see it either.

"So *you*," she said, pointing her finger at Joliffe, "are going to *fix* that, aren't you?"

Still backing away, his hands already up in surrender, Joliffe said, "I'm trying. I swear I am."

Basset and Ellis nodded in hurried agreement. Rose swept them all with a look of disgust, as if even their surrender was insufficient apology for being men, and turned away to tend the fire.

Leaving Basset and Ellis to what they would, Joliffe retreated all the way to his corner beyond the cart, taking his writing box with him. There must be some delay at the kitchen, that the boys were not back yet, and he made a show of having out paper and pen and ink as if at work already to meet Rose's demand. He would have worked gladly, too, but his thoughts slid away to the worse thing in his mind.

If, as he feared, it was incest between Sir Edmund and Mariena, what different look did that give to what he so far knew? For one thing, it could explain the prolonged dealing before agreement was made for John Harcourt to marry Mariena. If Sir Edmund intended to keep Mariena for himself, it could also explain why Harcourt was murdered. But then why move on so quickly to dealing for another marriage? And why was it Will, rather than Amyas Breche, who had come close to grief these several times, while nothing had befallen Amyas?

Yet. There was still time for it to happen. Not much time, though. Not with only three more days until the wedding.

But there was still the possibility that Harcourt's death was only by chance, or even—if purposed—it was for some other reason than Sir Edmund's secret. What that purpose might have been, Joliffe had no thought on at all, but either way, it would mean Amyas was in no danger. That did not mean he wasn't, though; and none of those possibilities answered why Will was having "accidents." Could they be for someone's revenge against Sir Edmund for John Harcourt's death or some other reason? To increase Mariena's inheritance? For some reason to which Joliffe had no clue?

Did Lady Benedicta know what was between her husband and daughter?

That was a thought Joliffe had been keeping shy of but now faced. Because if Lady Benedicta did know, then complications only increased. It would explain the lack of love between mother and daughter—or, no, it didn't, because it was said they had never done well together. But it could explain Mariena's sudden sickness the other night. Lady Benedicta could have poisoned her. It was a possibility. There was enough else apparently awry here, it was not that far from reasonable to think she might.

But why only slightly poison her? Or why at all? Lady Benedicta reputedly had no attachment to either her husband or daughter. If she knew, or suspected, what there was between them—if there really was something—would she care enough to bother making Mariena suffer for it? Or, to take it another way, would she have been satisfied with making her suffer so little? Or could there have been another reason to do it?

Such as Will's bad fall that day.

Looked at from that way, there was some sense to what had been happening, both to Will *and* about Mariena's sickness. She was the one who would most benefit from her brother's death. Let him be dead and she was heir to Deneby. That she would be willing to his death was an ill thought, but Joliffe found he could think it of her fairly easily. And if Lady Benedicta suspected the same about her, then, yes, he could readily see her warning Mariena off her purpose with threat of death against herself.

But why John Harcourt's death? To judge by how readily he had set to talks so soon after Harcourt's death, Sir Edmund apparently had no objection to Mariena marrying, so he was unlikely to have killed the man. And Mariena was said to have been eager to the marriage, with no apparent gain by his death. And Lady Benedicta reputedly would be glad to have the girl gone. So if Harcourt's death had not been murder at all, then Amyas was safe enough, and what business did Joliffe have in wondering about the rest?

Maybe no business at all, but he knew, regretfully, that was not going to stop him now. They had all, except for Will, become suddenly fools to him. Sir Edmund. Lady Benedicta. Mariena. They were all carrying on like poor actors in a bad play. Cold, angry mother. Hot-loined, possibly murderous daughter. Incestous father. Joliffe supposed that if he were a priest he'd have to take them seriously. And if someone wrote a play of them, it would have to be a tragedy. But to him—looking at their miserable blundering about without a clear thought about the rights or wrongs of anything they felt or did—the whole business looked a farce.

Unless John Harcourt truly had been murdered and someone truly was trying to kill Will and there was actually incest between Sir Edmund and Mariena.

Not farce then, no. Plain tragedy.

When Lord Lovell came, he would have to be told it all, Joliffe supposed, to make of it what he would. Joliffe only hoped to be well away from here as soon as might be after that.

Piers and Gil came back with deep bowls of stew, thick brown bread, lumps of cheese, and a tale of an irate cook and the kitchen in chaos, all plans upset because of the two knights and their ladies who had arrived before their time.

"If it was my household," Rose said as they finished their meal, "I'd not be doing somersaults to make them think the better of me. They'd have what we were going to have and be happy with it or not, as pleased them."

"Ah, but that's because you are perfection itself," her father said. "Whatever you do is beyond the bounds of others' hopes and no more could be desired than what you give."

Rose rolled her eyes, and Ellis lightly slapped the back of Piers' head before Piers had more than opened his mouth to make some bright comment back at his grandfather.

"You do but speak the truth, good sir," Joliffe said, standing up and brushing bread crumbs from the skirt of his doublet. "Shall we make ready?"

Rose helped Joliffe into Marian's gown and with the long wig, then held the small mirror while he colored his face. Basset and Ellis saw to Gil, and Piers took care of himself. By the time they were ready to head for the hall, Gil was looking as if he was working not to be ill, and Basset said bracingly as if to them all, "We know what we're doing. We've done the play here. We can do it there. Simple as that. Onward!"

At the hall, at the play's beginning, Joliffe and Ellis entered the hall first, leaving the others waiting in the screens passage. Gil still looked ill and was standing stiffly, as if waiting for the worst to happen, but when he came in behind Basset, he came with firm stride and hand on sword hilt, just as Basset had been teaching him; and he took up his stance with enough swagger but not too much, said his line out loud and clear when he was supposed to, made his move on Marian on the sixth blow of the swords, and died without excess from Robin's perfectly placed sword thrust. He could not have done better if they had rehearsed him for a week, Joliffe thought, nor their audience been more approving, with even a few cries of "down-with-the-sheriff" among the clapping and thumping on tables afterward, so that the whole company returned across the yard in high and merry humour, Rose with them because she had slipped into the passage to watch with the servants, wanting to see how it went.

Too over-pleased to contain himself, Gil strode ahead with Piers, talking and talking about how it had gone. The rest of them followed more slowly, as pleased but too tired for much more than wide smiling, except Basset said thoughtfully as they went, "I maybe better take up Lord Lovell's offer of an apprentice's contract for him. Otherwise, the first greater company that sees him will hire him away from us before I can say, 'Wait!'"

At the cartshed, they found Rose had been to the kitchen before coming to the hall and had brought back a pitcher of ale and plate of small seedcakes. "Because you'd either be in need of comforting if all went wrong," she said, "or else we would want to feast your triumph."

"Feast it is!" said Basset, and for good measure they built up the fire, too.

Tiredness wasn't far behind them, though, and they were beginning to ready for bed when Joliffe said, "Someone is coming."

They all turned and looked into the darkness, waiting, half-wary, until the maidservant Avice came out of the shadows into the little lantern-light. Not cloaked for the chill night, she had her arms wrapped around herself and was not looking happy to be there as she pulled one hand free, pointed at Joliffe, and said, "You. My lady has a headache. She wants you to play your lute for her until she sleeps."

"Lady Benedicta?" Joliffe said, with a sinking feeling in his belly already telling him otherwise.

"Mariena." Avice shifted from foot to foot. "She's gone to her bedchamber. She'll have wanted you there five minutes ago. Make haste, won't you?"

Chapter 18

With his lute slung behind his shoulder by its strap, Joliffe followed Avice not back to the hall or even to the tower but farther along the yard to the wooden stairs leading up to the open gallery that ran outside the wing of rooms there. It being evening's end, most of the lanterns around the yard were out, only the ones at the hall door, the top of the stairs to the tower, and the outer gateway still burning. Glints and hints of light showed at window shutters' chinks and cracks here and there along the wing, but he and Avice were in shadow where she stopped at the stairfoot, and he only faintly saw her pause at rubbing her arms to point upward as she said, "You want that door there at the near end, where the light's showing around the shutter's edge, and if she has a headache, I'm a lark on the wing. Good luck to you."

She started to leave but when, startled, Joliffe said, "What?" she turned back, came close to him, and hissed,

"She has an itch like a she-cat on the prowl, does our Mariena. The sooner she's married and somebody satisfies her, the better for everyone." She moved closer, her breath warm on his cheek as she said even lower, "Look you, no matter how willing she gives out to be, don't you think you'll get more than some kisses and an ache in your loins from her, that's all. Meanwhile"—her own hands found him in the dark—"give us a kiss, there's a sweetheart."

Thinking, Why not? Joliffe pulled her to him; and when he had done and let her go, she went on leaning against him a long moment before finally giving a deep sigh of contentment and stepping back.

"That," she murmured, "will warm me to my bed." She laid a hand on his chest. "Just you be careful up there. Don't give her any kisses like that or you'll find yourself in trouble you won't get out of easy."

With that, she was gone away into the shadows before Joliffe could promise he meant very much to stay out of that kind of trouble.

More worried than he wanted to be, he went up the stairs and along the open-sided gallery, instinctively quiet-footed in the settled-for-the-night quiet of the manor. Because of his quiet, he surely was not heard as he neared Mariena's door—instead heard a man's voice from inside that stopped him where he was. If Mariena had a man with her, then . . .

Angrily, loudly, in answer to something Mariena said, "I'm to marry him in three days! You said—"

The man's voice interrupted hers, and Joliffe moved quickly to the window, getting his ear near to the shutter in time to hear, ". . . not give you up. What does married have to do with it? Because you're married doesn't mean you'll stay married."

Silence answered that for a long moment before Mariena said slowly, "Oh." And after another pause, sounding as if she were smiling, "You mean that I'm to have him for a pretty while and then—"

"And then we pray," Sir Edmund said, his voice cold and quelling, "that your wedded bliss goes on for a long, long while. Yes?"

Again there was a pause from Mariena before she said again, as if just catching up to his thought, "Oh." And then with sudden false brightness, "Yes." And on a note of laughter, "Oh, yes!"

A silence followed that Joliffe tried not to fill with any thought of what the two of them might be doing together. To count on it lasting long, though, was hardly safe. Sir Edmund must have come to her unexpectedly. He was not likely to linger long, and this not being a place to be caught overhearing, Joliffe had one foot raised toward retreat when Sir Edmund said in a suddenly harsher voice, "One thing, though. Leave off on Will."

Mariena began what sounded like a protest but broke off on a yelp of pain as Sir Edmund went on, "Let one more thing happen to him and you'll have bruises to explain to Amyas on your wedding night, along with your missing maidenhead."

"You swore he wouldn't know," Mariena said, sounding half-way to angry and at the same time afraid.

"He won't know," Sir Edmund said coldly. "I'll have him so fumble-brained with drink, he won't know more than that he's had you, if he even knows that much. But bruises he won't miss. If not that night, then the next. So you leave Will alone."

Mariena started, "I haven't done . . ." but broke off with a squeak of surprise or pain.

"Leave him alone now and ever after," Sir Edmund said, his voice flat with threat. "He's my son. He's my heir. You leave him alone. If ever he's hurt and I think it's your doing . . ."

He left the threat for her to imagine for herself. Or maybe he showed her again the pain he had in mind if she disobeyed him, but Joliffe was in full retreat by then, having heard enough. His thought was to go back to the stairs and down, to wait in shadows until Sir Edmund was gone, but the door's latch rattled, telling someone was coming out, and he vaulted the gallery's railing, hung by his hands for the hairsbreadth of an instant before he let loose and dropped soft-footed to the ground just as the opening door spilled light in a narrow band across the gallery walk. Out of sight in the darkness below it, he moved swiftly into the deeper darkness under the gallery and pressed himself to the wall there, holding his breath. His thought was that Sir Edmund would go along the gallery to the tower and his own chamber. If he did not . . . if he came down the stairs to the yard and was carrying any kind of a light . . .

Joliffe began to breathe again as Sir Edmund's footfall went away toward the tower; but he stayed where he was until he heard the tower's thick door shut and even then he moved only to the edge of the deeper darkness under the gallery, keeping from sight while he looked to be sure there was no one to be seen anywhere. Unseen watchers he could do nothing about. If they were there, they had already seen him and worry about them was useless, and taking a deep, steadying breath, he left hiding and—this time not quiet at all about his going—bounded up the stairs. For good measure, he whistled an uneven, seemingly absent-minded tune as he neared the door, meaning to sound like a simple man with nothing to hide. In the same quick, easy way he started to rap at the door, but before his second knock fell, it was snatched open and a frightened-faced woman looked out at him.

For a moment he stared at her, startled. As a knight's daughter, Mariena was of course companioned almost everywhere, certainly in her bedchamber. The woman would be her waiting-maid. But with what he had just heard, he had thought to find Mariena alone. That she was not unsettled him in a new way. If this woman was not a complete fool, she had to know what was between Mariena and her father, just as the man who had held their horses in the woods this afternoon had to know. How wide did the corruption spread in this place?

On the instant, though, he turned his own startlement into a wide smile and a small, flourished bow; and the woman said over her shoulder, "It's the player, my lady. You sent for him, remember."

"Of course I remember," Mariena snapped. "Let him in and close that door. It's cold out there."

The woman was already stepping aside, opening the door wider for him to come in. He did, more outwardly bold than he inwardly felt.

Mariena's room was far smaller than her parents' in the tower but as comfortable in its way. The shutters and door and roof-beams were painted a forest-green. The bedhangings were a strong blue. A woven mat of golden rushes covered some of the floor, and on one wall a painted tapestry of flowers and trees showed dimly in the shadows beyond the light of the small oil lamp burning on a square table between the bed and a small fireplace in the farther wall.

Mariena was standing there, her back to the low fire, already in her bedrobe of some dark, green fabric that fell in heavy, loose folds from her shoulders to the floor. Her hair was loose, too, a dark, soft frame to her white face; but she was cradling one arm against her as if it hurt and Joliffe hoped it did. What had Amyas Breche ever done that she should so look forward to being his widow?

The pity was Sir Edmund was probably in no pain at all, despite he surely deserved to be, probably even more than Mariena did.

But presently Joliffe was more worried about his own

plight than Amyas'. Even without Avice's warning, he would not have been happy to be there, as good as alone with Mariena. Nor did the way Mariena was presently staring at him make him any happier.

For one thing, he could not tell whether she was looking at him with lust or anger. For another, he did not know what he would do, whichever it was. Anger, he decided as he made a low and sweeping bow to her, would be the better. With anger she might be satisfied simply to send him away. If it was lust, he would have to forestall her, whatever the after-cost of her displeasure might be.

Without taking her eyes from him or smiling, Mariena ordered, "Wine, Lesya. For both of us." And at him, "Come here."

Joliffe went, stopped before he was very near, and bowed again. "My lady."

She let go of her arm, put one hand to her throat at the closed front of her bedgown, and with the other shifted the bedgown's long folds away from her feet as she moved toward him. Even under the bedgown's loose flow, the graceful, deliberate sway of her hips showed. She was, beyond denying, beautiful. She was also not for him even to touch except at his peril, and he was judging at what point he could step back from her without giving offense, when she stopped far enough from him for propriety's sake but too near for his comfort. Her smile at him was bright and young with innocence, but he no longer believed in her innocence in any sense of the word, and keeping his own face as bland as might be, he slipped his lute from behind his shoulders to in front of him and said, drawing his fingers across the strings in a gentle, low strum, "I grieve to hear you're troubled with a headache, my lady, but pleased you thought my lute and I might do you service."

Mariena took another step toward him, too near now. She put out a hand and stroked it down the neck and along the body of the lute, stopping just short of his fingers. Softly she said, "I hope you may. Do me service." She looked up at him from under her lashes. "You played the damsel in your play tonight very well, but I think from what else I've seen of you, there's nothing of the damsel truly about you."

To weave words with a woman toward a mutually desired end could be a pleasant pastime, but just now words were his only protection against Mariena, and with no pleasure at all, he said carefully, "I'm pleased the play pleased you, my lady."

"The play pleased everyone," she said. "But *you* pleased *me*."

Her eyes, raised to his face, were inviting him to kiss her, and though he had pleasured women before now because his playing had pleased them—had pleasured himself, too, or he'd not have done it—everything about Mariena was too dangerous for even so slight a matter as a kiss. Besides the plain peril of making sport with a knight's unmarried daughter at all, he was become frightened of Mariena herself. Women driven by lust could, in their need, be either dangerous or tedious, depending on who they were and how many or few wits they brought to the business. At worst they could be both dangerous *and* tedious, and he had begun to think Mariena was one of that kind. But he had no wish to find out further and for certain, nor did he want to give her any claim on him in any way.

But neither did he think he could afford to offend her, since her smallest accusation against him would suffice to ruin him and probably take the rest of the players down with him. A *great* accusation would likely have him dead, and he did not want to find out which she would make if he refused whatever she was about to ask of him, but refuse her he surely had to do, despite her eyes were large and dark in the lamplight, her lovely mouth curved in a small smile, as she leaned closer to him and said softly, "Won't you please me some more? Here? Now?" She raised her hand, made to touch his cheek.

Joliffe had decided he was going to have a violent coughing fit right *now*, but by some small movement or look he maybe betrayed his unwillingness toward her more openly than he meant to, because Mariena's face changed on the instant from lust to anger and her hand flew aside from his face and came back in a hard slap that jerked his head to the side.

Then she flung away from him, exclaiming like a small child denied an expected treat, "Oh, I'm not in the humour for it. I don't want you. Go away." She threw herself onto her bed, her back against her pillows, her dark hair fanned out across them, her arms crossed tightly like a barrier between him and her. But with equal sharpness she ordered, "No. Stay. Play me something. That's what you're here for." And at her waiting-maid, "Wine, you slow-footed whore," despite the woman was already crossing the room to her with a silver-gilt goblet.

Joliffe, his face stinging from the slap, took the first song that came into his mind, a half-bawdy tavern song. Mariena had seized the goblet and begun to drink before she caught the words of what he was singing. He saw her eyes go startled over the rim of the goblet. Then she choked and had to sit up, laughing and choking together, snatching the napkin Lesya brought, wiping at her chin while ordering Joliffe, "Go on. That's what I want. Something that isn't this place."

He sang and she drank. He followed the first song with another like it, and while Lesya filled her goblet again, Mariena waved him on to a third. He obeyed with a song that at the start seemed like the others but shifted into a quieter way before it finished, and from that one he went into a yet quieter one. His hope was that the music and wine would work together to lull her into sleep while he sang, and indeed as he softened his voice into "When the nightingale sings, the woods grow green," Mariena settled a little deeper against her pillows, her eyes closed, the goblet resting on her stomach, held in both her hands.

Lesya hovered not far off, probably to rescue the goblet should Mariena's hold on it slacken, but Mariena's hold held firm; and when Joliffe finished, "Sweet love, I pray you to love me an hour. I sing sadly of the one for whom I long," on a soft and fading note, hoping she had faded to sleep with it, she patted the bed beside her without opening her eyes and said, "Come sit here."

He looked at Lesya, asking for help. She shrugged, then beckoned her head toward the bed. That was not the help he wanted, but keeping hold on his lute and his lute firmly between him and Mariena, he went to the bed and sat not quite so near as she had bade him. She opened her eyes and stared at him with an owlish effort that made him think she must have had more to drink than he had thought.

"You play very well, player," she said.

He knew he played well enough, not very well; but if Mariana knew no better, well and good, and he made her a small bow and said, "Thank you, my lady."

Keeping her eyes on him, she held her goblet out to the side. Lesya stepped forward and took it, then stepped back. As if the goblet had removed itself and no one else was there at all, Mariena slid her hand onto Joliffe's leg and asked softly, "Do you play women as well as the lute?"

Evenly, he said, "I have been known to, yes, my lady."

Her hand slid over the curve of his thigh. He was just the little way too far away for her to reach where she plainly wanted to go but rather than order him nearer, she whispered, "Will you play me, player?"

There were only two ways to go from that question, and since he most assuredly did not mean to go the one, he went the other, meeting her boldness with his own. "No, my lady, I will not."

Her hand, which had begun to stroke up and down his thigh, stopped. She went on staring at him, but rather than the harshness he had feared would come with his refusal, after a moment a small smile eased the tightness of lust from her mouth and she took back her hand, laid it with the other on her belly, and said, "Fairly answered," closed her eyes again, was silent a moment, then said quietly, "Tell me, player, do you ever grow tired of being alive?"

The question and its quiet threat took him by surprise, keeping him from any answer.

Still quietly and without opening her eyes, Mariena said softly, "Don't you grow tired of it? Tired of all life's mess and disappointments?"

He realized she was not making a threat. Instead, blur-brained with wine and sleepiness, she was maybe giving away her own most inward thoughts. Thoughts someone so young should not have. And he said, matching her quiet, "I've wearied many times over of life's disappointments, yes. But of life itself? No, of that I've never wearied."

Mariena made a small sound that might have been a disbelieving laugh if there had been more strength to it. "The more fool you," she murmured. She half-opened her eyes, smiled at him so slightly he hardly saw it, and said, "I wish you loved me, player," before her eyes closed again and she rolled over and curled in on herself, gone suddenly, completely, into sleep, it seemed. But he did not move, nor did her waiting-maid until Mariena's breathing had evened into what could only be sound sleep; and even then he only turned his head, careful not to shift the bed at all just yet, as he looked at Lesya and asked softly, "Well? What did you give her?"

The woman shrugged. "A sleeping draught. Sir Edmund

orders it." She turned away to the table and started to pour some wine into a cup there.

"Should you be drinking that?" Joliffe asked.

"The potion is in her goblet before ever I pour the wine. It's only to make her sleep, anyway. It does no harm."

"And it forestalls her craving after men," Joliffe ventured, to see what the woman would say.

Lesya had lifted the filled cup to her mouth but stopped, set the cup down, and turned on him in one swift movement, hissing, "Don't ever say that. About her craving men. Don't *ever* say it."

Joliffe held up his hands as if to show he surrendered and was unarmed.

Lesya still stared at him, suspicion unassuaged, and snapped, "What makes you say it, anyway?"

Joliffe stood up from the bed and strolled toward the table with an easy smile. "I've none so great opinion of myself that I expect women to fall into a passion for me as easily as she seems to have. That wasn't love for me in her eyes just now. That was lust, and likely any man would have served." And did Sir Edmund know how willing she was to lay hands—and maybe more—on other men and was that why he had her sent senseless to sleep at night to contain her wantonness? And be sure no one had her but himself?

Eyeing him over the cup's edge, Lesya drank deeply, lowered the cup, and said with another shrug, "Well enough then, yes. She has a lust for men maybe beyond the ordinary." She shook a finger at Joliffe. "But if one word about her gets out, I'll see to it it's your guts that Sir Edmund gets."

Given that almost any man who came into Mariena's reach probably knew about her, Joliffe thought that was hardly fair but did not say so, only caught Lesya's hand and kissed it before she could pull away. "Her secret is safe with me." Until he had chance to talk to Lord Lovell, he silently added. "And so is yours."

"Mine?" Lesya had been enjoying his kiss but now snatched her hand away. "What do you mean—mine?"

"She doesn't know you give her this sleeping draught to drink every night, does she?"

"Of course she doesn't! She'd tear my hair out if she knew I did it! And who says I do it every night?"

Joliffe grinned as if they were sharing a particularly good jest and said lightly, "I'd have you do every night if she were my daughter." Since it seemed unlikely Lesya was going to offer him any of the wine, he sat down on the long-legged stool beside the table and started to stroke a quiet song from the lute, asking as if interested more in what his fingers were doing on the lute strings than in his question, "Does Lady Benedicta know what Sir Edmund has ordered?"

"Lady Benedicta?" Lesya had finished her cup of wine, was starting to fill it again. What she had already downed was maybe serving to loosen her tongue. Or maybe she was just past caring what she said. "Lady Benedicta gives me the potion to give her." She sat down on the chair and took another long drink. "There's no harm in it. Lady Benedicta uses it herself."

Joliffe wondered if the woman was simple enough never to wonder what Lady Benedicta could do with that draught if she chose to change it. *Did* Lady Benedicta know what her daughter was—although she surely didn't know what was between her and her father—or did she simply do her husband's bidding without asking why?

All outward innocence, he asked, "Lady Benedicta sleeps badly?"

"Lady Benedicta? The nights she doesn't have her draught she spends more hours walking the floor than in her bed, so Felicie, that's her woman, says. It's been worse lately, too. That John Harcourt was the image of his father, Felicie says."

"What's his father to do with it?"

Lesya gave a wary glance toward the bed, but the wine well and truly had hold on her tongue now and she leaned toward him to say in a lower voice, "He was her lover. Lady Benedicta's. Years ago. John Harcourt's father. It didn't last long and the man's dead, but it must have stirred her, to see his son that looked so much like him when he was something to her. And this John going to marry her daughter and then dying all sudden that way." Lesya sat back and wetted her second-hand sorrow with a long drink.

"Small wonder she doesn't sleep well," Joliffe said. "But John Harcourt's death wasn't an unlikely death, was it? I heard he was sickly youth and took a chill." Lying through his teeth as he said it.

Lesya hiccuped on unswallowed wine, swallowed quickly, and said, "Sickly? Not him. Fit as a stud stallion." She gave a nod at Mariena. "Couldn't keep her hands off him, she couldn't, and you could see he wanted her, oh, yes."

Putting on a scandalized voice, Joliffe started, "But they never . . ." He made a suggestive gesture.

Lesya scorned that thought. "Never. Sir Edmund knows my lady Mariena too well to give her chance for that." The wine's momentary ease went out of her. Her face fell into downward lines and she reached for the wine pitcher again, muttering, "Knows her far too well, he does."

Pretending he did not hear that, Joliffe asked lightly, "So how did he die then, this stallion-ready John Harcourt?"

Lesya had enough wits left to turn willingly from Sir Edmund to that. "Nasty, it was. He started with a pain, then a flux that nothing stopped. Lady Benedicta did all she could but nothing helped. She's good with herbs. If she couldn't find a way to save him, there wasn't any."

And if there was a way to kill him, she'd know it, too, Joliffe thought, but said, to keep the maid talking, "Did Mariena help nurse him?"

"Her? Not so's you'd note it," Lesya scoffed. "She's never bothered to learn aught like that." Another deep drink of wine. "Never one for learning anything. Except of one sort. And that comes natural, like, no learning needed."

That raised another question to which Joliffe could guess the answer. In the usual way of things, servants weren't given unstinted wine, supposing they got any wine at all, costly and troublesome as it was to get. Yet Lesya had no pause at downing this pitcher of it all by herself. Probably it was part of her payment for keeping secret what was between Sir Edmund and Mariena. Had Sir Edmund thought ahead to when the balance would shift from wine enough to keep her quiet to too much wine and a tongue she no longer controlled? Joliffe would wager he had—and about what would have to be done with her when that time came.

That time might not be so far off, either. Lesya was sighing over her cup now, shaking her head as if under a weight of sorrow. "They would have been lovely together, my lady and John Harcourt. I'd have gone away with her when she left with him, too, and that would have been good. Good to be away from here. You don't know. My brother is Sir Edmund's man and he says we're onto a good thing here, but I'm not . . . not . . . not"—shaking her head back and forth on each "not"—". . . liking it anymore."

She was drinking herself drunk past being useful to him, Joliffe judged. She was not likely to tell him any more of much use before she was soused out of her wits into weeping uselessness, and readying to make his escape as gracefully as possible, Joliffe ran his fingers in a quick, closing way across the lute strings, gave a huge sigh of seeming-regret, and stood up, slinging the lute around to his back. "Well, I'd best be going. Tomorrow will be here soon enough."

Lesya caught hold of his doublet's edge and smiled up at him. "My bed's not as soft as hers," she said, "but I can make it as warm for you."

Saint Mary Magdalene, save me, Joliffe thought, rather desperately smiling at her as he stepped back far enough that she had to let go his doublet or be pulled forward off the chair, saying while he did, "Alas, sweet maid, I am expected in my own bed. Otherwise . . ."

Still retreating, he kissed his hand toward her and left "otherwise" hanging between them as he got altogether away, out the door and safe into the mist-cold night.

Chapter 19

With the mist and the hour's lateness and carry—
ing too much knowledge unsafe to have, Joliffe
crossed the yard's thick darkness between the few lanterns'
light with a constant watching all around him and a crawling
unease up his back. Going into the thick, narrow blackness
between carpenter's shed and stable to reach the cart-yard
was an effort of will because anything—anyone—could
be waiting unseen in the dark there, dagger in hand. All of
which was fool-worry because no one here knew that he
knew anything beyond what he should, and so no one here
had interest in having him dead; but that did not stop him letting out his pent breath when he came into the cart-yard and
in sight of the low red glow of the players' fire.

He was surprised, though, that it had not been banked
for the night before now. Was surprised, too, to find Basset
sitting hunched almost over it, wrapped and hooded in his
cloak. Everyone else seemed to be asleep, and when Joliffe
had laid the lute into its case and into the cart, he went to

sit on his heels beside Basset and ask, quiet-voiced, "All's well?"

"Well and very well with us," Basset said back. "With you?"

"Well enough." But he said it too slowly, weighted with his thoughts.

"You've learned something," Basset said.

"I've learned something," Joliffe agreed. Several things, including how discouraging other people's lust could be and to what depths of foolishness lust like Mariena's could take someone. He had known something of foolishness' faults before this, but none so deep as these. "Most importantly, Amyas *is* in danger."

"From whom?" Basset asked.

"From Sir Edmund and Mariena both. But not until after he's married her."

"Not before?" Basset asked. "You think then that Harcourt's death was only chance?"

"To my mind he was likely murdered, but I don't have any proof he was, nor know why, and couldn't swear to who did it."

"Ah," said Basset dryly. "That's helpful, isn't it? What of Will?"

"He's probably safe for now." But only if Sir Edmund was right in thinking Mariena was to blame for everything that had befallen the boy and she believed his threats. But if he was wrong? What if it was someone else than Mariena? Who? Lady Benedicta? Joliffe was certain against that—and equally certain she had used the bedtime draught to make Mariena ill as a warning after Will's last "accident."

But if not Lady Benedicta, then who?

"So you think Harcourt was indeed murdered," Basset said. "But Will is safe for now, and Amyas in no danger until after he's married. Is that the way of it?"

"Probably." But only probably. The trouble was that he was more than half-way sure Lady Benedicta had poisoned John Harcourt to his death but did not know *why* and so there was no telling but what she might choose to kill Amyas, too, before his marriage, whatever her husband's intention. But still the question was why would she want to prevent Mariena's marriage. The more especially if she knew about the incest. But did she know? And even if she did, that did not answer much. The dislike between her and Mariena went back for years longer than the incest could have, and why, with finally the chance to be quit of Mariena, would she kill Harcourt? But if she had—or someone else had for a reason Joliffe equally did not see— then Amyas could be in danger the same way. Just as Will might still be if Sir Edmund was wrong about Mariena harming him and it was someone else entirely set on hurting, if not killing, him.

Basset sighed and held his hands out over the fire's glow. "It's something to tell Lord Lovell anyway. He'll do something about the marriage, I suppose. What to do about the rest will be his choice, too, and better him than us."

"Better never us at all," Joliffe said. He was suddenly in a savage anger at everything. "I've had a vile, ugly evening." Faced with lust he couldn't return and wine he wasn't offered. "I'm for sleep and to hell with it all."

He left Basset banking the fire, undressed barely enough, and slid into his blankets still seething with frustration and anger. The pieces of whatever was happening here were taking shape but they didn't yet fit together. It maybe should have been enough that Amyas and Will were probably safe for now and the rest could be left to Lord Lovell, just as Basset had said, but that did not stop his thoughts from circling. There was Mariena's frightened waiting-maid. She plainly served Sir Edmund rather than Mariena. She had to know their secret and probably saw to

it that Sir Edmund knew whatever she knew of Mariena.
That meant Sir Edmund would hear what had passed between her and Joliffe, so thanks be given to every celibate
saint that he had done no more than what he had. Unless
Lesya told Sir Edmund about the questions he had asked.
Would it matter if Sir Edmund knew he knew about the
sleeping draught? Maybe not, if Sir Edmund didn't know
Joliffe understood it was meant for a way to keep
Mariena's lust in check, and surely Lesya would keep that
part of their talk to herself. He hoped. Did Lady Benedicta
know the draught was for that, or did she truly think it was
simply to make Mariena sleep well? Did she know her
daughter lusted beyond the ordinary for men? Did she
know of Mariena's and Sir Edmund's sin? Did she agree
with her husband on what he intended for Amyas Breche, or
did she know nothing of it? Had Sir Edmund wanted John
Harcourt's death, or had that been Lady Benedicta's doing
alone? Supposing she had done it. Supposing anyone
had done it. But if she had done it, did Mariena know
it? Was Mariena's sin with her father partly in revenge for
that treachery? Or had their lusting started even before
that? How wide and deep did treacheries go among these
people?

All that was a circle Joliffe went around more than once
but all the answers stayed uncertain and the questions did
not change and he fell asleep still circling.

He awoke to heavily falling rain and pity for Mariena
and was not happy about either one. He was tired of rain,
he was tired of mud, and he didn't want to think about
Mariena or anyone else at Deneby now or ever again. Lying
tightly rolled into his blankets, refusing to open his eyes,
trying to deny morning was come, he burrowed deeper into
his bedding. Even at the least guess, there looked to be so
many wrongs—either done or intended—here that he
doubted anyone could any longer sort out one as separate

from another. And if some of the wrongs went back to whatever had gone amiss between Sir Edmund and Lady Benedicta years ago, there was likelihood no one even remembered for certain the how or why they had begun.

One thing was discomfortably clear, though. Whatever wrongs Mariena had done, was doing, meant to do, she was as much betrayed as she was a betrayer. From every side she was wronged beyond measure—by her father, by her mother, by even the waiting-maid who should have been her own. If ever there had been goodness in her, no one had ever done anything to help it grow. He disliked her too much to want to pity her, but he did, without pity in the least lessening his wariness and dislike. Pity did not change the fact of her lust or her greed or that her own father thought she had tried for her brother's life. She had certainly shown no scruple in thinking of Amyas dead. No, Joliffe did not choose to be such a fool as to think she was not dangerous to anyone she turned on.

An unkind toe prodded at his back and Ellis said, "We're not bringing your breakfast to you. Rise and gloom with the rest of us or go hungry."

Joliffe rose, looked out at the rain, and said, "I think I'd rather be hungry than wet."

In a heroic voice Basset declaimed, "Be brave, my heart, and face the worst the world can give!"

"Just now the worst is having to look at Ellis," Joliffe growled.

Intent on being away to breakfast, even Ellis ignored that, and Joliffe did go with them, silently hunched into his cloak. Gil and the rest of them were still riding high and happy from last night's play. Joliffe, unable to give up his thoughts and unwilling to spoil their pleasure, let himself be drawn into talk of what changes he could make to the plays they had been doing and what plays they could do again, now they were one more man to the good. Gil had more training ahead of him but no one doubted now he would be one of them, and the talk gave Joliffe reason, when they returned to the cartshed, to go away to his corner with his writing and the script box as if he meant to see what could be done. And that gave Basset reason in a while, when he had set Ellis to teaching Gil more about using his voice—"The deep growls strengthen your throat cords, the high cries keep them loose, and everything in between gets you from one to the other," Basset told him cheerfully—to join Joliffe, bringing a cushion and sitting down on it with a stiffness that made Joliffe ask, "How go the joints?"

"Better." Basset gave a soft grunt of discomfort as he settled. "By fits and starts," he amended. Forgoing the grumble to which he was probably entitled, he started to talk plays. He had some thoughts that were the same as Joliffe's and some that Joliffe had not had, and warming to the talk, Joliffe let go his worries for the while. Only when Basset asked, "So how does *Dux Moraud* come on?" did everything drain flat again, so quickly Joliffe was unable to hide it.

Basset, reading his sudden silence and his face, said, "As bad as that?"

Joliffe tried, "Not . . . the play so much," but had nowhere to go from there except where he did not want to go. When he had begun to work over that play, with its incestuous and murderous father and daughter, it had been a story, just a story, to be pulled about into whatever shape met the players' needs, his only great problem with it his quest to give it some grace and sense beyond the readily seen ugly pleasure of the tale. Face to face with such ugliness in truth, there was no pleasure in it at all. All the answers he had considered giving to the play for his own satisfaction were no answers at all when faced with the harshness of lives lived in just such ugliness.

Slowly, watching his fingers twirl his pen and keeping his voice too low to be heard beyond the cart, he gave way and told Basset what he had seen in the woods yesterday, had learned last night, and now suspected. Basset listened, with occasional looks to be sure no one else was near enough to hear, and at the end gave a low, long, almost silent whistle before saying, "You're for it, my boy, if anyone knows you know all that."

"Thank you," Joliffe said with heavy mockery. "I needed to hear that. It adds to my mind's peace."

"Pleased to be of comfort to you." But for all his words' lightness, Basset was frowning with thoughts probably no more pleasant than Joliffe's. "At least we can tell Lord Lovell something of what he wanted to know concerning this purposed marriage. How much he'll thank us for the rest, I don't know. Once it's done, though, it's no more our matter. He's the one who'll have to sort it out, thank all the saints."

Joliffe nodded silent agreement with that, but Basset was too skilled at reading what the body betrayed of unsaid thoughts to accept that for all his answer and asked, "Is there something more?"

Joliffe started to answer, stopped, tried again, and finally said, irked at himself, "I have this clutter of questions all churned together in my mind and they won't stop churning. I've found out too much and not enough. There are too many pieces that could go together too many ways and I can't stop shifting them around. There has to be some way it all makes sense and it doesn't yet."

"You're asking a lot of life, if you want it to make sense."

Most of the time, Joliffe was of the same opinion, but he shook his head against it now like against a fly's buzz and said nothing, frowning at the pen he was still twirling.

Basset watched him a moment, then said, "Well, if you can't let it go, go at it as if you were trying to make a story of all these pieces you have. Shift them around and fill the gaps until they make the sense you want."

Joliffe nodded without looking up, still twirling the pen. Basset waited a few moments, heaved a sigh of business done, patted Joliffe on the knee, and labored up from the cushion. When he reached the other side of the cart, he said to someone, "Leave him be for now. He's thinking."

To which Ellis said, "Ah. Let's hope he doesn't hurt himself too badly, then."

Chapter 20

Joliffe kept to himself most of that day. Save for mid-day dinner and afterwards a quick through-run of that evening's play, he stayed beyond the cart, chill but needing his thoughts more than he needed the fire and the others' talk. Piers and even Gil moaned at having to take Tisbe out to her grazing when the rain eased off to hardly more than a misting, and Joliffe gathered from their half-heard talk when they returned that the last reading of the banns must have gone without trouble. Not that that much mattered. Given what he had to tell Lord Lovell, the marriage was unlikely to happen. What held him was what he was untangling by way of little scribbled thoughts on paper and lines drawn from one to another—lines often scratched out and replaced by others going other ways.

Finally he sat for a long while without adding anything or scratching anything away. If the few guesses he had added in were right, it was all there. Nor were the guesses wild. They were come out of what he knew for certainty, and because they made everything else come together, he was afraid he now had the right of it all. Nonetheless, he straightened, finding his back hurt with being bent too long, drew in a breath to the very bottom of his lungs, and let it out with a deep relief. It helped to know. Or to think he knew.

Putting his work away, he made to rejoin the others, shuffling from behind the cart, his legs as stiff as his back, and was surprised to find Will was there, sitting beside the fire with Basset, Rose, and Ellis. Everyone had been keeping so quiet—and must have signaled Will to the same before he was across the cart-yard—that he had not known the boy was come. Basset had apparently been telling him a story, their heads close together. Rose was mending a shirt. Ellis was carving something from a thick stick. But they all alike looked up at Joliffe questioningly, and he smiled in what he meant to be an easy way and said, "All's settled. No more trouble."

Ellis muttered, "That will be the day," and went back to his carving.

Rose watched Joliffe join them, her worry showing. He smiled better, just for her, and said, "Truly. All's well."

He didn't know if she believed him, but she smiled in return and went back to her sewing. Standing between Ellis and Basset, Joliffe held out his hands to the fire that was blazing more merrily than was its wont. "This is a goodly fire. Did someone bring us wood?"

He cocked an eye down at Will, who beamed with pleasure. "My lady mother said I should. I'm best out of the way just now, she said. She said I could stay, too, if no one minded. There's more guests come and everybody's busy with readying for tomorrow when the rest of the guests will come. The day after that is the wedding and then next day there's to be more feasting before everyone starts home and Mariena goes away. Now Basset is telling me a story about Sir Lancelot."

"Then I shall let Basset get on with it," Joliffe said, "and sit myself down to enjoy your lady mother's gift. Add my thanks to everyone else's, if you please."

With Will there, Joliffe was safe from whatever unwanted questions he might have had from Ellis about what he had been doing and any talk with Basset; and as Will was leaving, Piers and Gil and Tisbe returned. Joliffe took Tisbe to tie her up again and wipe her dry, while the boys were sent to fetch the players' supper, and when they had eaten, it was time to ready for that evening's play. Or, rather, two plays—*The Baker's Cake* and *St. Nicholas and the Thief*—in place of *Robin and Marian*. Both were ones they had done so often that they could all have done them in their sleep, but in the hall that evening they wholeheartedly put themselves into their playing, to do honor to Lord Lovell in front of the increased guests and because they owed Sir Edmund fair return for their good meals and good shelter. Their playing won laughter where they wanted it and silence where there should have been and at the end a hearty hand-pounding as they made their bows. Tired, satisfied talk saw them all to bed, and Joliffe would have been grateful for how quickly sleep took him except that he was so quickly asleep.

If he dreamed, he did not know it and was kept from his thoughts the next morning by practice both for that night's play, *Griselda the Patient,* and the two farces they would do tomorrow at the wedding banquet. Supposing the wedding happened, Joliffe thought once, then pushed the thought down and covered it over with the work of teaching Gil how to take a blow from a padded bat as if he were being hit "with a hunk of oak wielded by a giant," Basset said. "In a farce, if it isn't over-played, it won't set them laughing."

Twice through the morning a hurrying in the yard told when more guests arrived, but the hour for dinner came without a meal to go with it because Lord Lovell had sent word that he and Lady Lovell and their people would be there soon after mid-day and all was being held back for them.

"Which should put the cook into a foul humour," Rose said. "Trying to keep the dinner from spoiling and holding up work on everything for tonight and tomorrow's feasting, too."

"At least Lord Lovell looks to have dry riding today," said Ellis, unpleased himself at the delayed meal. "That should help *his* humour anyway."

Yet more rain had pattered to an end sometime toward today's dawn, and although the clouds still held, the day was dry above if not underfoot, with puddles among the cobbles of the yard and the cart-yard's packed mud slick with wet. The hint of a mid-day sun showing through the clouds made no difference to that, and when a trumpet sang out distantly, telling that someone of importance was nigh, Rose warned, "Don't any of you dare slip and fall," as she straightened the Lovell tabard over Gil's shoulders.

They meant to be in the yard with the rest of the household to greet Lord Lovell when he rode in. For that they were putting on their tabards, but Basset had decreed that Gil should have Piers' because, "It will please my lord to see Gil has become fully one of us."

Piers, not happy, tried, "It'll be too small for him. It won't fit him."

"It's a tabard," Rose said calmly. "It doesn't fit, it hangs."

"It'll be too short," Piers warned.

"Lady Lovell considered you would be growing rather than shrinking," his mother returned. "There's a hem in it I can let down in a trice if need be."

"And it won't look a tent on Gil, the way it does on you," jibed Ellis.

Because Ellis, tall and broad-shouldered, wore a tabard with easy grace, Piers was still looking for a quick come-again at him when Basset said, "What you'll have is your cap with its feather and you shall stand at the end of our line and flourish it to my lord and lady."

Ever-pleased for a chance to show off himself and his feather, Piers ceased troubling, fetched his hat from where he safe-kept it in the cart in this wet weather, and followed the rest of them out to the yard happily enough. Because they were wearing Lord Lovell's livery, no one contested their right to line up not far aside from where Sir Edmund, Lady Benedicta, their family, and guests were hurriedly gathering outside the main door to the hall, just in time as the Lovells rode in with their attendants behind them and probably several baggage-laden horses bringing up the rear somewhere. Lord and Lady Lovell themselves were in brown traveling cloaks whose lower edges, as well as their horses' legs, showed how muddy their travel had been, but they were both smiling as they drew rein in front of Sir Edmund. He and everyone else bowed or curtseyed, and Lord Lovell answered with a raised hand and smile to everyone and, "Well met, Sir Edmund," to his host.

"My lord," Sir Edmund returned, coming forward to hold his bridle while he dismounted.

One of the men guests went to help Lady Lovell likewise, with Lady Benedicta coming forward to greet her. As lord and lady, host and hostess all moved toward the hall's doorway, there were more bows and curtsies among all the lookers-on, but Piers gave a particularly great flourish of his cap that brought Lord Lovell to look straight at the players. He took in Gil standing with them in a tabard and as he passed by nodded to Basset in acknowledgment, so that afterward, going back to the cartshed to put the tabards away before going at last to dinner, Ellis said in the triumph they all were feeling, "That nod! Everyone saw it. He noted us and everyone saw it!" Rose, smiling, tucked her arm through his, and Piers risked his cap by a high toss into the air, and Basset clapped a grinning Gil on the back.

Joliffe, trailing behind them all, had on a matching
smile and said enough right things to be a part of their
pleasure, but inwardly he was darkly waiting for when
Lord Lovell would want to know what he had learned. He
didn't doubt that would come before the day was out, but
he had to wait some several hours and the day was drawing
into late afternoon, with rain threatening again, when a
Lovell servant brought word that Lord Lovell wished to see
Master Basset and the player Joliffe.

"We're at his service," Basset said as easily as if being
summoned to a lord were an every-day and always-
pleasant happening for him.

Rose hurriedly straightened their collars and smoothed
their hair, smiling, but Joliffe saw the worry in her eyes as
she brushed something imaginary from his doublet front
and he was sorry for it. She had worries enough in her life
without he gave her more. He could argue, he supposed,
that this one was not his fault; but despite he could argue
anything almost any time, including whether good was bad
upon occasion, he just now did not feel like arguing anything and smiled at her with what he meant to be assurance.

He only wished he felt as assured as he tried to seem.
What he had to tell Lord Lovell was truly not his fault, but
messengers had taken blows for ill-received messages before this. And what if Lord Lovell simply refused to believe him?

Lord Lovell's man led Basset and Joliffe not to the great
hall or the tower or even the galleryed wing of rooms but
past there to a gate in a wooden wall across the space between the wing's far end and the sheds and workshops
along the manor wall beyond it. Until then, Joliffe had
vaguely thought the gate led probably to a woodyard or
some such serviceable place and was surprised when he
followed Basset into a small garden of four squared flower
beds divided and surrounded by narrow, graveled paths. It

must have been meant for a lady's pleasure garden, but the place had a drowned, brown air of being little cared for that Joliffe thought came only a little from the weather and not much from autumn. It was a place unloved, here but not truly wanted or cared for by anyone.

Very like Lady Benedicta, he thought.

Another time he might have followed that thought, but there was no time now. Besides the soaking ground, the only place to sit in the garden was an unsheltered wooden bench, where Lord Lovell had chosen not to sit. Instead, he was standing, looking down at a crumpled plant long since beaten by weather into nothing recognizable, and he gave up his contemplation of it without probable regret as he turned, waved that his man could leave them, then waited where he was while Basset and Joliffe came to him, saying as they bowed low, "I ask your pardon for meeting you nowhere better than this. It seems to be the only private place on the manor at present, but it's a condemnedly damp and cold one, so let's make this go quickly. I gather from Sir Edmund that you've well pleased everyone here."

"We've hoped so, my lord," Basset said.

"Has Gil given satisfaction? Or is he as hopeless as you feared he would be?"

So he had not been fooled by the good front Basset had put on taking the boy, but giving that part of it no outward heed, Basset said full-heartedly, "He's all and perhaps more than could be hoped for. He learns quickly and does well. In truth, he bids to be so good, I've considered again your offer to apprentice him to us and think to accept it now, if your lordship allows, lest he be wooed away to another company before his time."

"He's that good, is he? His mother hoped he'd have failed by now and I would bring him back to her. She'll be displeased." But Lord Lovell was not. Far from it. "Yes, I think we can draw up apprentice-papers for him. What of the other matter?"

"That's best told by Master Ripon," Basset said and stepped aside with another bow.

Left facing Lord Lovell, Joliffe thought: Right; take the good, leave me the bad.

But he had to admit the bad was fairly his, and as Lord Lovell's heed shifted to him, he bowed again, playing for time despite he knew that time would make no difference. Whether said soon or late, what he had to say was not going to be welcomed.

"You've found out something?" Lord Lovell prompted. "Or nothing?"

"Something," Joliffe said, and there being no way into it but straight, went on, "But about much more than John Harcourt's death." From there, keeping his voice flat and bare of outward feeling, he told it all as nakedly as he might, both what he had learned outright and what he had made of it, including warning that he might have it all the wrong way on.

After a time Lord Lovell ceased to watch his face, instead stood looking at the path between them, and went on looking at it a while longer after Joliffe had finished. Joliffe and Basset exchanged glances but waited in silence, until finally Lord Lovell looked up from his thinking and said, "God's blood and bones. Should it be Lady Benedicta we first talk to, do you think?"

Joliffe was unused to being asked by a lord what he thought, but since he agreed that was where they should begin, he said, "If your lordship wishes it."

Already started for the garden's gate, Lord Lovell said, "Come then. You'll have to be there for it."

In some small corner of himself, Joliffe thought he would rather not be there for it, but mostly he would not have missed learning how true his guesses were for half the world. For the whole world he might have forgone it, but not for less—and since no one was offering him the world or anything else, he followed Lord Lovell from the garden, with Basset now coming last. Lord Lovell's man was waiting outside the gate, and Lord Lovell sent him off to find where Lady Benedicta presently was, saying, "Tell her I'd have private word with her."

The man went at a run toward the hall. Following at a steady stride, Lord Lovell was just past the steps to the tower when his man came running back to say Lady Benedicta was taking the air atop the tower with Lady Lovell. Should he go up and bid her come down?

Lord Lovell gave the doubtful sky a doubtful look—the mid-day hint of sun had faded away behind lowering grey clouds—but said, "No. I'll go up to her," and turned aside for the stairs up to the tower doorway.

Joliffe, mindful it might be better if Lord Lovell did not know of Basset's aching stiffness, said quickly, "By your leave, my lord, would it be best if less rather than more were there when you talk with her? Would Master Basset do better not to come?"

Lord Lovell paused, then granted, "Yes. She might talk the easier. Master Basset, if you would be so good as to leave us."

"My lord," Basset said with a bow; and gave Joliffe a single small nod of thanks when Lord Lovell was turned away again. Joliffe returned the nod before following Lord Lovell up the stairs and into the tower. Inside the doorway, Lord Lovell said at Joliffe, "You lead." Joliffe bowed and started up the long curve of stairs while behind him Lord Lovell turned back long enough to say something to his man still following them. In answer the man bowed and disappeared out the door, and with Lord Lovell at his heels, Joliffe kept on up the stairs.

Passing the open doorway to Lady Benedicta's chamber, Joliffe glimpsed why she might have chosen to go to the tower's top for a time, crowded as the room was with the bright talk and quick laughter of a great many—or maybe only six or so—women come as guests for the wedding. If Lady Benedicta was as little given to laughter and talk as Joliffe had thus far seen her, that merry group could well have been wearing on her.

As he stepped out on the tower's roof, though, he saw that it was more than weariness had taken her there. The roof, round like the tower, was low-pitched, coming to a point in its middle, with around its outer edge a narrow walkway made of wooden slats fixed to wooden rails over the guttering that carried rainwater away to drain through the holes through the base of the outer wall. Since no Deneby lord had ever paid the royal fee for right to embattle his tower, that outer wall was not the high and crenellated battlement it might have been but merely low, with its flat top making a goodly place to sit, which was what Lady Lovell and Lady Benedicta were doing there. Almost as far from the door as they could be, they were seated side by side on cushions they must have brought with them, Lady Benedicta with her head bowed, one hand covering her eyes, with Lady Lovell holding her other hand and looking worriedly at her.

They both looked toward Joliffe as he came through the doorway, and knowing he was not going to be welcomed for himself, he stepped quickly aside for Lord Lovell to go past him. Lord Lovell did and the women stood up to curtsy, his wife looking faintly surprised but Lady Benedicta's face blank of anything but courtesy, not even sign of the tears Joliffe had thought she must be hiding behind her hand.

"My lord?" said Lady Lovell, still holding Lady Benedicta by the hand. From what Joliffe knew of her, she was a lively, kindly woman. If her kindness held good against what was coming, he would be glad she was here, sorry as he was for everything else.

But sorry saved no one, and when Lord Lovell said, "My ladies," in a way that warned he was not pleasantly here, his wife took double hold on Lady Benedicta's hand with both her own and asked, "What is it?"

"A question first," said Lord Lovell. "Lady Benedicta, is Mariena your daughter?"

With a little bewilderment and open surprise, Lady Benedicta said, "Yes."

"And Will is your son?"

"Yes." Firmly and even-voiced, with her guard now up between her surprise and him.

"And John Harcourt the elder was your lover years ago."

Braced for many things, she was not braced for that. She stiffened, then lifted her head higher and said, "Yes. And for it I've done such penance as my priest required of me."

Lady Lovell seemed unsurprised by that, but Joliffe had already gathered that Lady Benedicta and her lover had never been much of a secret. And now others were coming up the stairs, their voices ahead of them, and he moved well aside from the door, around the walkway's curve, as Lord Lovell, hearing them as well, turned toward the doorway.

Will came out first, bounding with eagerness but pausing to make a creditable bow to Lord and Lady Lovell before his mother held out her free hand to him and said, "Come here, Will."

Will started to obey, turning sideways to go past Joliffe on the narrow way between the slant of the roof and the outer wall, but maybe suddenly not certain everything was well because he stopped half-way between Joliffe and his mother, just as Mariena came out the doorway in her turn. She took in everyone with quick-eyed curiosity even while she curtseyed to Lord and Lady Lovell before she had to shift toward Joliffe, who had to shift farther along to make room for Sir Edmund now following her onto the walkway. He, too, bowed, and said with the ease of a man with an open conscience, "We've quite a gathering here." Adding with a glance cast at the sky, "We're likely to be wet before long, though, my lord."

Lord Lovell, not diverted by either courtesy or weather, said, "A question, Sir Edmund. Is Mariena your daughter?"

Openly taken a-back by the question, Sir Edmund said, "Sir?" Then, as certainly as Lady Benedicta had, he answered, "Yes. Of course she is."

"And Will is your son."

More strongly despite he was beginning to look confused and maybe wary, Sir Edmund said again, "Yes."

Lord Lovell looked from him to Lady Benedicta and back again. "Then the lies have begun."

"I think Will should not be here for this," said Lady Benedicta.

"I didn't ask for him to come," Lord Lovell said. "Sir Edmund?"

"Since you'd asked for Mariena and me, I saw no harm," Sir Edmund answered. "Now . . ." He looked quickly between his wife and Lord Lovell. Whatever he saw there, he seemed to change from what he had been going to say and said instead with a kind of muted defiance, "No. Let him stay. Let's all hear whatever this is." He looked at Joliffe. "But what's he here for?"

"For my reasons," Lord Lovell said. "Now. Sir Edmund, the man you first chose for your daughter to marry was the son of your wife's lover, yes?"

That seemed to take no one by surprise, not even Will. Stiffly but with no sign he was uneased, Sir Edmund said, "He had not been her lover for a long time past, and anyway the man is dead."

"So is his son now." Lord Lovell looked to Lady Benedicta. "That was your doing, wasn't it?"

Her face became a rigid mask, Lady Benedicta held silent, not even protesting her innocence.

But Lord Lovell had not waited for her answer, had returned his look to Sir Edmund and challenged, "The thing is—Mariena is not your daughter, is she?"

Sir Edmund had taken talk of his wife's lover with no particular feeling, but drew a sudden inward hiss of breath before declaring sharply, "She is, sir."

"What you intended," Lord Lovell said as if he had said nothing, "was to marry your supposed daughter to her own half-brother. In deliberate revenge for your wife's faithlessness, yes?"

Joliffe was maybe the only one near enough to Mariena to hear her soft gasp at that. Standing aside as he was from everyone, he was able to see them all save Mariena, turned too much away from him for him to see her face, but her rigid back and that soft gasp told much as Sir Edmund said fiercely, "That's a foul thing to say, my lord. I protest it."

Lord Lovell, ignoring his protest, turned back to Lady Benedicta, challenging her now with, "To keep your daughter from that marriage, you poisoned young Harcourt. You killed him. Gave a cruel death to a young man who'd never done you harm."

After a moment of silent stare at him, Lady Benedicta said, "You claim to know much, my lord."

"I know enough," he returned. Despite he knew little, he sounded very otherwise.

It was as fine a play of feigned confidence as Joliffe had ever seen. Whether it would have sufficed against Sir Edmund and Lady Benedicta he didn't have chance to learn, because Mariena cried out at her mother, "You know you killed him! We all know it! You hated I'd be happy with him and so you killed him!"

Like a taut-held bow set suddenly free by its bowstring breaking, Lady Benedicta turned on her, snarling, all the mask gone. "You blind, idiot fool! I did it to keep you from mortal sin! From incest with your own brother!" She pointed at Sir Edmund. "A sin he meant to set you to for yet more revenge on me."

"I loved John Harcourt!" Mariena screamed at her.

"You lusted for him," her mother flung back scornfully. "You've never loved anything. All you've ever felt is lust. You even lust for him." She jerked her head at Sir Edmund. "And he..."

Sir Edmund cut sharply into her words. "I didn't know Harcourt was her brother. If you had told me..."

"You knew," Lady Benedicta said back at him. "You've always known Mariena isn't your daughter. You knew better than anyone that we shared nothing but a bed in the while when she was conceived. Or for years afterward."

"You'd sworn you'd never see Harcourt again," Sir Edmund said, cold and harsh. "But you went off that one more time, like a bitch in heat, and—"

"You *knew* she's not your daughter," Lady Benedicta flung back at him. "From the very first you knew. That was the only forgivable part of your starting to lust for her when she was barely twelve. Too proud to bed servants, oh, yes, you were that. But your twelve-year-old daughter..."

"Your bastard!" Sir Edmund said. "And for all she was hot and ready even then, at twelve, I never had her!"

Raw with scorn and anger, Lady Benedicta said back, "I'll grant you that. You had me instead. Instead of her, you rutted me and I had to let you, to keep you from her."

"At least it finally got me a son!"

In their freed hatred for each other they had forgotten everything else. Even when Sir Edmund made to move past Lord Lovell, to circle the roof toward his wife, and Lord Lovell put out an arm, stopping him at the same moment Lady Lovell moved away from Lady Benedicta to put herself as barrier if Sir Edmund had come farther, neither Sir Edmund nor Lady Benedicta gave either of them heed except Sir Edmund stayed where he was, still hurling his hatred at his wife with, "That's the one good thing you've ever done for me. My Will."

"He's mine, too!"

"But after that all you've been good for is dead babies. Making love to you was like making love to a log, and all I got for it were dead babies. And her?" He flung a hand toward Mariena without looking at her. "That precious daughter of your lover? I caught her, age fifteen, with a squire's hand in her gown and her own hand between his thighs. I beat him and—"

"And probably had yourself in Mariena's bed before the day was out," Lady Benedicta said at him. "That's about when it started between you, wasn't it? Though I didn't know until far too late. It's *you* I should have killed instead of John Harcourt!"

"But they burn wives who kill husbands, don't they?" Sir Edmund said back at her. "And nobody would believe it was any accident if I suddenly sickened and died. You'd have been burned within a month. Besides"—he jerked his head toward Mariena—"she enjoys it. She's as hot for it as you are cold."

"She enjoys it and it keeps you out of me!" Lady Benedicta said. "But to marry her off to her own half-brother . . ."

Sir Edmund laughed. "God's blood, I loved the thought of that! I would have married her to him, let them have their sport, and then told the world I'd found out too late they were brother and sister, half and half. He'd be ruined by the foulness. I'd never been able to ruin his father but that would have done for the son! And you I'd finally be able to put close-confined into a nunnery, no one to say me nay, and Mariena I'd have back all for myself again for as long as I wanted!"

"But I wanted John Harcourt!" Mariena cried out. "I loved him!"

Sir Edmund and Lady Benedicta both looked at her almost blankly, as if only now they remembered there was anyone but themselves here to hear their hatred. Then Lady Benedicta cried back at her with angry despair, "He was your brother! Don't you understand that? You couldn't have him! It would have been *incest!*"

"Incest is nothing! I'd already done incest!" Mariena pointed at Sir Edmund. "With him. I . . ." She stopped, turned her look from her mother to Sir Edmund to her mother again, then back to Sir Edmund, staring now, her mouth open in a way that would have been laughable any other time or place; and Joliffe realized that only now had she caught up to what they had been saying. Still staring at Sir Edmund, she said almost blankly, "You're not my father."

He laughed, cruel and hard at her. "No, my dear fool. I'm not your father. It's never been incest between us. Only lust."

"But we . . . when we . . ." She looked back to Lady Benedicta. Her voice and face hardened. "It was supposed to hurt you, what we did. That I'd bed with my father. But you knew he wasn't."

Lady Benedicta shook her head and said with sudden, crushing sadness, "Mariena, the only thing that hurts me, besides you hate me, is your foolish lusting, and from that I couldn't save you."

"You knew he wasn't my father!" Mariena shrilled. "You knew it and you've been laughing at me for it!"

"Mariena, there has never been anything about you I've laughed at," Lady Benedicta said with the weariness of a heart and mind worn almost to nothing with enduring. "I swear, believe me, that I've never laughed at you."

But Mariena was beyond hearing anything except herself. She shoved past Joliffe as if he were a thing in her way, not a person; pushed him so hard aside with a hand on his chest that the back of his knees caught on the low wall of the battlement and he sat abruptly down as she passed him, crying at her mother and back at Sir Edmund, "You've both laughed at me! Both of you! You've laughed at me and used me!" And at Sir Edmund, "You *never* loved me!"

No more than she had ever loved either of them or done other than use them, too. But what she did was always different than what was done to her, Joliffe thought. At least in her own mind. But she was near to Will, still standing caught between all the angers around him. And she grabbed him and with her anger's strength swung him onto the wall, facing outward, a shove away from falling, crying out in her rage, "All you've ever cared about is him! I've always wanted him dead and now he's going to be!"

But she was still saying it, was only beginning to shove him outward, as her mother flung forward across the few yards between them and had Will by the arm and was wrenching him aside, out of Mariena's reach and back to the walkway in a single desperate swing that carried her outward in his place. As he hit the wooden walkway, she was falling, stretched sideways over the battlement, not gone yet, the wall wide enough that almost she might not have fallen if the force of throwing Will aside had been less, if her hand cast out toward Mariena had been seized and she'd been jerked back to safety.

There was time for that. Mariena's hands were already out, caught useless now Will was snatched from her reach. Only the slightest sideways grab was needed to catch hold of her mother's hand.

But Mariena jerked back, hands and body both, and Lady Benedicta was gone. Without outcry. Simply gone.

She was there and then she was not. Where she had been there was nothing.

Until the sickening single thud of flesh hitting stones in the cobbled yard below.

But by then Mariena had grabbed her skirts clear of her legs and was taking the single step needed to put herself onto the wall, turning back to sweep everyone with her angry, tear-filled gaze, screaming out at them, "You're all hateful! I hate you! *I hate you!*" And swung away from them and leaped outward even as Joliffe, scrambling to regain his feet, grabbed for her. Too late. All he could do instead was catch Will as the boy staggered up and toward the wall, too, as if meaning to see over it. Could only catch him and hold him back but not cover the sound of another body hitting stones.

Chapter 21

It was Lady Lovell who took everything in hand in the first terrible moments after that, first coming at haste to take Will from Joliffe, clasping the boy to her while saying over his head at her husband, "I'll see to him. Go down to the yard. Take over there. All that need's saying is that Sir Edmund and Lady Benedicta and Mariena were arguing. Mariena was going to push her brother off the tower. Lady Benedicta saved him but fell to her death. Then Mariena jumped. That's all we need say. Just that. Sir Edmund, you might do best to stay here, out of the way."

"She's in the right," Lord Lovell said at Sir Edmund. "Best you stay here." And added at Joliffe over the outcries that were started in the yard below the tower now, "You come with me."

He turned and disappeared down the stairs and Joliffe followed him, shoving past Sir Edmund, who had not moved and did not move, stayed standing frozen, staring at where his wife and Mariena had last been.

Joliffe overtook Lord Lovell as he paused at the door to Lady Benedicta's chamber, stopping the women just starting to come out its door with order they should stay there. Past their rising questions, Lady Lovell, coming with Will, said crisply behind him, "I'll see to them. Go on."

"Stay and help her," Lord Lovell said at Joliffe and went on.

Joliffe stayed, not certain what he was expected to do but more than willing not to see what lay in the yard. For choice, he simply stayed beside the door to keep anyone from leaving, while the women gathered to Lady Lovell as she went to sit on the chest at the bedfoot, some of them from the window where they had still been leaning out to see. With Will gathered in her arms on her lap, his face hidden against her neck as if he were a much smaller child, Lady Lovell repeated what she had said on the roof. The women's horror and exclaims were broken with cries of pity for Will, and though some of them kept going to the window to look out again, most busied themselves with bringing him wine and stroking his hair and making much of him while asking Lady Lovell questions to which she gave the same answers and they exclaimed and cried out again.

Only when Father Morice came did she get respite. With priestly authority he shooed the women away from her, sat down beside her, and said to her over Will's head, "They've been moved into the lower chamber here. I have one of her women finding sheets to shroud them. Lord Lovell has already sent someone for the crowner. He wants to know if you can go on seeing to things here."

"Of course. Yes," Lady Lovell said with her great calm. "Has anyone seen to Sir Edmund?"

"No," Father Morice said, sounding surprised, as if Sir Edmund had been forgotten until then.

Lady Lovell looked to Joliffe. "If you would, please."

"My lady," Joliffe said with a bow and went out; but not immediately up. Instead, he waited on the stairs above the door for Father Morice, and when the priest came out, closing the door behind him, said at his back, "How much of all this did you know, Father?"

Father Morice spun around. "Know? I wasn't there. You were there. You—"

"About Mariena and Sir Edmund and whose daughter she truly was and that he meant to marry her to her half-brother. How much of all that did you know?"

"Those are matters of the confessional," the priest said stiffly. "Not mine to divulge."

"Dealing over the marriage agreement was not 'of the confessional,' so tell me something: you dragged out the dealings with John Harcourt for as long as you could. That's what I've been told. Because you knew, yes? You understood what Sir Edmund meant to do but you didn't dare face him with it. What would you have done when the time came they were at the altar ready to say their vows? Did you plan to let them commit mortal sin? Would you have blessed the bridal bed that night and left them to it?"

Father Morice sagged backward against the wall. "I don't know what I meant to do. No. I wouldn't have let it happen. I couldn't have. I hope. I . . ." Despair edged his voice. "I don't know. And now she'll have to be buried in unconsecrated ground. Mariena will. Because she killed herself." He looked suddenly frightened. "It did happen that way, didn't it? She jumped? He didn't . . ."

Words failed him, the way his courage had when most he needed it, and for truth's sake, not comfort because he had no urge to comfort the man, that Joliffe said, "He didn't push her over. Not by *present* deed. Only by every-thing he did to her before." And he swung away from the priest and went up the stairs, back to the tower's roof.

The rain had come back, was a thick-falling mist greying and blurring the world. Sir Edmund had not taken shelter from it, though; was sitting on the battlement, hunched and slumped like an old and weary man, staring down between his feet at the runnel of rainwater in the gutter under the wooden walkway. He did not look up or show any sign he knew Joliffe was there; and Joliffe, when he had stood for a while with the rain brushing across his face and beginning to run down his neck, said ungently, "The rain will help to wash the cobbles clean of their blood anyway."

Sir Edmund gave a small grunt of pain and pulled his head lower between his shoulders. So he could hear what was said to him and he was in pain. Good, Joliffe thought, and said at him, "Your wife's last act was one of love. Your daughter's last acts were all of hatred." Sir Edmund started to shake his head, probably against Mariena being called his daughter, but Joliffe lashed at him, "She *was* your daughter. In everything but blood. In cruelty and coldness of heart, she was all yours, and now she's damned her soul to Hell. You, though, will likely repent of everything and save your soul. If not Heaven, you'll at least have Purgatory. But I hope you're put through hell here on earth before you die. I hope Lord Lovell sees to that much for you."

Sir Edmund a little raised his head, enough to say, "I never meant . . ." He waved one hand vaguely sideways. "Never meant her . . . them . . . to die. To . . ."

"No," Joliffe snapped. "It was Amyas you meant to kill."

That brought Sir Edmund's head up. A little wild-eyed he stared at Joliffe, who said, unrelenting, "Or did you mean to betray Mariena that way, too, and leave her married to him? Though any man who married her was as foul betrayed by you as man could be. And, yes, Lord Lovell knows what you planned for Amyas, too."

Sir Edmund had started to rise but at that sank down

again and put his head between his hands. "I never meant their deaths," he mumbled. "I swear that. I never meant that."

"No," Joliffe agreed coldly. "You preferred them alive and tortured. You left the killing to your wife and Mariena. I think there's not much absolution in that."

He went back inside and down the stairs at dangerous speed, leaving Sir Edmund to the rain. With any luck the cur would take the lung sickness and die. Or, better yet, despair and fling himself to damnation from the tower.

But he wouldn't, Joliffe thought bitterly. He was a man with no courage for anything except cruelty—the coward's pastime.

The rain had driven people to shelter under and along the farther building's gallery and under the pentice over the tower doorway. Joliffe shoved through the latter and down the stairs, already too wet to care about the rain, crossing the yard long-strided toward the cart-yard, slowing only for Basset, coming out from among the household folk sheltering in the hall doorway, to join him. Basset asked him nothing, but when they joined Ellis, Piers, and Gil huddled under the eaves of the carpenter's shed, Ellis started to ask, "What . . ." only to break off, either at the shake of Basset's head or the look on Joliffe's face as he went past them.

In the cartshed, Rose was tending the fire but must have known something of what was happening but likewise broke off the start of a question, instead saying at Joliffe as she laid more sticks onto the fire, "You're cold and you're wet. Sit down. Take off your doublet. Father, bring his cloak. Take off your shoes, Joliffe."

He had meant to escape into the corner beyond the cart but suddenly wanted not to be alone; wanted the fire and warmth and Rose's care; and he shrugged out of his doublet and flung it aside, sat down on a cushion, and leaned toward the fire, his hands held out to it.

"Shoes," Rose reminded.

As he pulled them off, Basset laid his cloak over his shoulders. Joliffe huddled it around him, leaning to the fire again. Rose set his shoes where they would dry without the heat shriveling their leather and hung his doublet over the ever-ready drying rack. "He should have something hot to drink," she said.

"I'm well. There's no need," Joliffe said without looking up from the flames at play among the sticks. They were warmth and light and like something alive, and just now he very much needed warmth and light and things alive.

Quietly Basset asked, "Were you right in what you told Lord Lovell?"

"I was right."

He began to shiver. Rose brought a blanket and wrapped it around him over his cloak. Piers had come to crouch on the other side of the fire, his hands out to the warmth, but Ellis and Gil had stayed standing just inside the shed's shelter, and Ellis now demanded of Basset, "What did he tell Lord Lovell?"

Still quietly, Basset told them. While he did, Rose sat down on a cushion beside Piers, put her arm around him, and held him close while watching Joliffe still staring into the flames. When Basset finished, Ellis swore softly, briefly, then demanded at Joliffe, "That's what you made out of what you found out here? All of that?"

Not looking up, Joliffe said, "It was the only way of things that made sense of it all."

"You told Lord Lovell that and he believed you?"

"Yes. Believed it enough anyway," Joliffe said tersely. "Enough to follow it through."

"So then?" Ellis demanded of Basset again.

"Then Lord Lovell went to challenge them with it, to see what they would answer," Basset said. "About that only Joliffe can tell you. I wasn't there."

"Joliffe?" Ellis said, only it was an order more than question.

Still watching the fire, where the sticks were now breaking down into glowing coals, Joliffe told them the rest and how only part of it all was being told to everyone else; and when he had finished, there was quiet among them all, with only the drizzling of rain off the thatch until finally Rose said, "You saw it from the yard, Father?"

"I saw them fall, yes. Then I looked away and didn't look back."

Rose signed herself with a cross. "God have mercy on them both." And after a moment, "On all of them."

Hushed, Piers said, "Poor Will."

Ellis, equally hushed, muttered, "Poor everyone."

Though there would be no play tonight, Ellis and Gil fetched the players' supper from the kitchen along with what was being said there. It seemed Lady Lovell's telling of what had happened on the tower was the one that would hold, though no one seemed clear on what had set so desperate a quarrel going or for certain what the quarrel had been.

"Sir Edmund has shut himself away into some room in the tower, with only Father Morice going in or out," Ellis said. "Amyas is in grief and only keeps saying, 'But why? Why?' Most of those who knew much seem to think this all was something that was a long time coming and almost bound to come, one way or another. Lord and Lady Lovell are giving all the orders that have to be given."

"What's being said of Will?" Rose asked.

"'Poor boy' sums it up," Ellis said. "Lady Lovell has kept him with her, so no one's had chance at him."

"Hasn't Sir Edmund asked for him?" Basset asked.

"Someone said he had and she'd refused. Whether that's true or not . . ." Ellis shrugged.

Then a servant with Lord Lovell's badge of a dog on his doublet came to say Lord Lovell wanted to see Basset and Joliffe. Rose did her usual quick straightening and smoothing of them before they left, and when Joliffe forced a smile of thanks at her, she patted his arm like he was Piers and said, "It will be all right."

Since he had finished telling his side of what had happened, he had not spoken at all nor did he now, only kept the smile on his face for her sake until he was turned away to go with Basset after the servant.

Lord Lovell was in a small chamber off the great hall that looked to be where Sir Edmund carried out manor business, with tables at which he and a clerk could work and a chest against the wall for keeping documents; but there was also a backed, comfortably cushioned bench in front of a fireplace, and a fire burning there against the damp of the evening now drawing in, and Lord Lovell was seated there; and when Basset and Joliffe had bowed to him, he gestured them to come stand near the fire, taking a long, searching look at them both before asking, "You can keep quiet about all of this?"

"We can, my lord," Basset said.

"Master Ripon?" Lord Lovell said.

"Yes."

"It's a miserable business," Lord Lovell said. "But you did as I asked and I'm well pleased." He held out a small pouch to Basset. "This is for your trouble."

Basset took it with a bow that accepted the dismissal that came with it, but Joliffe asked, "What's to be done about Sir Edmund?"

Lord Lovell frowned, not at Joliffe, only at his own answer. "Whatever his priest decrees for him. There's no proof he had intent against Amyas' life. For the rest, to make public the whole ugliness would serve mostly to hurt Will hereafter, which seems to me wrong, he being the one innocent in all of this."

"You won't leave him here with his father, my lord?" Joliffe asked.

That was impudence, which Lord Lovell acknowledged with a level look before he answered anyway, "I mean to take Will into my household until he comes of age. He'll leave here with my lady and me. As for leaving . . ." He paused, then seemed to make up his mind about something. "It will be best, I think, if you and your company leave in the morning, Master Basset."

"My lord?" Basset asked, surprised and showing it.

"In a day or so, hardly more, the crowner will be here with his questions about the deaths. If you're not here to answer questions, you won't have to lie to him. You're my company of players. I'll answer for it that you knew nothing beyond what I myself can tell him and that I sent you on your way because your skills are unsuitable to a place now in mourning and your places at table would be better used for other people."

Basset bowed. "We'll be gone at first light, my lord."

"Good. Tell young Gil I'm sorry to have no chance to speak with him, but he's to go on serving you well. I shall expect to see your company at Minster Lovell at Christmastide."

That was complete dismissal, and with another bow, they took it; but crossing the yard, Basset weighed the pouch in his hand and said, "I'm liking this lord more every day."

At the cartshed the rest of the company took the news in good part, no one minding to be away from here; but it wasn't until the morning, when Deneby Manor was behind them and there was a hope of sun behind the clouds, that

Ellis said across Tisbe's back to Joliffe as they walked along, "Anyway, this will surely stop you trying to make something out of that grievous *Dux Moraud*. That's the one good thing from all of this."

Joliffe, having had the long, unsleeping hours of the night to come to some terms with yesterday, feigned large surprise at him. "What? By no means whatever! In truth I've finally seen my way clear to the end that had me stopped until now."

"Please," Ellis pleaded. "No."

"Yes," Joliffe said blithely, his spirit rising with the familiar pleasure of irking him. "I've been trying to deal with Moraud as a villain of great daring and great sins—sins so great his repentance was a thing beyond believing. Or at least beyond my being able to write it well."

"Humility," Ellis said. "I like that in you."

"But," Joliffe said grandly, "now Sir Edmund has shown me the way. There was nothing great or daring about anything he did. All his sins were small-hearted and petty. Petty lust. Petty hatred. Petty greed . . ."

"If those are petty sins," Ellis said impatiently, "what exactly do you consider a *great* sin?"

"Pride," Joliffe said promptly.

Ellis gave a bark of laughter. "That makes you a great sinner, then. You've enough pride for—"

"My pride is honest and proportionate pride," Joliffe said with dignity. "There's no sin in pride at filling my humble place in the world as best I'm able. In using well what talents God has given me. In—"

"Sir Edmund?" Ellis said quellingly.

"Sir Edmund," Joliffe said, unable to keep a hard edge from his words, "is a hollow-hearted coward who has never seen beyond what *he* wants, what *he* feels. Other people's grief or pain or hope or happiness don't matter to him. Only *his* grief, *his* pain, *his* hope and happiness count for anything. If he comes to repentance now, it's not because his heart has truly changed but because he's frightened to his hollow core that he'll otherwise be made to suffer for what he helped to happen." Joliffe heard the anger building in his own voice and shifted back to deliberate lightness. "If I do him wrong, may I be forgiven. But there I have my Moraud. A petty man sniveling his way into repentance. I think—"

"You think too much," said Ellis.

Author's Note

Lord and Lady Lovell are historical. His effigy can be seen on his tomb in Minster Lovell church in Oxfordshire, close by the ruins of Minster Lovell manor house. The site is a lovely one to visit, with its remains of golden Cotswold stone buildings beside the Windrush River under Wychwood Forest.

The Denebys and all about them are imaginary, but the story of incestuous father and daughter is an old one, to be found in many sources and forms through the centuries, including the contemporary *Confessio Amantis* by John Gower *and* the actual play of *Dux Moraud*.

Unfortunately, the play presently exists only in fragmentary form, written in the 1400s on a damaged and reused parchment of the early 1300s. We have the Duke's speeches, no one else's. This brief remains of the play can be found in *Non-Cycle Plays and Fragments,* edited by Norman Davis for the Early English Text Society, Oxford University Press, 1970, or in perhaps more generally accessible form (if somewhat less accurately and under the title *Duke Moraud*) in Joseph Quincy Adams's *Chief Pre-Shakespearean Dramas*.

Two-Time Edgar® Award Nominee
MARGARET FRAZER

A Play of Isaac

When his band of traveling players are taken
in by a patron, Joliffe and company find that
murder has taken the spotlight—and it's up
to them to catch a killer in the act.

0-425-19751-4

pc882

From Edgar® Award-Winning Author

MARGARET FRAZER

The Dame Frevisse Medieval Mystery Series